Wiley Michael
Black Hammock

BLACK HAMMOCK

BLACK HAMMOCK
Michael Wiley

Severn House Large Print
London & New York

This first large print edition published 2017
in Great Britain and the USA by
SEVERN HOUSE PUBLISHERS LTD of
19 Cedar Road, Sutton, Surrey, England, SM2 5DA.
First world regular print edition published 2016 by
Severn House Publishers Ltd.

British Library Cataloguing in Publication Data
A CIP catalogue record for this title is available from the British Library.

ISBN-13: 9780727895097

Severn House Publishers support the Forest Stewardship Council™
[FSC™], the leading international forest certification organisation. All
our titles that are printed on FSC certified paper carry the FSC logo.

MIX
Paper from
responsible sources
FSC® C013056

Typeset by Palimpsest Book Production Ltd.,
Falkirk, Stirlingshire, Scotland.
Printed and bound in Great Britain by
T J International, Padstow, Cornwall.

To Julie, Isaac, Maya, and Elias

Acknowledgements

My thanks to Keith Cartwright for introducing me to Black Hammock Island, to Mary Roach, Norman Cantor, and Ruth Richardson, whose books have guided me through the morgue, to Julia Burns and Clark Lunberry for reading and advising, to Christine Kane for spinning the web, to Philip Spitzer, Lukas Ortiz, and Jennifer Woodason for always knowing the best way through, and to Kate Lyall Grant, Sara Porter, and Charlotte Loftus for making it happen.

In *Black Hammock*, Lexi reads from Nathaniel Hawthorne's 'The Birthmark,' Stephen Crane's 'A Dark-Brown Dog,' and Mark Twain's *The Adventures of Huckleberry Finn*.

Note on the Daniel Turner Thrillers

In each of the Daniel Turner thrillers, Homicide Detective Daniel Turner plays an important secondary role. He is the common element in others' lives and deaths, getting caught in the spirals of crime that he investigates. These are North Florida city, swamp, and island thrillers – set far from the well-traveled crime fiction of Miami Beach, Disney World, and the Everglades – and the people who star in them are city, swamp, and island characters.

In writing about them, I dig into the psychologies and motives of heroes and antiheroes, persecutors and victims, criminals and seekers of justice (legal or vigilante), the beautiful and the ugly. Daniel Turner is a character in *their* stories. He is their brother, their childhood friend, their enemy, and their protector, and they love him or hate him – or sometimes think barely at all about him – as we do the people in our lives who hurt us and save us.

Emerging from others' shadows, Turner is the man who, at the end, wears a badge showing his right to use deadly force and to order the world. When the dust settles, *if* it settles, he embodies the law – shaky, just or unjust, sometimes arbitrary but generally necessary.

Let your story be that you are a stranger.
                              Sophocles, *Electra*

One

Oren

The land south of Atlanta turned fast enough to scrub forest and waste and big flat timber tracts that looked like a brown wind had come through and other tracts that were still uncut and green to the edge of the road. High-wire power lines, hanging from metal towers, stretched through channels cut in the green parts of the forest like wire straps that could hold the earth down if gravity forgot itself. The sun was shining so bright it seemed it would twang those power lines.

We had set out from Atlanta to kill my mother and her husband. A slow kill. An orchestrated kill. A slow-motion war of obliteration.

Why not just shoot them and be done with it? First, if I pointed a pistol at them, they would point theirs at me. Second, they took me apart piece by piece, so I would take *them* apart piece by piece. Then I would blow them from their house. Big bad wolf.

Paul's Ford Taurus groaned when he accelerated on I-75-southbound, and a truck blasted its horn as it slid past. We kept the air conditioning on full, but my T-shirt and jeans were wet with sweat. Paul didn't sweat, though he was a big man, three hundred fifty pounds, which he carried mostly in his chest and thighs. He leaned over the steering wheel, his forehead close to the windshield, and asked, 'What will you say to your sister and brother?'

I said, 'How about, *Once upon a time . . .*'

'That's it,' he said. 'Keep it simple. Don't freak them out. Make it traditional. Nice and clean.'

'Nothing's clean,' I said. 'It never was.'

'Pretend it is,' Paul said. 'Pretend it *was*. Just pretend. Every word is good if it takes you where you're going. Let your story be that you're a stranger.'

Paul was tall too, so tall his knees rubbed the dashboard and his hair buffed the inside roof. 'Tell the story straight and they'll get it,' he said.

'It's not a straight story,' I said.

'Didn't say it was. I said, *tell* it straight.'

'I don't know,' I said.

I'd met Paul at a bookstore in East Atlanta Village. I was there with my girlfriend Carol when Paul walked in. Carol said, 'If I ever want to do it with a giant, that's the giant I want to do it with,' and I said, 'Thanks a lot,' and she said, 'Did I say I want to do it with a giant?' and I said, 'Just the same.'

He went to fiction and picked up William Faulkner's *Sanctuary*.

I asked, 'Is he really that good-looking?' and Carol said, 'Uh-huh.' She went and stood by him and said, 'That's a nasty book,' and he said, 'I know, so I'm doing the world a favor,' and slipped it into his pocket without paying. Not to be outdone, I held my hand for him to shake and said, 'My name's Oren.' His hand swallowed mine and he grinned the biggest grin, because

2

when he wasn't driving around in his Taurus or training security dogs, which is how he made his living, he was smiling the sweetest smiles – the kind of smiles that would make the neighbors say afterward, *He was good at heart.*

'Paul,' he said. 'My name is Paul.'

And it was all downhill from there.

Was this trip to Black Hammock Island his idea? Not strictly speaking. Strictly speaking, it was my idea. But he encouraged it. Encouraged, conspired, and weaponized. He had a hand in it – two hands, the giant hands of a man the Greeks would have called a god and the Romans would have thrown into a ring with lions. Old story.

The July sun shined high and hard over I-75-southbound. It bleached the pavement. It flaked the green paint on Paul's hood. It sparkled off the roofs of other cars, turning them into a thousand wandering stars. Dogwoods and hollies and sourwoods and scrub oaks hunched on the sagging highway shoulders, their leaves spangling. Kudzu draped a stand of deadwood like sheets on furniture in an old house after the owners are dead.

'What?' Paul looked at me sidelong.

I must have been staring at him. 'You could hit the gas,' I said.

'I thought you wanted to do this slow,' he said.

'There's slow and there's backwards.'

'We don't want to lose the others,' he said.

The others. Carol drove behind us in her jacked-up yellow Silverado pickup. Three of Paul's German shepherds – Cereb, Stretcher, and Flip – rode in

3

crates in the truck bed. In the cargo box mounted between the dog crates and the truck cab were the guns, big and small. Seventeen of them to go against the forty or fifty that my mother and her husband Walter took from my dad. Behind Carol, Jimmy drove his red Tacoma pickup with a red BMW F800 motorcycle strapped on – the F800 because it rode well on pavement and great in the dirt. In *his* cargo box were jugs of gasoline, fireworks that Jimmy had bought in South Carolina, and a stick of dynamite that Paul had found wherever he found such things. Behind Jimmy, Robert rode a Honda NC700 because cabins and insides gave him the shakes.

'What's the plan when we get to the island?' Paul asked.

He knew the plan. He'd helped make it.

'What's the plan?' he asked again.

He'd had me repeat it a hundred times. 'I'm not saying it again,' I said.

He gave me the sidelong look. His eyes belonged in a baby seal, not a six-foot-eight, three-hundred-fifty-pound gladiator. His eyes made women think they might like to do it with him.

'Speed up, will you?' I asked.

He eased his foot off the pedal. We hung in the right lane with Carol and Jimmy and Robert drifting along behind us, the German shepherds barking because they could.

I said, 'If a golf cart comes on to the highway, slide to the side so it can pass, all right?'

He eased the gas again.

I said, 'The plan is set them up, make them dance, and knock them down.'

'That's not the plan,' he said. 'That's an outline.

4

Not even an outline – it's an outline of the outline.'

'I know the plan,' I said.

'Tell it to me again. Reassure me.'

'I'm not telling it to you again,' I said.

'It's theater, you understand?'

'It's not theater,' I said. 'It's war.'

'It's a theater of war,' he said. 'It's a goddamned five-act play. If you forget your words – if you step left when you should step right – they'll kill you. Tell me the plan.'

I told him the plan. I'd gotten to the point where we would have basically ended my mother's painting career, wrecking the self-portraits that had given her a name beyond Black Hammock Island, and we would have her and Walter locked and helpless inside their own house. We would have taken or destroyed their guns. We would have their yardman Tilson working with us. We would have their neighbor Lane Charles too.

Then Robert opened the throttle on the Honda, cut into the center lane, raced up alongside, and stared into the puttering Taurus, as if to say, *What the hell?* I kept telling the plan, and Paul kept his eyes on the road, but he gave the car enough gas to take it to the speed limit, and Robert dropped back.

'The end,' I said, when I finished the plan.

'The end is the beginning,' Paul said.

'Like a circle,' I said.

'Nothing like a circle,' he said. 'But like a revolution.' Paul was smart too. He was as smart as he was big. For a man who looked like a gladiator, he was psychologically astute.

5

I agreed with him, more or less. 'Like a circular revolution.'

Then my phone rang. Caller ID said, *Mercer School of Medicine*. If I had answered, the caller, a bird-voiced woman, would have asked – again – *Where's our shipment?*

I would have said, *It went out this morning. I'm terribly sorry for the delay.*

She would have said, *Anatomy begins in two weeks. We need prep-and-process time.*

I would have said, *Of course you do. Look out your window. The trucks are coming.*

She would have said, *Next session, we'll be looking for a new supplier.*

I let the call ring through to voicemail, which said, *We're currently out of the office. Please leave a message.* It wasn't that I was uncaring. I'd been preoccupied.

We drove past the city of Forsyth, dropped into an area of farmland and back into the forest before Macon. Traffic thinned and we shared a stretch of southbound with a refrigerated semi-trailer truck that looked as closed and tight as a black beetle.

When Paul caught me staring at him again, he said, 'You know we'll do anything for you. Anything to make this right.'

'I know,' I said.

'You just ask it,' he said. 'We love you. We all do.'

'You're already doing it,' I said.

We got off the highway at Tifton at two in the afternoon. The signs said, *Visit Historical Tifton*, said, *Visit the 19th-Century Village – Farmhouse!*

Sawmill! School House! Turpentine Still! Grist Mill! said, *Tifton is The Friendly City*. But Tifton was a bunch of roadside businesses with boarded windows – and other places, still kicking, that said, *Speedy Cash, New Fashion, Georgia Auto Pawn, Titlebuck Title Pawn*. A city to pass through, not to visit.

My phone rang again. It was Jimmy and he said, 'Lunch?'

So I called Carol and said, 'Lunch?'

We swung into the Ole Times Country Buffet, a restaurant with blond-wood paneling that looked sickly in the overhead lighting. Carol squeezed between me and Jimmy on one side of the booth because Paul had the other side to himself and Robert borrowed a chair from another table. Carol asked, 'How far to where your dad grew up?'

'Don't know,' I said. 'Maybe an hour.'

She sawed a slice of ham four ways like a tic-tac-toe game and forked the middle square into her mouth. She said, 'I don't get it. We could be on Black Hammock tonight.'

'If you dig up the dead, you've got to do it right,' I said. 'You want to consult with the relatives beforehand or, if that's impossible, at least honor them. It's the right thing to do.'

'It's respectful,' Paul said.

'Oren's always been respectful,' Jimmy said.

'Disrespect is bad karma,' Robert said.

'What goes around comes around,' I said.

The road from Tifton to Waycross passed cotton farms and sugar cane fields, algae-slicked ponds, and half-painted houses with screened-in front porches and open carports. We drove through the

7

cotton and lumber town of Enigma, passed more farms and fields and miles and miles of slash-pine timberland, then rolled through Willacoochee, with an old Lockheed T-33 Shooting Star airplane perched on the roadside in front of the Masonic Lodge. My dad taught me many lessons before my mother and Walter killed him, among them to remember names and places.

Then after another slash-pine forest we came to a neighborhood of red-brick apartment houses and red-brick churches, a Coca-Cola distributor, a bunch of clapboard single-family houses, and a line of automotive shops. A sign said, *Welcome to Waycross*.

I asked Paul, 'You know where you're going?'

'Sure,' he said.

We stopped at Sapp's Florists and drove on to Hazzard Hill Cemetery, which had no hill, no trees either, just a big scorched-grass field that would have been fine for football except for the white stone markers. Carol offered to go with me, but I left her with the others and scuffed across the dead lawn until I found the stones for my grandparents. I pulled half of the daisies and black-eyed Susans from the bouquet and laid them on the grave of my grandfather, deceased December 25, 1968. I said to his stone, 'If you ever cared for your son, and I understand that you did once, then watch over me now because I'm going to get him what's coming to him.' Talking to dead people had never bothered me, and I added an *Amen* because it couldn't hurt. Then I laid the rest of the flowers on the grave of my grandmother, deceased also December 25, 1968, and said, 'You too. Amen.'

When I went back to Carol and the others, Paul said, 'That was quick.'

'It was a one-sided conversation,' I said.

So Paul let the three German shepherds out of the crates and they ran across the cemetery, biting at each other's haunches, lifting their legs on the gravestones. Cereb, Stretcher, and Flip had fallen into the category of *unrentables* at Paul's security company, which meant they attacked business owners more often than protecting them. Other trainers would have put them down, but Paul took them home and called them family. Sometimes they bit him too, though they also came to him as if his low whistle gave them an electric shock. They were vicious and unpredictable, but Paul towered over them and they knew an Alpha when they saw one. After a while he'd taught them to treat Carol and me with vicious respect, if not affection.

Now when Stretcher tore a clump of yellow chrysanthemums from a pot that a mourner had set on a grave, Paul said, 'Come' – almost too softly to be heard – and the three dogs spun, ran back, and raised their hard eyes to him for praise or punishment.

'Those aren't animals,' Robert said. 'They're machines.'

'Careful or they'll eat you,' Paul said, and he crouched and let Flip lick his cheek.

While Jimmy, Robert, and Paul checked in at the Econo Lodge east of downtown Waycross, Carol and I drove to the house where my dad had grown up until he was seventeen and my grandparents died and he left town. The house was one of the

9

few remaining in the historic district, and a law firm had converted it into offices some time ago. It was a big wooden place with a wide front porch and a wide second-floor balcony. Antique gas lamps burned on the sides of the front door, though the sun hung high in the afternoon sky. Roses bloomed in the garden between the front porch and the street.

Carol pulled the truck to the curb and stopped.

'Do you want to go in?' she asked.

From my dad's stories, I knew the pre-conversion layout of the rooms, upstairs and down. I knew the smells – the sugar and fruit of the kitchen, the cigarette smoke in the den where my grandfather paid bills, the rankness of the bathroom where water sometimes backed up through the plumbing. I knew the bedroom upstairs in the back, where my dad slept and where he shelved the books he had bought in the order in which he had read them, as if the line of books was a timeline matching the years of his own life, and where he also kept an empty silver box that his mother had given him on his fifteenth birthday. I knew my grandparents' bedroom, where they slept in side-by-side beds, and the yellowing Chinese screen that my grandmother set between the foot of her bed and the bedroom door. I knew that a middle step on the stairway to the second floor sagged when one stepped on it. I knew that the banister wiggled at the top where a bracket had come loose. I knew the house as my dad had described it, but while the outside structure still stood and roses still bloomed in the front garden, my grandparents had been dead for many years and even

10

their ghosts would be painted back into the walls or gone altogether.

'Let's go to the motel,' I said.

'Are you sure you want to go through with this?' Carol asked.

I said, 'Don't I seem sure?'

'You seem sad,' she said.

'No,' I said. 'Not sad.'

'Then what?'

'I guess I'm just lonely,' I said. 'I can go into an art gallery and see my mother's paintings of herself, and even though she's hundreds of miles away, she seems more real to me than I do. I thought that coming to this house, I would see something of myself. I don't. This place is nothing to me. I'm nothing to it.'

'That gives you a kind of freedom,' Carol said.

'Does it?' I asked.

Carol had said she would do anything for me. Paul too. They loved me, they said. And Jimmy and Robert owed me. I had lied to save them from the police – as their mom had broken all the rules to save me. Jimmy and Robert had been screwing around up on the Beasley Knob mountain trails, riding their dirt bikes drunk and coked-up, which was a bad idea even on the open road, much less on rocks, ruts, and tire gullies. I was taking photos as they came up Blue Rock Trail and launched into the air over a dirt lip, doing no-footers, fender grabs, and whips, while Jimmy's wife Diana, who should have been used to this kind of thing, kept calling him a *fucking idiot* and telling him he was going to *break his*

11

fucking neck and she didn't want to be a *fucking widow*. Finally, he got *fucking sick* of it, threw his helmet into the trees, brought his dirt bike beside her, and said, 'Get on.'

'I'm not getting on that bike with you,' she said. She'd spent a year on the women's motocross circuit and knew when the drop got bigger than the rise.

'One ride, baby,' he said.

She said she wasn't a *fucking baby* or a *fucking fool* either.

He whispered something to her. I don't know what it was – he never would tell – but she climbed on the back of his bike with a laugh and threw her head back so her hair fell on her shoulders. He hollered, 'Fuck, yeah,' and gave the bike gas. They rode halfway up the path doing a wheelie, dropped to two wheels, accelerated, and shot over the dirt lip.

Why Jimmy decided to try a no-hander with Diana on the bike behind him, I can't say.

Why Robert, who'd been sitting on his bike above the jump, chose that moment to race down the trail, cutting off Jimmy's landing, I don't know either.

But, flying through the air, Jimmy's bike pitched forward.

He grabbed at the handlebars.

He threw his weight backward.

He did everything an experienced freestyle biker can do to pull out of a crash.

But Diana launched into the sky over him and the expression on her face was *I fucking knew it*.

She landed headfirst on a boulder.

And that was that.

When the Blairsville police arrived, Jimmy was cradling Diana's bloody body in his lap. If I had said what really happened and then the police had done toxicology, Jimmy would have faced manslaughter at the very least, and maybe Robert too. With their prior records, that could have meant fifteen years.

How much was my made-up story worth to Jimmy and Robert? My story of Diana riding over the dirt lip *alone* on the dirt bike, the sun glinting on the metal, the sun catching in her eyes, disorienting her, seeming to melt the dirt bike out from under her.

'It was nothing,' I said, after her funeral.

'It was everything,' Robert said.

'We'll do anything for you,' Jimmy said. 'We love you like a brother.'

'*Anything*,' Robert said.

I said, 'Well, now that you mention it.'

They owed me their lives, and so they asked, 'When do we go?'

The truth was, though, I would have lied for them no matter what – would have done anything for *them* too. Their mom had taken me in during the worst days. When my family thought I was dead and gone, buried in the woods behind their house, Jimmy and Robert treated me like one of their own.

After we ate dinner at Ranchero's Fresh Grill, we went to the Econo Lodge, and while Jimmy and Robert got high behind the motel, and Paul flirted with the Dominican woman who was pushing a cart of towels down the breezeway,

13

Carol took my hand and led me into our room. She pulled the shades and said, 'Get in bed.'

I stripped to my boxers and climbed under the sheet. But she didn't come to me, not right away. She went into the bathroom and turned on the shower. I waited, alone, which was part of the game she liked to play when I was feeling sorry for myself and she knew she could make my world gleam, and when she came back out naked, her pale skin shined with water and her wet black hair rained on her neck and shoulders. She said, 'You should never feel lonely when I'm with you.'

She was almost pretty. Something wasn't quite right with her face, something in the eyes and the nose. But I loved that not-quite-right something more than the rest of her. In Atlanta, she acted in training videos and, in good months, TV commercials that aired in the metro area. In the safety video that they showed to new MARTA drivers, she pretended to trip in the bus aisle and break her arm. Wearing a red uniform, she demonstrated how to empty a deep fryer into a grease trap in the video watched by every fry girl and fry boy who worked at the Big Buster Burger restaurants. But when we went out on a date, the people who recognized her knew her as the *Whee-Girl* from a commercial she did for Norm Thomas Toyota, in which, wearing a black bikini and red high heels, she slid down the windshield of a Camry, squealing, *Wheeeeeeee*.

I had met her at a video shoot for Emory University Medical School. They'd called me in because they needed a cadaver – middle-aged male, no evidence of external trauma – and that's

14

what *I* did for work – that and supplying live-transplant organs. They called in Carol because they needed an almost-pretty actress who could pretend to be a first-year med student queasy at the sight of a dead middle-aged male.

Now in the yellow glow of the motel room lamps she came to the bed, pulled back the sheet, and put her hand in my shorts. I reached for her damp skin, but she said, 'Don't move.'

So she pulled off my shorts and mounted me. Her face looked pained and happy, her neck flushing pink. I reached again, and again she said, 'Don't.'

She rose and fell, cupping her breasts in her hands as if she was in a movie, and made a sound that was more engine than human. She closed her eyes. Then she screamed, as she liked to do, a thread of drool stringing between her lips, and collapsed on my chest.

'Can I move now?' I asked.

She pulled herself from me and got on to her hands and knees, her ass facing me. 'Go for it,' she said.

Afterward, as we lay in bed with the lights out, she said, 'Tell me about the place again.'

The room was hot, even though the air conditioner buzzed. 'It's an island, is all,' I said.

She said, 'An island paradise.'

'You know it's not like that,' I said.

'It could be,' she said. 'I can picture you as a little kid running naked on the sand.'

'It's not like that,' I said.

With her finger, she drew a line down my sweaty chest. 'It can be. It'll be whatever we make it.'

15

'Not this place,' I said. 'It's about as forsaken as you'll ever see.'

'Then why are we going?' It was a tired question, with a tired anger. She was sick of being the *Whee-Girl* and wanted some place better.

'You know why I'm going,' I said. 'It's not a choice.'

'It's all a choice,' she said. 'We can turn back.'

'*You* can turn back,' I said. '*I* can't.'

She leaned over and kissed my nipple in the dark. 'Then we'll make it a paradise.'

I closed my eyes and tried not to dream the old dream of myself when I was eight years old, hugging my dad's dead body, swimming in my own hot tears and his hot blood. I had dreamed that dream so many times that it no longer felt like a nightmare – the blood, the tears, the hot night as Tilson carried me out of the house on Black Hammock Island into the dark where I should have died but instead lived. The dream felt like a video of my life, and the fear that I felt was *another's* fear – the fear of an actor who was playing me – as much as my own. The hole-like loss that I felt was real *and* unreal, so familiar that I could look at it as in a mirror and study it from different angles like a wound that existed more in cold reflection than on my own hot skin.

A knock on the motel room door woke me. The lamp was burning on the night table. Carol was already sitting on the side of the bed, pulling on her pants. She looked at me, one eyebrow raised. 'You were yelling in your sleep again,' she said.

'Sorry,' I said.

16

Another knock on the door. Paul, standing outside in the dark, said, 'Time to go.'

'What time *is* it?' I asked Carol.

'Time to go,' she said, as if Paul was an oracle and all she could do was repeat after him.

'Should we worry about his power over us?' I asked.

'Huh?' she said.

The night was hot, and sweat slicked my hands and neck as I climbed into the passenger side of Paul's Taurus. 'Why do we need to leave in the middle of the night?' I asked him.

'I was restless,' he said. 'Couldn't sleep.'

So we drove east out of Waycross, Carol in her Silverado – the German shepherds sleeping in the back – Jimmy in his Tacoma, Robert on his motorcycle. Through the windshield, the night under the back-road tree cover was so dark it seemed a mist hung in the air. We drove with the air conditioning on as if it could ease the heat that rose inside us.

An hour later, we arrived in the little oceanside city of Brunswick. It was three in the morning, but we crossed the causeway to St Simons Island, parked where the pavement disappeared under a layer of fine white sand, and ran on to the beach. A half-moon floated in the western sky, and the light played on the white of the waves as they broke and foamed and rushed. A hot night-breeze picked up the ocean spray and laid its stinging salt on our skin.

Carol whooped happily.

'Shut up,' Robert said, as if he was afraid the

17

neighbors would call the police and then the police would find our load of weapons and explosives, and then what would we do?

But the rushing water hushed Carol's voice, sucking the edges off the noise, and all that remained was as chiming as night-birds. So she whooped some more and jumped and did a cartwheel on the sand where it turned hard from a receding wave, and she ran into the ocean with her pants and T-shirt on and dove into the black water. Then we all were tumbling and swimming, licking the salt off our lips as we came up from the Atlantic for a breath of air.

After some time, we crawled out and lay on the beach, watching the sky as the moon and the stars clocked to the west and the hot breeze dried our salty skin.

'If this is forsaken, I can handle it,' Carol said.

When the sun rose, we drove back across the causeway and ate breakfast at a Denny's, then found a business called Hot Weld Auto and Truck and bought a roll-bar kit, which they promised to install on Carol's truck by noon, and a set of high-powered flood lights, which they would hook to the roll bar. Jimmy and Paul drove to a Lowe's and came back with a portable generator – 5,500 running-watts, enough to power the floodlights and anything else we might think of.

Then Jimmy unstrapped his motorcycle from the bed of his Tacoma, and he and Robert rode off looking for whatever trouble they could find at ten in the morning, and Paul went into the Hot Weld front office, with its oil and metal smells, to pass time with the counterwoman. So Carol and I walked to a picnic table on the side of the building that had morning shade. Traffic hummed on the street, and inside the garage a metal saw sang as the blade touched steel. But the air smelled of the ocean and of trees and flowers that grew near the ocean and of the rivers and muddy swamps that surrounded the city on two sides out of three – smells that reminded me of the island where I'd lived my first eight years and where I'd known the love of my dad, who had died and had taken part of me with him.

I must have looked sad again, because Carol said, 'We can still turn back. You don't need to do this.'

'Yeah, I do,' I said. 'I've always needed to.'

She watched me for a while.

'But *you* don't need to,' I said. 'And Paul and Jimmy and Robert. You still can turn around.'

'We're with you all the way,' she said.

'Why?' I asked.

She put a hand on my thigh, and she had the thinnest, strongest fingers. 'I'll go wherever you go.' She laughed. 'Up to a point.'

'This goes beyond that point,' I said.

'Let me decide that,' she said.

'And Paul?' I asked.

She said, 'He's always up for a bash.'

But I knew what kind of bash this would be. I had been gone for eighteen years, but Tilson had visited me in Atlanta and had sent messages about my family on Black Hammock Island, and he had always ended by saying, *Stay away, boy, stay away*. I'd also gotten a single note from our Black Hammock Island neighbor, Lane Charles, an old

19

civil rights fighter and journalist who reminded me of Paul, taking on battles that weren't his own. He'd once written a book called *Rough Justice* that said violence is justified in honorable battles. In the note he'd sent me, he had typed six words on a three-by-five card – *When are you coming home, child?* – and he had sealed the card in an envelope and given the envelope to Tilson, who, he suspected, knew what had become of me. I took those six words also to mean that life on the island was as bad as Tilson said it was and that Lane Charles would stand by me, as he'd stood by others in battles bigger than mine.

We drove south from Brunswick early in the afternoon, crossed the Georgia–Florida border, and hit the gas, speeding into the rising heat. As we crossed over marshes and winding rivers, thunderclouds started to stack in the western sky as they often did on July afternoons in this part of the South, but no wind blew and the sun shimmered on the pavement of the Interstate. When we saw signs advertising motels, we left the highway and got rooms for Carol, Jimmy, and Robert at a Red Roof Inn.

I went in with Carol, and I showered and changed into my white dress shirt and my blue suit pants and jacket. I pulled on my socks, put on my black dress shoes, and used a rag to make them shine. I tucked a white handkerchief into the suit pocket.

'The outfit will make a difference?' Carol asked.

I said, 'It's a matter of respect.'

'But you're going to kill them,' she said.

'Not right away,' I said. 'And anyway I always show respect for the dead.'

I had never seen Carol cry, and she didn't as I left, but she stood at the motel room door, skinny and black-haired and almost pretty, and said, 'Stay safe.'

'I'll try,' I said, though in *Rough Justice* – which I had read and reread in Atlanta, trying to touch anything from home – Lane Charles said he thought safety was overrated. He thought people should throw themselves back into a fight even years after someone hurts them. He wrote, *Justice delayed isn't justice denied. It might be a bastard cousin to a left hook while both men are still standing in the ring, but sometimes you need to heal after you take a blow. If a punch knocks you out or cracks your jaw, you've got to stop seeing double and get the dental work. Then you can climb back into the ring and break your opponent's neck.*

'See you soon,' I said, and kissed Carol, and then the wind that comes before afternoon thunderstorms in this part of the South blew across the parking lot, raising a plume of hot dust, and the first thick drops of rain darkened the concrete.

Paul and I drove out through the rain toward the ocean, weaving through backstreets past subdivisions of little bare houses and then factories and then nothing at all until we reached Sawpit Road, which ran alongside Clapboard Creek and took us through a stretch of timberland with scrub pine trees growing in rows as neat as field corn.

When the creek hooked east toward the ocean

and the timberland stopped as suddenly as if some god had used a knife on it, we drove out of the rain on to dry pavement, though clouds were chasing us from the west and the sunshine seemed like a mean lie.

We came to the old bridge to Black Hammock Island, and Paul slowed the car and looked at me. 'You ready?' he asked.

I just kept my eyes on the road, which had changed hardly at all in my years away.

As we crossed the bridge, Paul said, 'You're breathing hard.'

'Nope,' I said, 'just breathing.'

'They won't know you,' he said. 'They can't. You were only eight—'

'I know,' I said, 'but—'

'You're dead to them,' he said. 'You look nothing like—'

'If they recognize me, I don't know that I'll be able to go through with it,' I said.

'You're a good man,' he said.

'I don't think so,' I said.

'A good man,' he said. 'An honorable man. This is an honorable thing for you to do. For you. And for your sister and brother.'

'Fine,' I said.

'So take it easy,' he said.

'I'm glad to be back is all,' I said.

'Remember, when the curtain goes up, they deserve everything you give them,' he said. 'I wouldn't be here with you if they didn't.'

We drove for a mile past marshes, mudflats, weather-beaten trees, and dry ditches. Then we came to the driveway. A padlocked gate stretched across it, and a hill – a dune of sand that had blown across the island thousands of years ago and then had sunk and hardened into a soil almost as thick as clay – rose between the gate and the house.

'You sure about this?' Paul asked.

'I've been coming this way for a long time,' I said.

'What are you going to tell your sister and brother?' he asked.

Lexi had been about a year old when I last saw her, Cristofer a newborn. She would be nineteen now, he eighteen. We'd grown up without each other. What could I tell them that would make sense? I said to Paul, 'I'll tell them that once upon a time an eight-year-old boy jumped from the top of a pine tree. He made no sound as he fell past the first thin branches. He made no sound as he fell past the thickening and past old nests and fire scars. He made no sound as he cut the difference between himself and the dirt – ten feet to five, four to two. When an inch remained between him and the ground – a half-inch, a quarter – the people sitting under the tree suspected nothing. Although the boy had fallen a hundred feet or more, no one knew what was coming. Then, in the time between what was and what would be, the world ended in a catastrophe of blood and bones.' I opened the door and asked, 'You think Lexi and Cristofer will like the story?'

'You're hopeless,' Paul said.

'Ha,' I said, and as I got out of the car, the wind that comes before thunderstorms rushed up the road and rain broke from the sky. So I climbed over the gate and walked over the hill and into the yard. Lexi was sitting on the front porch as if she'd been waiting for me for eighteen years.

Two

Lexi

The man came over the hill in the afternoon. Vaulted over the gate. Came over the hill and into the yard. Black clouds stacked in the west. The sky held its breath. Breathed out. The wind whipped over the hill sweeping dust and sand off the dry ground. Rain pocked the ground. The sand and dirt turned into fish scales and then into a brown wash.

Because metaphors are one-way tickets. From here.

Lightning jagged the sky. The yard smelled like salt. Like a first world. If I closed my eyes I could believe it. The man came over the hill and up the driveway. Kicking wet sand and dust.

These things are hard to get a grip on.

But I know this much. Nothing on this island stops for rain.

The man wore blue suit pants and a blue jacket. A white handkerchief poked from his pocket. A cotton-white star. He'd polished his black shoes fine and hard. A beautiful man. I could see that much even through the waves of rain and the tar smoke and the spattering sand and dust.

24

Cristofer bounced on his trampoline in the side yard. Bounced and grunted. Skinny golden-haired angel. Bouncing. Reaching into the sky. All day long. Skipping meals. Rain or wind or sun. Mom painted in her studio shed. Walter washed tar off his hands and arms in the kitchen. As if. Tilson fixed the chicken fence. He'd fixed it a thousand times if one. Lane Charles stood at the side of his cane field. He knew better than to step across the property line. Walter had said he'd shoot him. He sometimes stepped across the line anyway.

I sat on the front porch. Reading 'The Tell-Tale Heart' out of the Bible that I'd cut the middle out of. So I could stick in a paperback book. Because that's what I did when Walter hid my dad's books in the attic and said, *Thou shalt not*. And Mom rolled her eyes but let Walter have his way. As if. But I could cut the middle out of a Bible. And I could climb a ladder to the attic and find Walter's hidey-hole.

I read 'Tell-Tale' from *Great American Stories*. And I stroked my leg under my dress. Higher and higher. Circling higher. Because there was happiness between the rainclouds and the sun and who deserved it if I didn't?

My orgasm and a man coming over the hill. The most exciting events of the day. Of any day. Around here.

So much was unclear until he came. We'd been ghosts. Ghosts in a fog in the night though it was a July afternoon. I know that much. Until the rain came the sun had shined so hot it could burn a hole in a bleached sheet if you left it out too long to dry. It had been a day to run off to the pine woods and sit in the shade. Or to find a porch swing and read a book. A place to escape the stinging hot July and the weed-and-holly smell and the tar smoke and the biting yellow flies.

The man in the blue suit came over the hill. He raised his face to the rain as if he was looking for directions. But if the rain was guiding him it was a cruel rain telling him to walk to our house. He was fine-looking though I couldn't see his eyes. And eyes as they say are the windows.

I took my hand out of my dress. Picked up the Bible. Walter gave it to me because I'd tired him with begging begging begging for my dad's books. Pastels of a shepherd and lambs. Jesus and Mary. The burning bush. Jacob wrestling. It had a red binding and a strap with a heart-shaped lock that held the cover closed even if you chucked it at a wall. Which I'd tried. I kept the key on a leather string around my neck.

I opened the cover and breathed the old-yellow-paper smell of *Great American* Edgar Allan. Closed it and locked the strap. Look at me. I was a girl on a front-porch swing with a Bible on her lap. Church mouse.

The man came to the porch. When he smiled each white tooth was a star in the sky. He took the handkerchief from his pocket and wiped the rain from his forehead. He said, 'Is this where Kay Jakobson lives?'

I gave him my best smile also. It was small change. 'My mom,' I said. 'Who wants to know?'

'An admirer,' he said.

26

'She's old for you,' I said. 'And married. And self-obsessed and not a very nice person.'

'I saw her paintings,' he said.

'You're not the first.'

'In Atlanta,' he said.

'And you came all the way down here to meet her?'

'I want to buy one,' he said. 'If she'll work that way.'

'Sorry to disappoint you,' I said. 'How did you get into the yard?'

He said, 'I climbed over the gate.'

'Bad idea to climb over a gate,' I said.

'I tried to call,' he said.

'No you didn't. I would've answered.'

'I tried—'

'You're a liar.' I said it nicely.

He smiled those teeth at me. 'I would have called if I'd known you would answer,' he said.

'I'm here all the time,' I said.

Three

Oren

When we started planning this trip, I told Paul, 'My mother's family has been on that land since the end of the Civil War. They're beholden to it.'

'*Beholden*?' he said. 'What the hell are you talking about?'

27

'I'm telling you, I need to blow them off that place,' I said, 'or they won't go.'

'Big bad wolf? You could just sneak up and kill them,' he said.

'It's not that easy.' I said. 'They would still be there. Something of them would.'

'Now you're talking about ghosts?' He was impatient with stupidity.

'Something bigger and realer,' I said. 'Something in *me*. If I don't go to war against them and blast them out of that house, they'll never be gone. Not for me.'

'There will be damage,' he said. 'Your sister and brother. Are you willing to live with it?'

'I don't know,' I said. 'Depends on what they're like.'

'You'd better figure that out fast.'

'I need to see what they're made of,' I said. 'Then I'll know.'

'Just don't start believing in ghosts,' he said.

Face-to-face, I said to Lexi, 'I guess this doesn't look like the kind of place I would expect Kay Jakobson to live.'

'I guess not,' Lexi said. She was nineteen but looked younger. Stunted. Did she look like me? Not even at a squint. She looked more like the pictures Kay painted of herself. What did they look like? *ARTFORUM* said, *Kay Jakobson's self-portraits, despite their pure, unforgiving lines, show the same desire that makes people scratch the scabs off their skin and reveal intimate secrets to strangers.* Lexi had the palest skin, but with her dress hiked halfway up one thigh and those

28

blue eyes, she seemed to have something craving that needed to get out.

The house hadn't changed since I'd been gone. It was two stories with just one door because my mother's great-great-great-grandpa thought a backdoor was an extravagance or wanted no one sneaking up behind him or both. When the roof leaked, they painted it with tar from the kiln. They nailed a new layer of shingles over the tar and smeared them with another coat to be sure. In the heat, the tar dripped from the eaves, and brown tears ran down the walls.

'Nice windows,' I said to Lexi.

Lexi put a hand on her bare thigh. 'Mom cleans them with Windex,' she said. 'When tar drips on them, she uses a razor blade.'

I wondered what Walter and my mother had done to her. I said, 'A lot of tar.'

'Yes,' she said.

'Why?' I asked. How much did she belong to this house? How much did she belong to my mother and her husband? Where would she stand when the fighting started?

'Why not?' she said. 'Walter makes it. My mom's husband. Pine tar is the best. Sand pine and slash pine and longleaf and loblolly. That makes the tar that everyone on the island wants when they want tar. Once a man drove from Charlotte to buy some. It's that good. Termites don't like it.'

'Oh,' I said.

'I could talk for hours about tar,' she said.

I couldn't tell if she was playing with me. 'It sounds like it,' I said.

'Everyone in my family can,' she said. 'Except

29

my little brother. He doesn't talk. At all. Did you know you can mix tar into your shampoo if you've got dandruff?'

'I don't have dandruff,' I said.

'I wouldn't think so,' she said. 'You can also disinfect a cut.'

'I didn't know that.'

'I could teach you a thing or two,' she said.

I smiled.

She said, 'You should come up on the porch. Get out of the rain.'

Instead, the screen door opened and Walter came out. He wore blue jeans and held a .22 rifle. Eighteen years had aged him thirty. He'd last seen me when I was a kid and he thought Tilson had killed me, but wouldn't he know me?

'Bad idea to climb over a gate,' Lexi said. 'And when someone lives on an island with only one old bridge, it's a bad idea even to cross that bridge.'

Walter asked, 'Who are you?'

If I went up the porch steps and took his gun, I could shoot him and then hunt down my mother. I said, 'An admirer.'

Walter screwed his face. 'An admirer of what?'

'I want to buy one of Kay Jakobson's paintings,' I said. 'I'm a collector – starting out.'

Walter said, 'You've got money, I suppose?'

'Some,' I said. 'Enough, I hope. For an artist of her kind.'

'What kind is that?' he said.

I stared down his stare. He showed no recognition, no worry. 'She's not for everyone,' I said.

'But she's for you?'

'I like self-portraits,' I said.

30

Then he eyed me as if he might know me. 'You know what,' he said, 'you've come into our yard uninvited. *I* don't like *you*. You can go back out the way you came in. You want a painting, buy it from the gallery.'

Lexi said, 'Walter is a Puritan of sorts. If you can believe that a man who likes nothing more than to screw my mom can be a Puritan. If you can believe that every morning a Puritan would sneak four eggs from our chickens and eat them plain. No salt. No pepper. And leave half a scrambled egg hanging in his beard. But Walter knows what he knows and he holds to it like God has told him it's so.'

Walter said, 'You've got a filthy mouth, girl.'

She looked down at her Bible.

I asked her, 'Will you introduce me to your mother?'

She pointed at the shed across the yard. 'That's her studio.'

'I'm obliged,' I said.

Walter said, 'The boy in the suit is "obliged"?' He pointed his .22 at the sky and fired it. The sound stung the air.

If I tried to take the gun, he would shoot me. I said, 'What's your problem?'

He said, 'I don't like strangers coming through the gate unasked.'

I said, 'There was no bell, no way to let you know I was here.'

Walter laughed. 'You want a doorbell? Where the hell do you think you are?'

'How do visitors let you know they've come?' I asked.

'They don't,' he said. 'That's why we have the

31

gate. That's why there's a lock on the gate. That's why there's a hill between the gate and the house. That's why we live on an island south of nowhere. We don't want visitors.'

I laughed at that.

But Walter chambered another bullet, metal sliding against metal. 'You'll be leaving,' he said.

I thought, *If he kills me now* . . . but I said, 'I've come to see your wife.'

'What makes you think she wants to see *you*?' he asked.

Lexi put the Bible on the floor under the swing and jumped off the porch. 'I'll take you,' she said.

Walter fired into the sky again, but Lexi and I crossed the yard, kicking mud and wet weeds. The stench of tar hung in the air. Tilson stood by the chicken fence and watched us, fear in his eyes, as if I was a ghost of myself. Next door, Lane Charles turned from his field and watched, grinning idiotically.

'What's your name?' Lexi asked me.

It was too soon. I said, 'Call me whatever you want.'

Lexi stopped and looked at me. Did *she* know me? She said, 'I'll call you Edgar Allan.'

Four

Lexi

Walter had built Mom's studio in the shade of a live oak. Spanish moss hung from the branches and lay on the ground and on the shed roof. Mom kept the door and windows shut in the July heat. An oven to bake her paint on the canvas.

I knocked.

'What?' she said. Which sounded like *Go away*. Mom had never learned manners.

I knocked again.

The door opened. *Fleshy* was the word for Mom. Paint flecked her skin and her hair. She smoked a cigarette. Sweat smelled from her body. But when she saw the stranger she pursed her lips. Asked, 'Who are you?'

'An admirer,' he said. 'A great admirer.'

She looked at him. Uneasy. I thought she would slide back into the shed and bolt the door as she sometimes did. But she said, 'You're welcome here.' She stepped into the yard as if she'd been waiting for him forever. The man in the blue suit looked at me like it was all a big joke. He was dangerous. A nameless man. A man of lies. But I didn't care. Didn't care. Didn't care. I *wanted* something. Needed something.

And he was something.

* * *

33

Mom told Walter to put away his gun and bring drinks. The way he looked at her she could have said to stick his hands into the fired-up kiln. But he went to the kitchen. He might argue and look like she'd twisted his balls but he always did what she asked. On his own he might have shot the stranger as easy as he slapped the backs of my legs with a strip of green pinewood. Which he did whenever Mom wasn't watching. As easy as he hit Cristofer when Cristofer got on his nerves. Which was always. But if Mom woke in the night and wanted a glass of milk he all but offered to drive to a farm up-island and squeeze a cow's tit so she could have it fresh. *True love* Mom called it. It smelled to me something like fear.

Now Mom asked the man in the blue suit, 'What do you do for work, Mr . . .?'

'Edgar,' the man said. 'You can call me Edgar.' Wink without a wink at me.

We sat on the front porch. Mom had put on a dress but hadn't wiped her face. 'What do you do for a living, Edgar?' she asked.

The yard was quiet except for the springs screeching on Cristofer's trampoline. Tilson had stopped hammering the chicken fence and disappeared. To get drunk. Or to visit the half-brained woman he called his wife. Though she lived in a different house. And he went to her only when her real husband was out. Whenever Walter nagged at him for disappearing Tilson would put on a pained face. He would point at his belly and say, 'I got stones.'

Edgar Allan looked at me. Looked back at

Mom. He said, 'A hundred years ago people would have called me a Resurrectionist.'

'Huh?' I said.

'That's what they called it,' he said. 'Now I'm a procurement specialist. I find organs for transplants and cadavers for medical study. I work with the dead for a living.'

'What a strange job for a young man,' Mom said.

'No stranger than anything else about him,' I said.

'I wouldn't say it's a calling,' he said to Mom. 'It's a paycheck. Most of my business is cadavers. Medical schools have certain times of the year when they need them. The rest of the year I work on my hobbies.'

'Collecting art?' Mom said.

'Sure,' he said.

I asked, 'Why did people call it Resurrection?'

'For a long time no one regulated it,' he said. 'Resurrectionists stole bodies from the morgue or dug them out of the ground. So they made people rise from the grave. Now we sit in our offices. I want to do something else though.' He said it like an afterthought. 'I want to start a theater.'

Five

Oren

I raised the glass of tea and toasted it. 'To Kay Jakobson.'

She raised her glass and said to Walter, 'Edgar digs up bodies for pay.'

'I'm a procurer,' I said.

Walter slapped a yellow fly that had landed on his neck. 'Drink your tea, buy your painting, and move along,' he said.

'We haven't even started talking, honey,' Kay said.

I said, 'I would like to stay a day or two, if that's all right.' *Act One, Scene One*, Paul called this. I called it *Poking Walter and Kay with a stick*.

'No, that's not all right,' Walter said.

I said, 'I'll pay for room and board. I don't want to put you out.'

Walter said, 'You sure as hell—'

I said to Kay, 'I want to know how you do what you do, and the thoughts that go into your work. For me, it's all about the method.'

She shook her head. 'We really have no room—'

'I'll sleep on a couch,' I said. 'Or here on the porch. I'll be no trouble.'

Walter moved close. I was taller than he was but I knew what he could do. He said, 'My wife said no.'

I put my tea on the floor and pulled a roll of bills from my pocket. I counted eight fifties and tried to give them to him. 'For two nights,' I said.

He looked at the money. 'You would pay four hundred dollars to sleep out on a porch?'

'Or inside on a couch,' I said.

He looked at Kay. She shook her head, but he snatched the bills from my hand. 'One night only,' he said. 'And then you go out the gate and down the road.'

36

I counted another three fifties and handed them to him. 'In case we want more time,' I said. 'If we're done after one night, I'll go, and you can keep the money.'

Walter stared at me as if he knew that I had tricked him. But he couldn't see the angle. He said, 'We'll give you the couch.'

Kay said, 'No, we'll give him Cristofer's room.'

I said, 'I don't want to inconvenience you.'

'You passed that marker a mile back,' Walter said.

'Cristofer can sleep in with us or on the couch,' Kay said. 'If we're putting you up, the least we can do is give you a bed.'

'The boy's room is dirty,' said Walter. 'Holes in the walls.'

I said, 'I'm sure I'll be comfortable.'

'The room smells,' Walter said. 'But the boy can't help it.'

'I'll open a window,' I said.

Walter shook his head. 'The window is nailed shut. And we've put locks on the door – the outside of the door. For his own good. We won't lock them while you're here.'

'I'll be no trouble,' I said, and the time seemed right to cause more trouble. I got my cell phone and started to dial.

'You won't get a signal unless you go out by the bridge,' Lexi said.

So I hung up and put the phone away. I said, 'Can you open the gate so my driver can bring in our things?'

Walter said, '*Our* things?'

37

'His and mine,' I said, like it was obvious. 'You didn't think I walked from Atlanta?'

Kay said, 'We thought you flew – or drove yourself.'

Walter said, '*You* can spend the night. Only you. One night only.'

'He'll sleep on the floor next to the bed,' I said. 'No trouble at all.'

'Send him out by the airport,' said Walter. 'There's motels. You can call him in the morning and he can pick you up.'

'I want to leave as soon as my business is done,' I said.

Open the gate, said the plan. *Then open it wider*.

I said, 'You won't even know he's here.'

'Let him stay,' Lexi said.

Walter turned on her. 'Did we ask you?'

'You never ask me,' she said. Her eyes glinted the way they did when she named me Edgar Allan.

'That's because your opinion isn't worth knowing,' he said.

'Let him stay,' Kay said.

Walter looked at her as if she was betraying him.

'It's just one night,' she said. 'They'll leave tomorrow. Isn't that right, Edgar?'

'If you want us to,' I said.

Walter said to Kay, 'Don't be a fool. You don't know who this man is.'

She said, 'He looks like a boy I used to know.'

I felt a shiver. 'I get that all the time,' I said.

'Shall I open the gate?' Lexi asked.

38

Six

Lexi

The driver was a big man in a little green Ford Taurus. He drove through the gate and waited while I closed it. Reached across the passenger seat and opened the door. Hunched to keep his head from rubbing the roof. His knees fat against the steering wheel. His eyes kind.

'You don't look like a taxi driver,' I said.

Only his lips were thin. 'What do I look like?' he asked.

A blue-eyed monster. 'I haven't decided,' I said.

'Well I'm a driver,' he said.

'How did Edgar Allan find you?' I asked.

'Who?'

I said, 'The man in the suit.'

'Right,' he said. 'I run a service.'

'A car service?'

'Uh-huh,' he said. 'And odds and ends.'

'What's your name?' I asked.

'Paul.'

'Really?' I said. 'What do you call your company?'

'You're a curious one,' he said. We drove up the rise and over the top of the hill. 'I call it *Paul's Car Service*,' he said. 'And the side business is *Paul's Odds and Ends*.'

39

'Right,' I said. 'What kinds of odds and ends?'

He leaned toward the windshield as we came down to the house. 'This and that,' he said. 'Mostly light lifting. Sometimes heavy. Comes and goes. Whatever needs doing.'

I said, 'Have you and Edgar Allan come to hurt us?'

A little laugh came from his big chest. He asked, 'Why would you think that?'

'Mom and her husband have been expecting it for a long time,' I said. 'They don't talk about it. But I can tell. Everything they do.'

'If you think we've come to hurt you, why did you open the gate?' he asked.

'A closed gate will keep you out?' I said. 'Anyway I don't mind if you've come to hurt us.'

'No one's going to hurt you,' he said.

We got out of the car. He took a black overnight bag from the trunk and carried it to the porch.

I said to Mom and Walter, 'This is Paul. He says he comes in peace.'

He grinned at them and went up the steps.

Walter looked scared. Big men did that to him. Mom said, 'I'll show you to the room.' She took the man into the house and said, 'I paint only self-portraits but if I painted others I could imagine painting you.'

Walter stared at Edgar Allan. Then rushed inside and up the stairs after Mom and the driver.

Edgar Allan sat on the porch swing. He patted the seat next to him. 'Join me,' he said.

But I turned and watched Cristofer on the trampoline. He wore blue jeans and two long-sleeved T-shirts and a gray windbreaker and a black wool

40

cap and boots. Though the thermometer had shot past ninety at noon.

Edgar Allan said, 'Sit with me.'

I said, 'Your driver says you won't hurt us.'

'Sit with me,' he said again.

'Should I be afraid?' I asked.

'*You?* No,' he said.

'Liar,' I said. But I sat with him on the swing. The chains that held it to the roof beam were hard with our weight. I kept my feet on the porch floor to keep from rocking.

'I have something to tell you,' he said. 'It's a story of a kind—'

But Mom yelled at Walter inside. Something about Cristofer's bed. Walter ran heavy-footed back down the stairs. He came through the screen door. He charged down the porch steps. He crossed the yard to the tar kiln that my dad built almost thirty years ago. Replacing the one that Mom's father and *his* father had used. It was four old General Electric ovens. Two stacked on top of another two. Bolted together and balanced over cinderblocks. In the middle a metal box collected the hot tar that dripped through holes punched in the ovens.

Walter opened the bottom door and shoveled out the mix of ash and soil and resin. Threw it on a waste pile. He picked up an armful of pine-wood strips from a stack behind the kiln and put it in. He covered the strips with Spanish moss and shoveled soil on to it. He closed the bottom oven and opened the top and crammed dry brush inside. He poured a quart of kerosene on the brush.

'That thing will blow up,' said Edgar Allan.

'It never did yet,' I said.

41

Walter sparked a kitchen match and threw it into one of the upper ovens. The kerosene and fumes roared. A ball of fire shot out and swelled. The fire wrapped around Walter. I never understood how he lived through that. He turned into a shadow that looked more like black smoke or a streak of tar than a man. Then the fire sucked back inside the oven and Walter closed the door. Vents would feed the fire until tar seeped from the pinewood into the box below. The tar would look as sweet as cane syrup but would taste like acid.

I said, 'Walter does that instead of hitting her.'

'Your mother?' Edgar Allan said. 'He lights fires?'

'Or else he hits me,' I said. 'The backs of my legs. And Cristofer. All over. We could show you. He's in love with the kiln.'

'In love?' he said.

'Some nights he doesn't sleep,' I said. 'Mom watches him from her bedroom window.'

'Where's your real dad?' he asked.

'Why?' I asked.

'Never mind,' he said.

'He ran off,' I said. 'When Cristofer and I were babies. That's what Mom says.'

'You don't believe her?' he said.

'I was too young to remember,' I said.

The kiln smoke hung low in the rain.

'Later a policeman used to come,' I said. 'He brought me candy and I would walk him around the yard. I showed him the chickens and the kiln and the woods and he fed me candy. He asked me about Mom and Walter and where my dad had gone. Then he stopped coming. Walter complained to someone.'

42

'What did Walter have to hide?' Edgar Allan asked. Then he picked up my Bible from the floor under the porch swing. He fingered the locked strap. Wiggled it as if to see whether it would break.

'Don't,' I said.

'Sooner or later everyone will stop hiding,' he said.

I tried to take the Bible. He screwed his lips and laid it in my hands.

'Who are you?' I asked.

As if answering for him a chicken screeched in the poultry pen. I knew that sound. I jumped off the porch and ran across the yard. A gray hen I called Goneril was going after one of the whites. Flesh hung from Goneril's bloody beak. She jerked her head back and swallowed the meat. Went after the white again. The white screeched. She had blood on her tail feathers.

I scooped mud from the yard and threw it at them. Goneril kept after the white. I threw more mud. Goneril jerked her head up and strutted away. I climbed into the pen and picked up the white. Cradled her in my arms

Edgar Allan came from the porch. 'What happened?' he asked.

In a bin by the pen we kept a shovel and a jar of vitamin feed and a pail of medicine. I got a can of tar from the pail. I said, 'The gray one's a vent pecker.' I handed the white to him. 'Hold her.'

He tried but the white screeched and fell to the ground. Left a streak of blood on his sleeve. I caught her and brought her to him again. 'Hold her like a baby,' I said. 'Tell her she can trust you.'

He tried and after a while she was calm.

I dipped my finger in the tar and lifted the white's tail feathers. I said, 'She won't like this.' I smeared the tar on her.

She flew up at Edgar Allan's face. She clawed at him as if he was lighting her on fire.

So I put her back in the pen. I said, 'The vent is how they lay their eggs. The gray one pecks the others.'

The white had scratched two pin-lines down Edgar Allan's cheek.

I said, 'She eats them and makes them bleed.'

'You've got to be kidding,' he said.

'Why would I kid about that?' I said. I touched the tar on my finger to each of his scratches. He took my hand in his own. 'Who are you?' I asked.

'It's a long story,' he said. 'You up for it?'

I looked at the yard. Walter worked at the kiln. Cristofer bounced on his trampoline. Mom watched us from Cristofer's window. In the poultry pen Goneril chased the white again. 'Let's finish this,' I said.

'Whatever it takes,' he said.

I caught Goneril and made him hold her while I got a bottle of reserpine from the pail. I drew some into a glass dropper. 'Hold tight,' I said. I took Goneril's head and craned it back and forced her beak open and squeezed a drop into her gullet. 'That'll slow her,' I said. I set her back in the pen. She shot across the dirt after the white. Then she lost interest. She wobbled on her skinny legs. She sat. She closed her eyes.

When Walter took breaks from the kiln he would ride his skiff into the inlets that surround Black

Hammock Island. He would drift down Clapboard Creek and out into the Sound. If red fish were biting we ate red fish. If flounder or sea trout were biting we ate flounder or sea trout. The last time he went fishing nothing was biting so he used a cast net to catch mullet which he brought home and smoked in the smoker. On the night that Edgar Allan came we ate the last of the mullet. By the time that he had cleaned his suit jacket and washed his face and come back downstairs Mom had put the plates and bowls on the table.

Paul and Cristofer were already in their chairs waiting. Most of the time Cristofer looked no one in the eyes but as he ate he couldn't stop watching Edgar Allan.

Mom said, 'You have a new friend.'

Walter said, 'With friends like these.'

When Cristofer wasn't kicking holes in his wall or keening he was gentle enough. But he was hard to know. He smelled. Not like sweat but what comes after it when a person hasn't bathed for months or years. His body had a stench between soil and a dying animal. Sometimes he did jump fully clothed into the seawater on the other side of the road. Afterward he let his jeans and shirts dry on his body and he smelled worse. When Cristofer was little Walter would strip him and soap him while Mom washed the clothes. Afterward he keened so long and loud that we gave up.

But Edgar Allan didn't seem to mind. He put an arm on the back of Cristofer's chair. Which most of the time would have set Cristofer keening. Edgar Allan asked Mom, 'Why do you paint only self-portraits?'

Walter said through a mouthful of rice, 'Stupid question.'

Mom said, 'Painting anyone else would be a lie. Suggesting that I know anyone else well enough to get them right would be.'

'But you know yourself well enough?' Edgar Allan asked.

'No,' she said. 'But at least I'm lying only to myself.'

'When did you start?' he asked.

Walter pried a piece of fish from the skin with his fingernail and put it on his tongue. 'Could we talk about something else?' he said.

'What would you have us discuss, dear?' Mom said.

'How about silence?' Walter said.

So we all ate for a while. Paul the driver pulled the platter of fish toward him. He unloaded half of it on to his plate.

Then Edgar Allan said, 'There's a party game that people in the organ transplant business play – a kind of puzzle. Let's say a man is going to be executed for killing another man and wounding the other man's son. Now let's say that the murdered man's son is suffering because of the wound. Let's say it's the kidneys. And then let's say that the organs of the guilty man are a match for the boy. Should the guilty man be forced to donate his kidneys to the boy for a transplant? Eye for an eye. Kidney for a kidney.'

'Maybe we should stick with art,' Mom said.

So Edgar Allan asked again, 'When did you start painting self-portraits?'

Mom sighed. 'My goodness. That must be nearly twenty-five years ago.'

'Is that when your first husband ran off?' Edgar Allan asked.

'Goddamn it,' Walter said.

Mom stared at Edgar Allan. 'No, it was some time before,' she said.

Edgar Allan ate a bite of green beans. Washed it down with a drink from his glass. 'How long did the court take to let you divorce him?' he asked. 'And how long after that did you remarry?'

Walter pushed his plate back. 'What's that got to do with—'

Edgar Allan said to Mom, 'I'm trying to understand how you do what you do. In the paintings that I've seen, the lines are always clean. The colors are always pure. Maybe you look older in the newer ones though I don't think so. Does nothing from your personal life get through? Or is that part of the lie? And if so how do you live with it? Or is that the illusion?'

Walter held his fork in the air.

'Whoopee,' Paul said.

Then Cristofer started laughing the way he sometimes did when he'd spent a whole day on the trampoline and had found a perfect rhythm. Bounce and grunt and bounce and grunt and bounce and grunt. A rhythm that made him laugh from his chest and his belly and his thighs. A breathless laugh. As if all the holes in his body would open and pour his insides out.

Seven

Oren

Walter shoved his chair from the table and charged outside, down the porch steps, and across the yard to the kiln. I wondered if he would come back with one of my dad's big guns. Kay looked unsure of herself. She got up and climbed the stairs to her bedroom. Paul grinned at me, reached across the table, and helped himself to the rest of the smoked mullet and a plate of tomatoes. 'Christ, this is good,' he said.

I locked eyes with Lexi. She seemed to have stopped breathing.

But when Cristofer's laugh died, she said to him, 'You can feed the chickens tonight. OK?'

He raced from the table and out of the house.

She said, 'He loves the chickens.'

'I see that,' I said.

'But he broke one of their necks,' she said. 'Then he did it again. So most of the time Walter doesn't let him near them.'

'But *viva la revolución*, right?' Paul said.

Lexi stared at him. Paul grinned at her, then ate the rice from the serving bowl. I wiped my brow with my handkerchief.

'What's he mean by that?' Lexi asked me.

I just folded the handkerchief, aligning the edges, and tucked it back into my pocket.

48

Eight

Lexi

That night in bed with the lights out I lifted my nightgown. And stroked my legs high and higher. Circling. Thinking about the man in the blue suit. Edgar Allan. The most beautiful man I'd ever seen. Personally. Asleep in the next bedroom. Or maybe as awake as I was and thinking of me. I thought of him getting out of Cristofer's bed. Leaving Cristofer's room. Entering mine. In the dark my ceiling fan turned and turned and I circled higher and higher.

I spoke his name out loud in the dark. The name we had made for him together. 'Edgar Allan.' If he heard me through the bedroom wall and understood that name as a beckoning. If he got out of Cristofer's bed and came to my room. Who was I to stop him? That question was all it took. A pin prick. A spark of light. A swelling as big and mean as the fireball that rolled from the tar kiln when Walter lit it with a kitchen match.

I fell asleep. Alone. Exhausted. I dreamed that Goneril vent-pecked the white chicken until the white was bloody. The poultry yard was a mess of blood and feathers and innards. The white lying on her side. Her black eyes glassy and unmoving. But then she started laying eggs through her open wound. Dozens and dozens of eggs. Hundreds of eggs. Endless eggs. Filling the yard. Piling on top of each other. Until the heap of them buried the white chicken. But still the eggs came and each one gleamed as bright as a star in the night sky.

Nine

Oren

I lay in the dark in Cristofer's room. On the floor Paul looked like a shadow mountain alive in the night, his big chest rising and falling with his big slow breaths, as if the earth itself was fattening and shrinking.

'Sure you don't want the bed?' I asked.

'I'm getting up as soon as they're asleep,' he said.

The room smelled like a dying animal too weak to leave its cave. *Cristofer can't help it*, Walter had said. I pulled the bed sheet over my face. Kay had changed the covers but the smell was deep – in the mattress, the bedframe too. The walls seemed to breathe it from the holes that Cristofer had kicked through the old plaster. In the afternoon I'd tried shaking the windows open, but, as Walter also had said, they were nailed shut.

'We could break the panes out,' Paul said in the dark. 'Get a breeze through.'

I said, 'Kay shouldn't have let it get this bad.'

'I like the kid, though,' Paul said. 'He's energetic. And' – he gave it some thought – 'honest.'

'Yeah,' I said.

'He deserves better,' Paul said. 'He deserves to have you here.'

'Yeah,' I said again. I made myself breathe in deep and long and slow. Then I breathed out and breathed in again, as big as Paul did, until the rancid smell no longer registered and I no longer tasted the bitter air on my tongue.

'He's a terrific kid,' Paul said.

'Yeah,' I said. 'He is.'

We lay quiet for a while. I didn't remember the silence from when I lived in the house. I remembered wind rushing through the tops of the back-acre pine trees or, on windless nights, insects chiming in the open windows. On stormy nights, the sound of breaking waves would blow across the road and over the hill.

'What about Lexi?' Paul asked.

'I don't know,' I said. 'She says Walter hits her. But I don't know if she . . .'

'Likes it?' Paul said.

'. . . if she's gotten used to it,' I said. 'I don't know if this is what's normal to her or what she'll do when the house starts to shake.'

'She seems to hate Walter,' Paul said. 'That's a start. So tell her your story. See where it takes her.'

A sound came from downstairs. Cristofer was making a noise between a high whining and humming. It was a glad, musical noise.

'He's singing,' Paul said.

We listened for a long time. He sang a word-less song and then sang it again, high and happy. After a while he lost a measure and then started

51

again, as if he was falling asleep and waking, and then the song pitched still higher, and it was the music of a child alone in the dark whining and winding toward slumber.

'It's lovely,' Paul said. He sometimes used words like *lovely*, which made me want to punch him until I realized he was serious.

'Yeah,' I said, 'it is.'

Then Cristofer was quiet.

Paul and I listened, and after some time he sat up and said, 'I'm going out.'

But then downstairs Cristofer laughed – at a joke in the dark or at the dark itself.

So Paul sat on the floor and I lay in the bed until the house became quiet again and stayed quiet.

Then I said, 'What's the plan?'

'Ha,' Paul said.

'You'll check the yard for my dad's guns?' I said.

'Close your eyes and let me worry about it,' he said. 'Big day for you tomorrow.'

'It won't be the last,' I said, and I sat up on the bed. I had no interest in sleeping.

He said, 'If they catch you, it's over.'

He was right. I lowered myself to the mattress. 'Don't get caught,' I said.

Then he was gone.

For a big man, he moved as quietly as a spider.

Ten

Lexi

In the morning our chickens were dead. Walter was first out of the house and he howled like he'd caught fire. I ran downstairs but Cristofer beat me out the door. I knew what would happen. I shouted at him to stop. But his messed-up brain told him to *go go go*. When he got to the poultry pen Walter hit him in the face with his arm. Which stopped him. Knocked him to the ground. His nose and lips bled. He didn't move.

When I got there I kicked Walter.

'Me?' he yelled. He shoved me away and pointed inside the fence.

The chickens were dead. Lying side by side. Goneril by herself. The four pheasant-brown campines in a row. The eight whites. No blood. Their beaks pointed at the hill. The yard smelled only of skunky smoke from yesterday's kiln fire. The sun was coming over the hill. The last damp hung in the morning air. The night had laid dew on the dead birds' feathers.

'A coyote?' I said.

Walter moved as if he would hit me. 'Cristofer fed them last night?' he asked.

'He didn't do this,' I said. I sat on the dirt next

53

to Cristofer. Cleaned the blood from his face with my nightgown.

Walter went into the poultry pen. He picked up Goneril and kneaded her body. Checked for broken ribs. He cupped her head in his hand and rolled it in circles.

'Broken neck?' I asked.

He forced open her beak. Smelled her gullet.

'What happened?' I asked.

He fingered through her feathers. Dropped her on the ground. Picked up the biggest white. Checked her. Dropped her.

Cristofer wiped his bloody nose with his hand and wiped his hand on my knee.

'What happened?' I asked again.

Feed was on the ground from last night. Walter picked it up and smelled it.

'It wasn't Cristofer's fault,' I said.

Walter went to the bin. He got the shovel and threw it into the pen. He looked inside the jar of vitamin feed. He pulled out the medicine pail and said, 'Oh Jesus Christ.'

'What?'

He took out the medicine dropper by the rubber-bulb. The glass tube was shattered.

Cristofer looked at Walter and keened low.

'Cristofer?' I said.

Walter pulled out the bottle of reserpine that I had used to tranquilize Goneril. He unscrewed the cap and turned the bottle upside down. It was empty.

'Oh Cristofer,' I said.

He keened louder.

Walter cocked his head and looked at Cristofer

54

the way you look at something disgusting when you're not sure what it is.

'You don't know that he did it,' I said.

But Walter kicked Cristofer in the ribs. He would have done it again but I grabbed his leg and hugged it until he pushed me away. 'This is insanity,' he said. And went across the yard and into the house.

'It was an accident,' I yelled.

Eleven

Oren

When Lexi brought Cristofer into the kitchen, I was sitting at the table. I had opened all of the downstairs closets but hadn't found my dad's guns. So instead of jamming them and stealing the ammunition, I had cleaned my jacket, put a crease in my pants, and polished my shoes. 'Good morning,' I said.

'No,' Lexi said.

Cristofer let her use a wet towel to wipe the blood from his face.

The chickens hadn't been part of the plan, but Paul was nothing if not an enthusiast.

In the front room, Walter sat on a green leather chair, his feet planted on the floor, his hands gripping the cracked leather on the arms. The chair had once been my dad's, but Walter sat on it as if it was a personal throne.

Kay came downstairs, and I don't know if she'd been watching the chicken pen from her bedroom window, but she went to Walter and kneeled on the floor. She whispered to him words that I couldn't hear, and after a while the anger fell from his face. He ran his fingers through her long hair, and she laughed and then he laughed too, a loving laugh that carved a space around them and excluded everyone else.

Lexi looked at the hem of her nightgown and Cristofer's blood on it. She looked at me. 'No breakfast this morning,' she said, then asked, 'Where's your driver?'

'He went for a walk in the woods,' I said.

'I didn't see him go,' she said.

'He was out before the sun came up.'

'The two of you missed the excitement,' she said. 'Some of it anyway.' She went into the front room and pulled the nightgown off over her head. She balled it up with the bloodstain on the outside, dropped it on Walter's lap, and went upstairs.

'Filthy girl,' Walter shouted after her.

Twelve

Lexi

In the middle of the morning Tilson came and Walter put him to work digging a pit for the chickens. The sweat on his black arms gleamed in the sun.

An ocean breeze blew through the tops of the back-acre pine trees but the hill kept it off the front porch. I sat on the swing with my Bible locked shut on my lap. Poe inside it. And Hawthorne and Charlotte Perkins Gilman and their kind. Their hearts beating fast. As if the Bible was a coffin and I had buried them alive.

Walter loaded an axe and his chainsaw and a can of gas into the wheelbarrow. And pushed it across the yard to the pine woods. Mom and Edgar Allan talked in the front room about lines and palettes and mirrors. I drifted off until Edgar Allan changed the subject.

'Who is this?' he asked.

I knew without seeing that he had picked up the one photo that Mom kept of my dad. It was the only picture in the front room. The only thing at all on the shelves by the fireplace.

'My first husband,' she said. 'Amon.'

She took the picture twenty years ago. My dad was in his forties then. Dressed in jeans and a black-and-red-checkered flannel shirt. Sitting at the dinner table. When I was twelve I stole the picture and put it on my dresser in my bedroom. Mom stole it back and put it on its shelf. She dusted it the same way she cleaned the windows.

Edgar Allan asked, 'If he ran off why do you keep the picture?'

'That's what he looked like when I last saw him,' Mom said. 'I keep it to help me remember what he did to me.'

'Your memory can't do that without it?' he asked.

'Some people's memories harden their

57

experiences,' Mom said. 'Mine has always softened them. I don't want to fall in love with him again even in my memory.'

'But you did love him?' he asked.

'Very much,' she said. 'For a time.'

'What happened?' he asked.

'We should talk of other things,' she said.

They were quiet. In the yard Tilson stripped off his shirt. Each time he sank the shovel into the sandy soil the grit scraped against the metal like a sharpening stone. Out in the pine woods Walter's chainsaw ripped and whined as he touched the blade to a tree.

Then Edgar Allan asked Mom, 'Did you ever hear from him after he left?'

She said, 'He's probably dead by now. I hope.'

'Why do you keep the rest of the shelves empty?' Edgar Allan asked.

She said, 'Does this really have to do with my painting?'

'I think so,' he said. 'You don't have to tell me if you don't want to.'

She said, 'Amon kept his books on them.'

'He took them when he left?' Edgar Allan asked.

'No,' she said. 'Walter didn't like them in the house.'

'What *did* he take when he left?' Edgar Allan asked.

I listened for what Mom would say.

Edgar Allan asked, 'Another woman?' Needling her.

Mom had had enough. 'Let's go see my paintings,' she said.

They came out of the house. Crossed the yard

58

to the studio and went inside. They looked like secret lovers. I itched to chase them across the yard and pound on the door until they let me in. Instead I opened the Bible and took *Great American Stories* from the cut-out. I read 'Tell-Tale' again. Thumbing the rough edges of the Bible pages where I had cut them. When I made the hiding place I had burned the insides in the kiln. The blackened paper had crumbled through the holes in the bottom ovens and into the box where Walter was collecting tar to paint the roof of the house. Now the ashes from Deuteronomy to the Book of John kept us dry when it rained.

Mom and Edgar Allan came out of the studio. She carried two of her paintings and he carried a hammer. They went to the side of the house so I locked the Bible and went to see. Edgar Allan hammered nails into the outside wall. Mom hung paintings on them.

'Why?' I said.

Mom said, 'He wants to see them in natural light.'

They went back to the studio and came out with more paintings.

'You're wrecking the wall,' I said.

'Nonsense,' Mom said.

Edgar Allan pounded nails. Mom went for paintings.

'Why are you doing this?' I asked him.

He said nothing.

I said, 'What's your real name?'

He said, 'Do you know how many paintings she has crammed into that shed?'

'Hundreds,' I said.

59

'Thousands. I want to see how they handle the sunlight.' He stepped back from the wall. 'If they can't take it what good are they?'

Mom came back and handed him two self-portraits. He hung them and they went for more.

Tilson stopped digging. Threw the shovel aside. Watched. Then he went into the poultry pen and picked up a chicken. He looked at it nose-to-beak and threw it over the fence into the pit. He picked up two more and threw them also.

Mom and the man laughed inside the studio. Sharing a secret.

Tilson held one of the white hens. He called to me, 'Miss Lexi.' Beckoned me with a finger.

When I joined him he said, 'Look at this.' He held the white by its neck. Turning its head so that the sun shined in its eyes. He thumbed apart the feathery down. He exposed the rough skin and a little hole which was one of its ears.

'What?' I said.

'Blood,' he said.

I saw nothing.

'Look close,' he said. 'You miss what need seeing if you keep blinking you eyes like a silly girl.'

I looked again and saw it. A prick of blood. As if a sewing needle had gone into the head through the ear. I asked, 'Could reserpine do that?'

'It only one side of the bird,' he said. He turned the chicken and showed me the other ear. '*Every* bird.' He threw the white over the fence into the pit. He picked up another and smoothed the down and showed me.

'I don't know,' I said.

He got mad. 'What don't you know?'

60

'I don't know what happened,' I said.

'I tell you what don't happen,' he said. 'Accident don't happen. These bird die because someone want them dead.'

'Why?' I asked.

'What I look like? I the man that bury the chicken when somebody kill them. Don't ask me why.' He picked up a brown campine. Thumbed the feathery down. Showed me a spot of blood. 'Look.'

'Who then?' I said.

He threw the brown over the fence and nodded to where Mom and Edgar Allan were hanging a painting on the wall. 'You watch out for that boy.'

'Him?' I said. 'Why would he—'

'He don't belong here,' he said. 'I know that. Not now. Not never. Good man don't climb over the gate in middle of the afternoon. No he don't.'

'He came to see Mom's paintings,' I said.

He snorted. 'Stop blinking, silly girl. You got stones in you eyes?' He picked up a chicken by the neck. Carried it out of the pen. Dropped it in the hole. Black flies sprayed from the ground. He said, 'Don't be surprise if when you done sleeping you open you eyes and see you house knock down.'

As I went back to the porch Walter and Paul the driver came side-by-side across the yard from the pine woods. Walter's wheelbarrow full of logs. Paul carrying more. Walter had a bloody gash over the bridge of his nose.

They dumped the wood by the kiln. Paul picked up the axe and started chopping and slashing. Walter looked dazed. So he wandered to the wall where Mom and Edgar Allan were hanging Mom's self-portraits.

61

Mom saw the cut on Walter's face and asked what happened. As if his bleeding annoyed her.

He wouldn't say. He stared at the paintings. Fourteen of them on the wall. 'What the hell?' he said. And said to Edgar Allan, 'You leaving yet?'

Edgar Allan smiled at Mom's portraits. 'We're just getting started,' he said.

Walter started to argue but Mom said, 'Edgar is going to stay one more night.'

When Walter called her a fool Mom said, 'He already paid us. I'm having a good time Walter. For the first time in a long time I'm having a good time.'

Early in the afternoon the first thunderclouds built in the west and Lane Charles came to the screen door. Everyone was inside except Paul the driver who was splitting logs into strips and ribbons and Cristofer who was sitting on the ground watching him. Walter answered the door and Lane Charles pointed his thumb at the poultry pen. 'Couldn't help but notice,' he said.

Walter left the screen closed between them. 'We've got company,' he said. 'Decided to butcher them.'

Lane Charles looked in the screen and saw Edgar Allan. 'Well, goddamn,' he said.

'Goddamn *what*?' Walter said.

But Lane Charles only laughed and said, 'You're eating egg layers? Meat's bad.'

'You ever try it?' Walter asked.

Lane Charles said, 'Can't say I ever wanted to.'

'Don't criticize then,' Walter said.

Lane Charles was eighty years old. His glasses

were dirty where the lenses touched his nose. Long ago he wrote a book and was a big reporter for one of the magazines. In the nineteen sixties he did stories on civil rights and sit-ins. Then outside his apartment building someone shot and killed the photographer he was sleeping with. The police charged *him* and kept him in jail for eight months until they figured out that two brothers had been driving around the country in a Dodge station wagon shooting sympathizers. But jail had broken Lane Charles. More or less. So he quit being a reporter and bought a farm that my grandpa carved out of our family land. Before Edgar Allan came only old civil rights workers crossed the bridge to Black Hammock Island. And young reporters writing *Whatever Happened to Lane Charles?* articles. 'His own damn fault,' Walter said when he told the story. 'Sticking his neck in other people's business.'

Now Lane Charles grinned through the screen at Edgar Allan and put a hand on the door as if he would let himself in. 'You cook your chickens by burying them in the ground?' he asked Walter.

Walter said, 'You should leave well enough alone.' He closed the door over the screen. There was a history of meanness behind his advice. Eighteen years ago Lane Charles had reported my dad missing. He hated the police but my dad was his friend and had been helping him put in pipes when he disappeared. And a missing man was a missing man. The police had come and that one policeman had kept coming back until I was six years old. Talking with Lane Charles.

63

Asking Walter questions. Bringing me candy. Walter never forgave Lane Charles for that.

So Walter sat in his green chair and said, 'The man keeps poking at wasp nests but he's surprised he gets stung.'

Mom looked like she had something to say to that. But thunder roared out over the ocean. Engine noise chasing a faraway jet. And Mom and Edgar Allan ran outside to move Mom's paintings back to the studio before the rain.

Walter glared at me. The nose gash he'd gotten in the pine woods was dark and swollen. He said, 'She thinks hiding them under a roof will save her but it won't.'

Late in the afternoon the sun split through the clouds and an hour later the sky was hard and blue. But rainwater still glistened on the metal fence around the empty poultry pen. And on the old black tar spills by the kiln.

Then the phone rang.

I picked up and the caller said he was a police detective. And, 'We've had a report of a disturbance.'

'Nope,' I said. 'Not here.' Mom and Edgar Allan were talking in the kitchen. Paul the driver was outside on the porch swing. Cristofer was sitting beside him.

The policeman said, 'We need to come and check.'

'I don't think so,' I said. I cupped the phone and told Walter, 'It's the police. They're coming to check on us.'

'Hell no,' he said.

64

I brought the phone back to my mouth. 'Hell no.'

'Is this Lexi Jakobson?' the policeman asked.

I felt the shiver you feel at moments like that. I asked, 'How did you know?'

'I used to come out your way,' he said. 'You were little. It must be fifteen years since I was last here.'

'You brought me candy?'

'Sure.'

'It was thirteen years,' I said.

'Right,' he said. 'Can you let me in? I'll see that nothing is wrong and then I'll be on my way.'

'Walter says no,' I said.

'I don't want to be a pain,' he said. 'But if you don't let me in my lieutenant will wonder what's going on. It would be easier if we just did this.'

'Hold on,' I said. I dropped the phone on Walter's lap.

I don't know what the policeman told him but when Walter hung up he said, 'He's calling from the bridge. Go let him in.'

So I ran up the hill. My dress brushing against my thighs.

A Sheriff's Office car was parked on the road. Windows closed. Engine running. I unlocked the gate and swung it open and the car pulled on to the driveway. The sun bounced off the windshield and blinded me. But when I opened the passenger door I knew him. He was older and heavier. Most of his red hair had fallen out or turned gray. But one side of his mouth curled higher than the other when he smiled and his eyes had a shine to them. Those things don't

65

change except when you die. A badge said his name was Daniel Turner.

I sat next to him and said, 'Did you bring me candy?'

He smiled that smile. 'That would be creepy.'

'Lane Charles called you?' I asked.

He flipped down the sun visor. 'I can't say.'

'Who else?' I said. 'What did he say was happening here?'

'How are your chickens?' he asked.

'You investigate chickens?' I said.

'Not usually.'

'Cristofer didn't do it,' I said.

He took his foot off the gas pedal. Gave me a look.

When he pulled the car next to the front porch Walter came out to the yard. He had picked at the nose gash and made it bloody.

Daniel Turner got out of his car. 'It's been a long time Walter,' he said.

Walter pulled at his beard as if he had spider webs. 'But now you're back,' he said. 'Like a seventeen-year locust.'

Daniel Turner laughed. 'Can't keep me underground forever.' He leaned a little to the left as he stood.

'I see that,' Walter said. He squinted as if the sun was too bright. 'But will you explain something to me? How does a man who's been on the homicide squad for – what is it – eighteen or nineteen years?'

'Twenty this past spring,' Daniel Turner said. And he crossed his hands over his belly.

Walter said, 'How does a man who has twenty

years get sent out on a call for a little disturbance? Killing business must be slow.'

'Business is always too good,' Daniel Turner said. 'But a nine-one-one operator who has been around for a long time – another locust like me – remembered your name and passed it along.'

'Because she thought you would be interested?' Walter said.

'She *knew* I would be,' Daniel Turner said.

Mom and Edgar Allan laughed in the kitchen. The policeman nodded at Paul the driver on the porch swing. 'Who are your guests?' he asked.

Walter said, 'Visitors is all. Is it any of your business?'

'I mean no disrespect Walter,' Daniel Turner said.

'We both know that's a lie,' Walter said. 'You drove through our gate for one reason only and that was disrespect.'

Daniel Turner jingled his keys. 'Everyone's all right here then?' he said. 'Your wife?'

Mom and Edgar Allan laughed again.

'You hear her,' Walter said.

'And Cristofer?' Daniel Turner asked.

'He's never been right,' Walter said. 'But you already knew that.'

'Looks like you've got no problems then,' Daniel Turner said. He walked back to his car. Favoring his left side. But he stared at Walter before getting in. 'The years haven't been good to you Walter,' he said. 'You sound as confused as you ever were.' He frowned at him. 'What happened to your face?'

67

Walter touched the gash and brought away blood. He said, 'I was cutting wood.'

'Looks like you put your face in front of the log,' the policeman said.

Walter said, 'Yep looks like it.'

'No disrespect,' Daniel Turner said.

'Then get off my land,' Walter said.

Daniel Turner got into the car. Started the engine. Rolled down the window. 'Stay well Walter,' he said.

But Walter was already climbing back up the porch steps. He went to the porch swing and glared at Cristofer. Cristofer glared back until Walter lunged at him as if he would bite him. Cristofer keened. Walter laughed. He looked at Daniel Turner. Showing both palms. Like they shared an opinion about Cristofer's idiocy.

Daniel Turner spun his tires in the wet. Slowed to get traction. Gassed the engine again and sped over the hill and out of sight.

'Goddamned fool,' Walter said and went into the house.

Paul the driver said, 'Come on.' And Cristofer puppied after him into the yard. Paul picked up Walter's axe.

When I came back from locking the gate he had given the axe to Cristofer and was teaching him how to split logs. When the axe struck wood Cristofer grunted. Everything else was quiet in the yard. Except for the chopping. And the grunting. And a low buzz by the poultry pen where black flies hovered like they knew there was something good inside the earth.

Thirteen

Oren

When Kay called dinner, Walter was sunk in his green chair as if no enticements of any kind would move him. She started to tell him again but thought better of it. She went out on the porch, called to Cristofer and Paul, and went back to the kitchen.

I had gone out to watch them chopping wood and had pulled Paul aside. 'Were the chickens necessary?' I asked.

'Close your eyes if you can't watch,' he said. 'But let it happen.'

'I'm just asking,' I said.

'Go inside,' he said.

So I went inside.

Now Cristofer, sweaty and grunting, came in with the axe.

Walter said, 'Leave it outside, you fool.'

But Cristofer gripped the axe handle like it was a baseball bat and swung it through the air.

'Goddamn it,' Walter said.

Cristofer's eyes lit up, he raised the axe above his head, and he bull-charged him. He swung the axe at Walter's head. Walter hollered and ducked and the axe handle bounced off the chair back.

Paul came through the door and took the axe

from Cristofer. He carried it back out to the porch and threw it across the yard.

Then Walter went after Cristofer. He cornered him by the bookshelves, seemed to rise up, and said, 'I'll kill you, you goddamned—' He couldn't decide *goddamned* what. Or there was no word for it, he was so mad. He said again, 'I'll kill you.' He might have done it or at least broken him, and Cristofer howled like he knew what was coming. But I moved between them. Paul had said, *Close your eyes. Let it happen.* But I wouldn't let this happen. I said to Walter, 'It was an accident.'

He stared at me, like *Who the hell are you?* He said, 'An accident? The boy tried to kill me.'

'Not very hard,' I said.

Walter said, 'Get out of the way or—' Again he had no word for it.

I grinned at him. Like I'd lost my mind. I said, 'Go ahead. But you won't touch him.'

Maybe he would have tried.

But Paul came in again. His face was red, as if he'd been choking on his own happiness. He grinned at me and asked Walter, 'What do you think of *that*?'

Cristofer looked at him and Paul opened his arms. Cristofer ran across the room and Paul pulled him to his chest, whispering, 'It's all right, it's OK.' Then Paul laughed a roar of a laugh.

Fourteen

Lexi

Most summer nights kids from both sides of the bridge met out on Sawpit Road by the boat ramp. To drink. To get high. To hook up and afterward go for a swim. On a night when Cristofer went axe-crazy I thought the less dreamtime the better. So I waited for the house to get quiet. Then I put on a dress and flip-flops and went downstairs and out.

The moon hung like a hook in the sky. The shadows bruised the ditches and the trees. The night had laid the heat thick on the ground. Sweat slicked down the back of my neck. I wiped it away and licked the salt from my fingers. At the first bend in the road an armadillo stood on the gravel shoulder as if it was afraid of pavement. I ran at it. Scared it back into the grass. I took off my flip-flops and carried them. Grit on my feet.

Four kids were at our meeting spot. On good nights we had as many as ten and our noise would make dogs bark. Martin was leaning against the *Road Narrows* sign. He was a blond-haired kid whose family had moved to Big Talbot Island but who kept coming back. I'd done him once when I was sixteen and sworn *never again*. Which was OK since most nights he didn't seem interested in repeating that catastrophe either. Martin's friend

71

Andy was lying on his back on the roadside. Looking at the stars. A can of Lone Star in his hand. A twelve pack at his feet. He was twenty and drunk most of the time. Sooner or later it might happen between us but not tonight. The Hendricks sisters were there. Saying over and over that they wished they had weed. Was Martin sure he had none? He was sure. He said over and over.

A cell phone rang. The Hendricks sisters jumped. You couldn't get a signal on the island except by the bridge. Even at the bridge it came and went. Sylvia who was the taller sister answered. Mouthed the name *Eric*. Walked off to talk in private. Andy saw his chance. Brought one of his beers to Kara. They wandered off too. I sat on the gravel where Andy had been lying. Martin sat beside me. He crossed his legs Indian-style. His blond hair hung to his eyes. 'Hey,' he said.

I tried. 'Hey.'

He cupped something inside his palm. Showed me a joint. A magician making a coin. 'Wanna get high?'

'The Hendrickses will hate you,' I said.

He blew the hair out of his eyes. 'I care?'

I said, 'I don't think I'm up to it tonight.'

'What's wrong?' he asked.

I straightened my dress so it came to my knees. 'Cristofer tried to kill Walter again.'

Martin pulled out a Bic. Flared it. Touched it to the end of the joint. Inhaled. Holding the smoke in his lungs he said, 'One day I'm going to get out of here.'

'Buy tickets for two,' I said.

He coughed. 'Why? You like this place.'

72

'I've never known anywhere different,' I said. 'That's not the same as liking it.'

'I don't see you leaving,' he said. And inhaled again.

I said, 'I don't see myself coming back like you when I've moved off island.'

He coughed and looked up at the sky.

So I got up and said, 'I'm going home.' It was a mistake to come.

He coughed again and called after me, 'Hey come back. I didn't mean it.'

'Mean what?' I asked.

I wished this was one of the nights when clouds covered the moon and stars. On those nights I would get so lost I could stumble off the road and into the grass. One night I tripped and fell. When I was lying on the ground an animal could have stood an inch from my face and I never would have seen it. The fear I'd felt had taken me out of the life I lived on the island. It had made me forget Walter and Mom and axes.

I wished this was one of those nights.

I had walked less than a quarter-mile back up the road when I saw Edgar Allan coming. He was talking on a cell phone. Or trying to find a signal. He looked as surprised to see me as I was to see him. He slipped his phone into a pocket.

'We're both out at the secret hour,' he said.

'Is that what you call this?' I said.

'Don't your mother and stepfather think you're home in bed?' he asked.

73

'I figure they aren't thinking about me one way or another,' I said.

He looked up at the moon. 'Some nights I can't sleep,' he said.

'And some nights you want to talk on the phone,' I said.

He lowered his eyes to mine. 'I check in from time to time,' he said. 'You know. The body business.'

'People keep dying?' I said.

'Always.'

'And someone needs to pick up the corpses?' I said.

'My competitors would if I didn't,' he said.

'You usually work at midnight?' I asked.

'You would be surprised,' he said. 'City morgues are open twenty-four hours and some of my best contacts are late-shift managers. They get lonely and need someone to talk to.'

'Uh-huh,' I said. And started walking home again.

'What's wrong?' he asked.

'Nothing. Your being here is making my mom happy,' I said. 'She also likes having someone to talk to.'

He caught up with me. Fell in beside me. He asked, 'Is there anything wrong with that?'

'Talking? No,' I said. 'But flirting?'

He took my arm in his hand. Gently mostly. 'If there's one thing I'm not doing it's flirting.'

I didn't mind him holding my arm. 'Your phone will work better if you go the other way,' I said. He said nothing to that. So I asked, 'You like working with dead people?'

'Most of the time I'm on my computer,' he

said. 'When I'm not on the computer I'm on the phone. People who need something call me and I call other people who have it. I'm a middleman.'

'You keep your hands clean?' I said.

'You're being sarcastic but I don't know why,' he said.

I said, 'She's flirting with you.'

'Is she?'

'You take her seriously,' I said. 'She doesn't get that from us. She likes it. She likes you.'

'The owner of the Atlanta gallery where I saw her paintings takes her seriously,' he said. 'The magazines do.'

He loosened his grip on my arm so I slid my hand into his. And asked, 'Do you ever touch them? The bodies?'

'Others do that part,' he said.

I said, '*I* would. Touch them. I wouldn't mind.'

'Some people don't mind,' he said. 'Others do but then they get used to it.'

'You can get used to anything,' I said.

'Sarcasm again? But it's not true,' he said. 'There's plenty that you can never get used to.'

'I don't think I would need to get used to touching bodies,' I said. 'Not after living in our house. Mom and Walter treat Cristofer and me like we're already dead. I touch myself sometimes and expect my skin to be cold.'

He pulled his hand from mine.

I wanted him to touch me. 'Do you like her more than me?' I asked.

'What? Your mother? No,' he said. 'It's not about liking.'

And I wanted him to laugh with me the way

75

I'd heard him laugh with her. But we walked quietly in the blue-shadowed moonlight. Our hands sometimes brushing. When we got to the gate I said, 'You can kiss me if you want.'

Fifteen

Oren

I took her hand again and said, 'Kissing would be a bad idea.'

She moved close to me. 'Are you sure?'

'Very.'

'Why?'

First: because she was my sister. Second: because I planned to kill our mother and stepfather. Third: because if she sided with them, I would need to kill her too. I said, 'Because I have a girlfriend.' And that was fourth: a girlfriend who was sitting by her phone at the Red Roof Inn, waiting for my call.

'I don't care,' Lexi said, and she tried to kiss me.

I pulled away and started walking back the way we'd come. 'I need to make my call,' I said.

She said, 'I figured you wouldn't kiss me.'

I asked, 'Why did you figure that?'

She said, 'Because you aren't who you seem to be.'

I felt a shiver of fear. 'Who am I then?'

'That's what I'm trying to figure out.'

76

'If I was who I seemed to be, I would kiss you?' I asked.

'Yes,' she said.

'You're smarter than your mother,' I said. *Our* mother – who thought I was dead and couldn't see in me the ghost of the child I'd been.

She said, 'So now we've established that I'm smart and you won't kiss me.'

'Smart can be dangerous,' I said.

'To me or to you?' she asked.

'Yes,' I said.

'Now who's being sarcastic?' she said. 'Tell me who you really are.'

'Tell you my story?' I asked.

'Unless you want to kiss me,' she said.

'It might be more than you can handle,' I said.

'The story or the kiss?' she asked.

'Yes.'

She said, 'I'll risk the story.'

I said, 'Once upon a time—'

'Cut it out,' she said.

I said, 'It's my story.'

'Fine. Tell it.'

'Once upon a time—'

A flashlight beam shined from the top of the hill between the gate and the house, and a man's voice called out, 'Who's there?'

'Damn it,' Lexi said.

The flashlight beam swung toward us. 'Who's there?' the man asked again. It was Tilson.

Lexi stepped toward the gate and said, 'It's me.'

Tilson came down the hill toward the road, the

flashlight shining on the driveway. 'What you do there, Miss Lexi?' he asked. 'Who you with?'

I said to her, 'I need to make my phone call.'

She squeezed my hand. 'Get close to the bridge.'

Tilson opened the gate and shined his light at her face, then mine. 'Who that you with, Miss Lexi?' He held the light on me.

'What are *you* doing here?' Lexi asked him.

'Watching the poultry pen,' he said.

'For what?' Lexi asked. 'All the chickens are dead.'

'Wouldn't a been if I been watching right,' he said. 'Don't want that spreading.' He kept the beam on me until I turned away and walked down the road.

Sixteen

Lexi

Up in my bedroom I kicked off my flip-flops. Unbuttoned my dress and let it fall to the floor. Pulled a chair to the window and sat in the dark with my feet sticking out into the hot night. The sweat on my skin clung to the wooden seat. I wanted to see Edgar Allan when he came back. I wanted to watch him come over the hill and cross the yard and come into the house.

But the night and the heat and the humid air and Cristofer's violence weighed on me and after a while I slept. And dreamed of hot white sand

78

on a hot white beach. Under a hot white sun. The white points on the ocean waves were as bright and hot as pins.

Until voices woke me.

Edgar Allan was talking with Tilson outside my window in the yard by the porch. The moon hung overhead. Tilson had gotten Walter's .22 and held it across his chest. He said, 'I caught you pissing when you was just this high. You come to make trouble you surely do. But I tell Miss Kay—'

Edgar Allan grabbed Tilson's shirt. Threw him against the house. 'You'll tell no one. You'll forget anything you think you know.'

'Take you hands off of me. Goddamn it. I save you life boy. You treat me right. I got stones.'

Edgar Allan threw Tilson down on the ground. And said, 'You've got what?'

'Stones,' Tilson said.

'What the hell are you talking about?' Edgar Allan said.

'Talking about you treating me right,' Tilson said. 'I got stones. In the belly. In the heart.'

'What are you—'

'You put me in water and watch me sink,' Tilson said.

Edgar Allan turned away from him. 'You're crazy,' he said.

'If I crazy it because a long time ago I take a boy that look like you but he ain't got no fancy clothes and he can barely sleep the night without wetting his blanket. I break all the rules with that boy.'

'Shh,' said Edgar Allan. But now he was soft. As if Tilson's words had crushed a bone inside him.

'Yeah?' Tilson asked. Now his voice got quiet too. 'You know about that?'

'Shh,' Edgar Allan said.

'Yeah I do believe you know that boy,' Tilson said.

Then Edgar Allan helped Tilson to his feet. 'Shh,' he said.

'I believe you do,' Tilson said. He sounded happy. 'You don't let us sink. Right? These reasonably good people now. You don't got to hurt nobody. You see what you want to see and then you go away.'

'Shh,' said Edgar Allan. 'Shh.'

Then Tilson pulled Edgar Allan into his arms. And they held each other like that. If they weren't crying I don't know what they were doing. In the moonlight. Holding each other. Then Tilson seemed to force Edgar Allan to his knees. And he put his mouth on Edgar Allan's forehead. His lips touching his skin. For the longest time. Then he said, 'You a good child. I always know it. You a good child.'

I could have yelled.

But I climbed into bed. And was awake. For the longest time.

Why did Tilson and Edgar Allan hold each other like that? How did they know each other? How did Tilson save Edgar Allan's life? Why did he call us good people? Cristofer was good if you didn't mind the keening and the violence. *I* was good some of the time or tried to be. But Mom was seriously questionable. And there was nothing good in Walter except his love for Mom. The rest of him was nasty from his boots to his beard. Why did Edgar Allan throw Tilson against the porch when Tilson said he was bringing trouble? Why did Tilson kiss him?

When I slept I found no answers and dreamed no dreams. No white hot beaches. No touching a stranger's hand or axe blood either.

I opened my eyes again when it was still dark. A dry breathing woke me. A dry heaving. A long breathing and a gasp. I thought my friend Martin had followed me home from the bridge. Climbed into bed with me. Was breathing out a mouthful of smoke. Then I smelled real smoke. Wood smoke. Burning-hair smoke. Smoke from cardboard and old rags and oil. It hung in the air over my bed and bit my throat. I left off the lamp as if the dark would make it a dream. Outside, the moon shined on curling blankets of gray and black. Then the sound of breathing turned into the cracking and hushing of a fire. As if the breathing animal had burst into flames.

I ran to the window. Mom's studio was burning. It looked like the balls of flame that swelled out of the tar kiln when Walter poured in kerosene. The fire spread into the Spanish moss on the branches of the oak. Sparking and flaring. Lighting the living wood of the tree.

I yelled. Like I also was on fire. Like the burning stars of the night were falling into our yard.

Walter and Mom and Paul the driver ran through the hall and down the stairs. Mom went into the yard and ran to the burning shed. Turned away. Ran to it again and away. As if pulled and pushed by the heat. She wore underpants and a bra. Walter

81

caught her and locked her in his arms. She hit and scratched him. Paul the driver went to the bin by the poultry pen. Dumped the medicine from the bucket. Took the bucket inside to the kitchen sink. Carried it to the studio and threw the water on to the fire. The fire drank the water and spat steam back at him. He threw the empty bucket on to it.

In the middle of the fire. Inside the black skeleton of the burning shed. The frames of Mom's paintings crumbled.

Edgar Allan walked downstairs from his room. His footsteps were easy. When he came into the yard his suit looked like he had cleaned and ironed it. The flames danced and gleamed on the toes of his polished shoes. He watched the studio burn and then turned and raised his eyes to me up at my window.

Seventeen

Oren

Kay raked her fingernails down her cheeks as if the blood underneath needed airing. She tried to do it again, but Walter grabbed her hands. 'No' – his voice was hoarse – 'no.' They stood in the yard, their faces grimy and their eyes red from the smoke, because what good would come from going inside the house? What good would come from going *anywhere*? Right now they were lost.

They were nowhere – which was where they belonged.

They wouldn't recognize me now. I knew that. Not until I pulled off my death mask. Smoke in their eyes. Fire in their eyes. Grief. They would see only themselves – lost.

The studio fire had burned inward as if seeking a pure point of light, and now, as the sun rose over the hill, dazzling on the damp haze of the night that had just passed, only a black scar remained on the ground, with a curl of smoke and then a hiss from an ember. The oak branches over the studio had flared, and the charred and blackened wooden stubs looked like deformities.

At the height of the fire, Lane Charles had run across the yard as if he could do anything. 'I called the fire department,' he said, as if *they* could do anything. When the two fire trucks came, all that was left of the studio was a pile of flames, nothing worth putting out. The firemen stood with the rest of us, watching the flames lick at the night, and then they climbed back into their trucks and drove away.

Then Lane Charles pulled me aside. Behind his glasses, his eyes were small and damp. 'This is a hell of a thing,' he said. 'A hell of a way to come home.'

'I read your book,' I said.

'I wrote that when I was a young man,' he said. 'I had sex in my blood.'

'It made sense to me,' I said.

'I see that,' he said. 'But you just burned a lifetime of work.'

I wasn't getting on that ride. I asked, 'Have

you seen Walter with my dad's guns?' Before walking downstairs and into the yard, I had gone into Kay's bedroom. I had looked in the closet and checked under the bed. I had opened the dresser drawers, Walter's and Kay's. I should have been happy when I found nothing, but a wave of fear had passed through me. Why hadn't Walter pulled out a big weapon? Unless he'd put the guns in the attic or hidden them in the pine woods, I didn't know where they could be.

'No guns except that pea shooter,' Lane Charles said. He stared at me with those damp eyes. 'I've come to wonder if there's any honor in vengeance. Maybe you should lance the wound and let it heal.'

I said, '*You* would do that after all they've done?'

'Me personally?' he said. 'I'm talking about you.'

He left then, promising to return later, and Paul came to me. 'Looks like a heavy wind blew through last night,' he said.

I was sweating, though the morning was cool. 'Sure,' I said.

'Looks like it tore your mother out by the roots,' he said.

'It's progress,' I said. I felt light-headed.

'No telling what a woman will do when she gets ripped out like that,' Paul said. 'No telling what Walter might do either.'

'I wouldn't mind having Jimmy and Robert and Carol here right now,' I said.

'Soon enough,' he said.

'Get Cristofer out of here for a while, will you?' I said.

'Right,' he said. 'And Lexi?'

'She stays,' I said. 'She's still undecided.'

Now, in the early sun, Walter put an arm around Kay and led her toward the porch. With tears in her eyes, she told me, 'I don't know *about* you.'

'What's to know?' I said.

'I don't know,' she said.

Walter said to me, 'You can leave.'

I said, 'I'll help clean up.'

'Unnecessary,' he said.

'As you wish,' I said, as if his wishes counted. I went upstairs and came back down with my overnight bag. But Paul was already gone with Cristofer. When I told Walter that my ride was missing, he went into the house, came out again, and called for Paul and Cristofer toward the pine woods. He looked at me as if he knew I had made them disappear. So I said, '*You* could drive me to the airport.'

He looked at Kay. She had raked her fingernails down her face again. He said, 'I've got my hands full.'

'Fine,' I said, and took my bag back upstairs.

When I settled on the porch swing, Lexi sat down next to me with her Bible. 'What did you do?' she whispered.

I took the Bible from her and fingered the locked strap. 'Too many secrets, right?' I said. 'Is it time to reveal everything?' I put a finger between the Bible and the strap and tugged.

'Don't,' she said.

But I tugged again and the strap broke. 'Now I know everything,' I said.

She tried to grab the Bible.

85

'Is it time to pull off the scabs?' I asked. 'Your mother likes to do that. At least she can't help doing it. Is it time to let the skin bleed?'

Lexi said, 'Give me the—'

I held the Bible away from her.

So she hit me in the mouth with the back of her hand. 'Give it back.'

I opened the cover. 'Ahh,' I said.

'It's mine.' She looked like she would cry.

I opened the book – *Great American Stories* – and read, '*As the last crimson tint of the birthmark – that sole token of human imperfection – faded from her cheek, the parting breath of the now perfect woman passed into the atmosphere, and her soul, lingering a moment near her husband, took its heavenward flight.*' I felt light-headed, from the smoke, from sleeplessness, from the wildness of the past night. I slapped the book shut and threw it off the porch.

Lexi jumped into the yard and got the book from the sandy dirt. Its old binding was broken. 'What's wrong with you?' she yelled.

Eighteen

Lexi

Cristofer and Paul the driver were still gone at noon. Edgar Allan walked out to the bridge to use his cell phone. When he came back he sat on the porch swing. Mom was lying on the ground by

86

the charred wood and ash where her studio had been. Dirt streaked her face. She'd scratched her cheeks bloody. Her eyes were red. Her legs were splayed. Tilson had come into the yard to see what he could do but Walter had sent him away. Now Walter was up on the house with a bucket of tar. Painting the roof with a thick slick black coat. As if that would repair the damage done.

Because tar had held the house together for a hundred and fifty years.

It had kept out summer winds and rain. It had warmed against the winter cold. Once it had blunted a pine tree that fell through the front roof in a lightning storm. Mom said it had held out a hurricane that swept over the island when her dad was a boy. Swept over but mostly stayed outside of the tar-sealed walls. Leaked in only through the rag-stuffed cracks between the door and the doorframe.

I answered the phone when the policeman Daniel Turner called again from the bridge. Then I walked over the hill without asking Walter. Daniel Turner drove in. Swung his car close to the porch. Walked over to the black fire scar. He scuffed the ashes with a shoe. A curl of smoke rose. He smelled the air like a hunter or tracker. He looked at Mom. Came back to the house.

He called up to Walter on the roof. 'You weren't going to report this?'

Walter looked at him. Looked at his tar-brush. Looked back at him like he was thinking of throwing tar on him. He said, 'The fire department knew. If they needed to tell you, they would. Is it a crime to burn down a shed?'

'Depends on how it burns,' Daniel Turner said.

'Depends on if it's insured or the paintings are. Depends on if anyone gets hurt.'

Walter said, 'It burned fast and hot. No insurance. No insurance. No one hurt.'

'Who started it?' Daniel Turner asked.

'It's got to be a *who*?' Walter said.

Daniel Turner had sweat on his forehead. The bottom of his neck was pink where the sun or his collar had bothered it. '*What* started it then?' he asked.

Walter pointed the brush at the hill. He said, 'You can let yourself out.'

'I don't know why you won't talk to me,' Daniel Turner said.

'The gate is where it's always been,' Walter said. 'Lock it behind you.' He dipped the brush into the can of tar and started painting the roof again.

Daniel Turner went back to Mom and sat on the ground. Her scratched face was raw. Her eyes seemed to look into her brain. 'Hey,' he said. Kindly. When she didn't answer he asked, 'Did you lose everything?' Still no answer. 'Where is Cristofer?' he asked.

That brought her back from wherever she was hiding. 'Don't blame him,' she said. 'He was sleeping when it started.'

He nodded. But asked, 'Where is he?'

She sank into herself.

'No one would hold him accountable,' he said. 'But if he's a danger . . .'

Nothing.

He stood and wiped the dust and sand off the seat of his pants. He said, 'A big fire for a small building.'

Mom cocked her head like she was just

88

realizing who she was talking to. 'I smoke,' she said. 'I use oil-based paints. I use turpentine.'

'You smoked inside the shed?' Daniel Turner said.

'All the time,' Mom said.

'In the middle of the night?'

'I smoke,' she said.

Walter stood at the peak of the roof. And said, 'Get off the property unless you have a legal reason to be here.'

Daniel Turner said back, 'Where's Cristofer?'

Walter said nothing.

Daniel Turner wiped the sweat off his neck. He went to the porch. 'What did *you* see?' he asked Edgar Allan.

Edgar Allan said, 'Last night?'

Daniel Turner sighed. 'Yes. Last night.'

Edgar Allan seemed to think about it. 'Nothing,' he said. 'I was sleeping. Then the shed caught fire.'

'And you didn't see what made it catch fire?' Daniel Turner asked.

Again he seemed to think. 'No.'

Daniel Turner ran his hand over his scalp. 'You're a bunch of fools,' he said. 'I should leave you to yourselves. You deserve no more.'

'Nothing we would like better,' Walter said.

But Daniel Turner spoke to Edgar Allan. 'What's your name, son?'

'These people call me Edgar Allan,' he said.

'Do they? And what do others call you?'

'Which others?' he asked.

'Don't be smart,' Daniel Turner said. 'What's your legal name?'

Once more he thought. 'I'm not sure I have one,' he said. 'Strictly speaking.'

Daniel Turner spit on the ground. 'You deserve whatever you get,' he said. He went back to his car and drove out over the hill. Kicking up a cloud of sand and dust so thick and yellow it looked like it should rain.

Walter said to me, 'Next time the detective comes you don't let him in the gate. I don't care if I'm dying.'

Nineteen

Oren

Cristofer and Paul were still gone when the afternoon thunderstorms rolled in and dropped wires of lightning into the ocean beyond the road and dunes, scattering the black flies that buzzed above the buried chickens, washing the ashes and soot from Kay's studio into little streams and pools that seeped into the sand. Kay stayed in the yard, a mound of grief in the rainwater, until Walter climbed down from the roof and took her inside. Lexi sat on the porch floor, her broken Bible by her side, watching me as I swung on the porch swing.

She said, 'You never told me your story last night.'

So I said, 'Once upon a time, a little boy disappeared – a little boy named Oren. All the adults asked, *Where is Oren?*'

'Is that your name?' she said.

'Do you want the story or not?' I asked.

'Fine,' she said.

I said, 'The adults searched the house and neighborhood calling for Oren, but he didn't come. It was as if he had become invisible, as if a magician had put him in a box and put the box in a room and turned off the lights and locked the door, and when the others opened the room and shined light in the box, the boy was gone.' I stared at her.

She showed no recognition. 'Go on,' she said.

I said, 'The little boy hadn't really become invisible, though you could turn on every light in the house and inspect the box from every angle using mirrors and probes. The trick was that he no longer was in the box or even the house. He had traveled to—'

'Forget it,' she said.

'You don't like the story?'

She said, 'I don't like how you tell it.'

'Don't blame me,' I said. 'The story tells itself.'

She leaped up.

I said, 'Or I suppose you *could* blame *me* . . .'

But Paul was coming from the pine woods through the heavy rain, carrying Cristofer. Cristofer seemed to be convulsing in Paul's arms. Lexi ran to him and I followed, slipping on the wet ground, the rain slapping our faces. Paul stopped and waited, with Cristofer jerking and flailing against his big body.

Paul was grinning. Cristofer was also – grinning and laughing so hard he made no sound. When Paul saw me, he laughed too and tossed Cristofer into the air and caught him. But when he noticed Lexi's worry, he tried to set Cristofer down.

Cristofer clasped Paul's shoulders and hugged his chest. His eyes were big and bright with rain or happiness or both.

Lexi asked him, 'Are you . . .'

He flailed and laughed in Paul's arms.

Paul said, 'You've got a terrific brother.'

Lexi yelled at him. 'Where have you been?'

Paul held Cristofer close. 'We went walking in the woods,' he said, as if she'd asked an unreasonable question. 'Everything got crazy here with the fire, so I thought we would get out of the way.'

'You were gone almost eight hours,' Lexi said.

'What's the problem?' Paul said. 'We hung out. Your brother told me about the trees and the animals. He knows everything about these woods.'

Lexi looked furious. 'Cristofer *doesn't talk*,' she said. 'He grunts and keens. Sometimes he signs yes or no.'

'Oh,' Paul said, and tossed Cristofer into the air.

Cristofer flailed and laughed a raw laugh. Rainwater flung from his cheeks and his hair.

'Put him down,' Lexi said.

Paul looked as if he might challenge her, but I also said, 'Put him down.' So he whispered something to Cristofer and set him on his feet. Cristofer stared like he knew he was in trouble.

Lexi asked him, 'Did you burn Mom's studio?'

He didn't answer.

'I'll keep Walter from you,' she said, 'but I need to know.'

A low keen came from his throat.

'Do you know who burned it?' she asked.

92

The keen grew louder.

'Leave him alone,' Paul said. 'He didn't do it.' The rain came down hard, splattering our legs with mud.

'*He* needs to let me know,' Lexi said. 'Cristofer' – she went to him and held his wet hands – 'did you or didn't you?'

He made a sound that could have meant anything. Then he pulled his hands from her and ran back toward the woods.

'Now you've done it,' Paul said.

'Go,' I told him, and he ran after Cristofer.

Lexi and I went back to the porch and sat on the swing. The rain was falling in sheets, fogging the air, and Cristofer and Paul disappeared long before they reached the pine woods.

I said, 'Once upon a time, there was a body snatcher.'

Lexi glared at me and said, 'I'm not up for it.'

I watched her and wondered whose side she would take when our mother and Walter started to bleed. She'd been a baby when they killed our dad – too young to remember him. As far as I could tell, she knew nothing of me. I said, 'Did you know that Keith Richards once told an interviewer that he snorted his dead dad's ashes? He mixed them with cocaine. I think it was deeply loving of him in a rock 'n' roll kind of way.'

'Goodbye,' Lexi said, and got up.

'These are the things you learn when you have a job like mine,' I said.

'Maybe it's time to get a new job,' she said.

'Maybe,' I said. 'Did you know that Ted Williams'

son preserved his dad's body? Cryogenics. He froze the old man. Stiff as a baseball bat.'

Lexi went into the house and let the screen door slap shut behind her, but I kept talking in case she was still listening.

'Baseball players use pine tar on their bats,' I said. 'It improves the grip. Ted Williams' son could have saved a few bucks by using pine tar on his dad instead of putting him in the deep freeze. That's more or less how the Egyptians did their mummies. Resin from the Cedar of Lebanon. Smear some on a hall-of-famer and he'll keep for three thousand years.'

Twenty

Lexi

An hour later the rain came hard. I was hungry. For more than food. I checked the cabinets anyway. Checked the refrigerator. Empty almost.

Outside an engine roared. Then hummed. In the rain. Like a song.

I looked out the window. Lane Charles was on his tractor at the side of his cane field.

'Goddamned fool,' Walter said.

Hard to argue.

Lane Charles turned the tractor. Turned it again. Started toward our yard. Ran into a muddy ditch. Could have been drunk.

'What did I say?' Walter said.

The tractor wheels turned in the ditch. Climbed the bank. Slipped. Lane Charles opened the throttle. Mud fountained from the tires. Stuck.

'Ha,' said Walter.

But Edgar Allan left the porch and walked into the rain. Went to Lane Charles and yelled at him something that sounded like rain and more rain. Lane Charles climbed down from the tractor. They walked to his barn together. Came back with a chain.

Lane Charles got on to the tractor and opened the throttle.

Edgar Allan tugged the chain. Shook like he was breaking his back. Edgar Allan in his blue suit. And polished shoes. Up to his ankles in mud.

'Stupid way to do it,' Walter said.

The tractor climbed the bank. Slipped back. Climbed again. Rose from the ditch. The tires gripping the sand and the dirt. Lane Charles hollering and laughing like a drunk man.

'That was nice,' I said when Edgar Allan came inside to dry off.

'That was goddamned foolish,' Walter said.

Twenty-One

Oren

The rain kept falling into the early evening, and when the clouds finally opened and exposed blue sky, Lexi called toward the pine woods for Cristofer to come home. Wedges of evening

95

sunlight glistened on the wet soil and swirled dark oily rainbows in the fresh tar on the roof. An egret flew over the yard. Lexi called for Cristofer again, and the wet land absorbed the sound.

Kay and Walter disappeared into their bedroom and closed the door. I stayed on the porch swing. Lexi went into the house, saying, 'Dinner in ten minutes.'

When I went inside, she had set the table with a loaf of sliced bread, a box of crackers, a stick of butter, a mostly empty package of cheddar, and three apples. She picked up the last of the cheese and put it in her mouth.

I took two slices of bread, buttered them, inserted crackers, and closed the sandwich.

'Sometimes you make do with what there is,' Lexi said.

'My philosophy too,' I said. 'Could be worse.'

She gave me one of the apples. '*I've* had worse,' she said.

'I know,' I said. 'I can tell.'

'Why are you still here?' she asked. 'Mom's paintings are gone. There's nothing for you. You could call for another car or a taxi.'

'I figure I can help,' I said.

'You can't.'

'Besides, I like it here,' I said.

She raised her eyebrows.

'Homey,' I said.

She laughed but asked, 'Did you burn my mom's studio?'

I took another bite. At some point, I would need to start telling the truth. But I said, 'You

96

know better than that. I love her paintings. I was asleep in Cristofer's room.'

'Why did you really come here?' she asked.

I chewed and swallowed. 'Did you know that it's actually illegal to buy and sell bodies – even for medical purposes?' I asked. 'So I charge for postage and handling, which is legal. But there's a black market. A lot of us use it. A few years ago, a guy at UCLA supposedly cut up about eight hundred cadavers with a hacksaw.'

'Please,' she said, and she carried her empty plate to the sink.

Twenty-Two

Lexi

I sat on the porch and waited for Cristofer. The moon edged into the sky. Climbing over the hill. In the yard an ember still glowed where Mom's studio had stood. A cool breeze came. Moths bounced against the screen door. Heat lightning flashed in the sky over the ocean. Tilson walked across the yard. I called to him but he didn't answer. I expected Edgar Allan to join me but he walked out across the yard. Following Tilson.

At midnight I went inside and picked up the phone. The Sheriff's Office operator said Daniel Turner was off duty. She asked if I wanted to leave a message. I said, 'No.' But changed my mind. 'Tell him that Cristofer came home but left again and hasn't returned,' I said. 'Tell him that the ashes are still smoking even though rain fell all afternoon. Tell him that's not a metaphor.' Then I changed my mind again. 'Forget it,' I said. 'Erase all that. Tell him nothing.' I hung up.

When I looked out my window the next morning, Cristofer was sleeping on the spot where Tilson had buried the dead chickens. I pulled on a dress and ran outside. The dead-bird smell seeped up through the sand. Stained the air. Cristofer was lying on the dirt. He'd spread his arms in a hug like he was in love with the earth and all that was inside it. Black flies walked on his face and hands. And churned in the air above him. His skin was covered with bites.

I pulled him away and held him to me. 'Where have you been?' I asked.

He opened his eyes. And grinned.

'Where have you been?' I asked again.

His eyes turned upward.

Clouds grayed the sky. The air was heavy and hot and smelled of rotting death and Mom's burnt studio. No one else was up and out. Next door Lane Charles's windows were dark. His tractor stood beside his cane field. His car was gone from his driveway. In the back acres a haze hung at the edge of the pine woods.

'Where's the driver?' I asked.

Cristofer stared at my forehead.

'Where is Paul?'

He looked at the sky.

So I took him inside to the kitchen. Found a bottle of turpentine that Walter had made from resin. Poured some on a towel. Cleaned Cristofer's broken skin.

He howled and howled.

'Yeah yeah yeah,' I said. 'That's what happens when you sleep with flies.' I dabbed again. He howled again.

Mom came to the kitchen wearing a blue night-gown. The scratches on her face had scabbed. Her hair looked more like shreds than something that belonged on a woman's head. 'What's wrong?' she asked.

I dabbed. 'Cristofer came home,' I said.

'You're waking Walter,' she said.

'Jesus Mom.' I dabbed a bite on Cristofer's chin.

His eyes flamed like he would hit me. I stared him down. He keened.

Mom turned to go back upstairs.

'We're still here,' I shouted. 'We still matter.'

Twenty minutes later Edgar Allan and Paul the driver came downstairs with the overnight bag. Cristofer grinned at Paul. Made a chirping sound. Ran to him. His puppy. Paul hugged him to his big chest. Said, 'Terrific kid.'

'You left him outside all night,' I said.

Paul said, 'This is a problem?' He carried the bag out to the porch. Cristofer behind him.

'You're going?' I asked Edgar Allan.

'We seem to be unwanted here,' he said.

'Right,' I said. 'We've got no breakfast. Just a couple of slices of bread. Sorry this didn't work out.'

He went to the counter. Got a slice from the plastic bag. Bit off a piece. 'It worked in its own way,' he said.

I asked, 'What way is that?'

'Your Mom answered some of my questions,' he said. 'She clarified my understanding.'

'All the paintings burned,' I said.

'There's that.'

'There's no bright side,' I said. 'Not around here.' I picked up the last apple from the counter. Took a bite. Handed the rest to him.

He took a bite also. He said, 'And I got to meet you.'

'And now you're leaving,' I said.

'Right.'

'You could stay,' I said. 'For another day or two.'

'What would Walter say?' he asked.

'Screw Walter,' I said.

He said, 'I've got to get back. Responsibilities. Business.'

'The dead can't wait?'

'They're surprisingly impatient,' he said.

I ran my fingers up my thigh.

He looked pained. 'That would be a very bad idea.'

'Why?' I asked.

'A long story,' he said.

I wanted to go to him. I said, 'You have a lot of stories that you never tell.'

'And you like stories.'

'For a long time they're all I've had,' I said.

He ate the apple. 'Where are the other pictures of your father?' he asked.

'What?'

'Other than the one your Mom keeps on the bookshelf,' he said. 'Did she throw them out?'

'What does that have to do with anything?' I said.

'Where are they?' he asked.

'In the attic,' I said. 'Mom put them in a box.' I'd seen the box when I'd climbed up to get my dad's books.

'You ever look at them?' he asked.

I said, 'What good would it do?' The truth was I was afraid to see them. Afraid of how I would feel when his face looked back at me.

Edgar Allan said, 'It would be doing something. That's all.'

The screen door swung open and Paul the driver and Cristofer came inside. I let my dress drop down on my leg.

Paul showed us his hands. Engine grease on his fingers. 'Car won't start,' he said.

'Can you fix it?' Edgar Allan asked.

'Someone cut the distributor cables and alternator belt. I don't know what else.' Paul looked at me like I might have done it.

I looked at Cristofer. He was staying close to Paul. He could kill chickens and he could light a fire. I didn't think he could cut up a car.

I called up the stairs for Walter and he came down in his tar-stained jeans. Shirtless. Barefoot. His hair and beard mashed. I told him, 'Someone wrecked their car.'

'What the hell,' he said. And he went to see. After he looked at their Taurus he went to his pickup. Sprang the hood. Looked inside. 'Goddamn it,' he said. He went to Mom's car and checked it too. All of the cables and belts and wires were cut. Snipped neat. Taken out. So you couldn't splice the ends together even if you knew how. Walter sucked his lower lip. Then he turned on Edgar Allan. 'You did this?'

Edgar Allan looked shocked. 'Why would I—'

'You come here uninvited,' Walter said. 'You all but break into our house.' Once a fury lit inside of Walter you had to let it die of its own. 'I know your game,' he said. He charged into the house.

'What now?' I asked.

Edgar Allan's face was red. He said, 'Call some tow trucks?'

But Walter came back with his .22. He sat on the porch steps with the gun on his lap. A guard against invisible armies.

'What good will that do?' I asked.

He stared at the cars and the pickup. Their hoods yawning. He looked at me. He looked at Edgar Allan. He chambered a bullet and sighted the rifle on the Taurus and pulled the trigger. A dimple sank into the passenger door. Green paint sprayed into the air.

That kind of thing could lead to blood. But Edgar Allan and Paul laughed. Cristofer looked at them. And laughed too.

Walter glared at Edgar Allan. 'I want you away from this house,' he said.

Edgar Allan grinned at him. 'I want to go,' he said. 'I'm *ready* to. But someone—' He pointed at the Taurus.

'Who?' Walter said. Like Edgar Allan had wrecked the car himself.

'I don't know,' Edgar Allan said. 'Why not *you*?'

Walter pointed the .22 at Edgar Allan's knees. 'Or your wife,' Edgar Allan said. 'She seemed

102

happy with me here until her studio burned. Maybe she doesn't want me to go.'

Walter chambered another bullet. 'You think this is funny?'

Edgar Allan said, 'Yeah. When someone reacts to a little vandalism by shooting a car, I'll laugh.'

Walter swung the gun. Aimed at the Taurus. Pulled the trigger. A crack jagged across the passenger window. He chambered a third bullet and said, 'It isn't funny.'

Edgar Allan said, 'Your neighbor dislikes you. Could he have done it?'

Walter said, 'Lane Charles may be a lot of things and he's got no fear. That's for sure. But he isn't a vandal or an arsonist. All these things happened after you came. I don't like you. And I don't believe you came here because of Kay's paintings.'

'What does your neighbor suspect you of?' Edgar Allan asked.

Walter cocked his head. Like he didn't know what he was looking at. He said, 'There are various kinds of stupid. Stupid ignorant. Stupid foolish. Arrogant stupid. It seems to me that you've cornered all of them.'

'Can I use your phone to call a tow truck?' Paul asked.

Walter turned on him as if he would take him on next. But he said, 'Call for three. And get a taxi for this sonofabitch.'

'I don't get paid unless I take him back to Atlanta,' Paul said.

'Your problem. Not mine,' Walter said. He turned back to Edgar Allan. 'Do what you want. Walk home if you need to. But you aren't staying

103

here another night. I swear to God I'll shoot you if you enter this house.'

In the middle of the morning the tow trucks came. They hooked up the cars and the pickup and drove out over the hill. Then Edgar Allan and Paul walked to the oak tree where Mom's studio had been and they sat in the shade of the trunk. Cristofer climbed on to the trampoline and started bouncing. High and higher. Like he was trying to go up to the sky and touch the stars. He grinned at Paul and laughed and laughed at the stretch and strain of the jumping mat and the screeching and groaning springs.

The clouds thickened and darkened. Mist started to fall. Walter came from the house and put wood in the kiln and fired it. The smell of tar filled the air. When Tilson walked into the yard looking like he'd spent a happy night in the arms of another man's wife Walter swore and sent him away. But as Tilson left he stopped at the oak and talked with Edgar Allan. It was all whispers. Tilson looked angry enough to kill.

Then Mom made a sound inside the house. A singing. A moaning. Something of both. I went in and found her in the bathroom. She was swaying in front of the mirror. Singing. Moaning. From deep in her throat. She had scratched the scabs off her face and was bleeding again. A bottle of Windex stood on the back of the toilet. The mirror glass shined under the overhead lamp. Mom craned her neck and looked at her reflection from different angles. As if the right one might show her something she was missing.

104

'This is messed-up,' I said.

'I have no paint left,' she said. Like that was an excuse. And she looked around as if searching for some.

'You need a doctor or a priest,' I said.

She saw her pack of Newports on a bathroom shelf and she shook a cigarette into her fingers. And lit it. She took a deep drag. 'No brushes either,' she said.

'We're out of all kinds of things,' I said.

She blew smoke out at the mirror.

'We've got no food,' I said. 'Except for canned stuff and about a half box of crackers.'

'Leave me,' she said.

'Food or paint,' I said. 'First things first.'

'Leave,' she said. 'Please.' She looked at the mirror and started swaying.

So I went back to the porch and got *Great American Stories*. I paged through until I found something I liked. Then I went across the yard to where Edgar Allan and Paul were sitting. I read aloud. If Mom could act messed-up so could I. I read, '*After a time, a little dark-brown dog came trotting with an intent air down the sidewalk. A short rope was dragging from his neck. Occasionally he trod upon the end of it and stumbled.*'

'I've never known anyone who has *trod*,' said Edgar Allan. 'Especially not a dog.'

'Shut up,' I said. '*The dog hesitated for a moment, but presently he made some little advances with his tail. The child put out his hand and called him. In an apologetic manner the dog came close, and the two had an interchange of friendly pattings and waggles. The dog became more enthusiastic*

105

with each moment of the interview, until with his gleeful caperings he threatened to overturn the child. Whereupon the child lifted his hand and struck the dog a blow upon the head.'

'Exactly,' said Edgar Allan.

When Daniel Turner called again from the bridge I said he shouldn't have come back. We didn't need him. And Walter had told me not to open the gate.

'I'll wait until you do,' he said.

'Hope you brought a magazine or a big crossword puzzle,' I said. And hung up.

He called again. Asked, 'Did your brother come home last night?'

I said, 'I told the operator to throw out my message.'

'She ignored you,' he said.

'Well he came home,' I said.

'Good,' he said. 'What's going on now?'

'Nothing,' I said. 'Other than someone cutting the wires on our cars.' I kept Walter's and Mom's latest craziness to myself.

'Let me in,' he said.

'I can bring you a snack,' I said. 'If you like crackers and canned beans.'

'Let me in,' he said again. When I didn't answer, he added, 'Something bad is going to happen. This is how it was before your dad disappeared.'

'What do you mean?' I asked.

'They had visitors,' he said. 'Your dad and mom did. Men with bad histories and records of violence. They came to see your dad. Then your dad's car was wrecked.'

106

I'd never heard of that. I asked, 'What happened to the car?'

'Something with an axle if I remember right,' he said. 'A week before he disappeared he rolled the car as he pulled from your driveway on to the road. If your next-door neighbor hadn't been coming home he would've drowned in the ditch.'

I'd never heard this either. 'Lane Charles saved him?'

'That time he did,' he said.

'*That time?*' I asked.

'Let me in,' he said.

'Can't.'

He asked, 'Who are your visitors?'

'They're OK,' I said.

'What do you know about them?' he asked.

Just what they'd told me. Not even that. I said, 'I've got to go now.'

'Let me in,' he said.

'Thanks for checking on us,' I said. And I hung up.

In the evening I ate a can of corn and a jar of artichoke hearts. I shared the last of the crackers with Cristofer. The garage had called and said the Taurus and Mom's car would be ready the next morning. The truck the following afternoon. They would call when they'd finished the work. The rain came down hard but died to a mist again as the sun set. My friend Martin called and asked me to meet him at the bridge. 'If you'll bring me a hamburger I'll meet you anywhere,' I said.

'What would you *do* for the hamburger?' he asked.

I said, 'Don't be an asshole.' But then, 'Anything.'

An hour later he called again. Said he was stuck somewhere with a keg of beer and could we meet tomorrow night?

'Asshole,' I said.

I went to bed. The wind had picked up outside and a hard rain started to fall. Edgar Allan and his driver were sitting in it. I felt like crying. I lifted my nightgown. Circled my fingers on my thighs. High and higher. Stopped. I was disgusted. With myself. With Mom. With Walter. Disgusted and disgusted. Mom had had three loves ever since I could remember. Her painting. Herself. And Walter. I couldn't really tell the difference one from the other. She painted self-portraits because she loved herself and she loved Walter because he loved her as much as she did. It wasn't that she didn't think about Cristofer and me. It was more like we were parts of herself that she didn't especially like. Extra hairs growing around her nipples. Sores on the inside of her lips. Not that she would cut off her nipples or lips to be rid of us. But she would prefer she didn't have such annoyances. And Walter? Ever since I could remember he had moved through the house with his tar-stained jeans and tar-stained arms like a mean spirit. Saying, *Thou shalt not.*

Me? Ever since I could remember I'd had an itch that started in my thighs and in my head. And no matter how I rubbed or scratched or scraped it the itch came back stronger than before. I knew I needed to do something to satisfy it. But I didn't know what that thing might be.

108

So the wind blew across the tar roof. And the rain fell. And tears filled my eyes. And disgust filled my belly.

I got up and went downstairs. Cristofer was lying on the floor by the green chair. A dog at its master's feet. Maybe no one had told him the bedroom was his again. When I opened the door to the porch the wind and rain stung my face and arms and legs. Black clouds rushed overhead. Shifting and changing shapes. One dark animal into another. Rain slapped the house. On the ground dark streams and pools rippled in the gusts.

I ran barefoot into the yard. When the wind eased and the head of the oak swung up toward the clouds I saw Edgar Allan lying in a puddle by the trunk. His knees pulled to his chest. His arms around his knees. His head tucked down. A black egg in the night. 'Hey,' I said.

He didn't move.

I put a hand on his wet neck and he jerked. Wild-eyed.

He breathed hard and shivered but when he saw me he said, 'Pretty – night.' Thick-tongued.

'Where's Paul?' I asked.

He looked around. 'Don't know.'

'Come on,' I said. I helped him to his feet and walked him to the house.

'We can't,' he said.

But I brought him on to the porch and into the front room. Got rags for him to dry his face. Led him upstairs to Cristofer's room. Water dripped from his pant legs. His clothes smelled like the wet earth. He looked at Mom's closed bedroom door. 'Where do they keep the other guns?' he said.

'What are you talking about?' I asked.

He said, 'Where are they?' He sounded confused.

'Be quiet and he'll never know you're here,' I said. 'In the morning I'll sneak you back outside.'

In the dark his eyes shined like a starving man's. He kissed my cheek. His lips wet and cold. Then he went into Cristofer's room and pushed the door closed.

I went back to my room. I put on a dry night-gown. Climbed into bed. I felt happy and tired. What if Walter found Edgar Allan in the house and hurt him? The nightmare that Mom had been expecting week after week and month after month as she Windexed the windows would have arrived. She would realize that she'd been sharing her bed with it all along. Daniel Turner would come back. Walter would be unable to keep him outside the gate. Other policemen would come too. They would poke and prod Walter. Would they arrest him? Maybe not. *A man and his castle* and all that. But they would turn him inside out.

I was getting ahead of myself. In the morning I would sneak Edgar Allan downstairs before Walter came out of his bedroom. Or if Walter got up first we would wait until he went out to the pine woods. There would be no hurting. No turning inside out. The garage would return the Taurus. Edgar Allan and Paul would drive out over the hill. Life would go back to the way it had been. For better and worse and worse and worse.

I slept. And when I next awoke the sky was still dark but the rain had stopped. I got up and

110

opened the window and watched the clouds sliding over the earth. The air smelled sweet of rain and salt and ash and wet soil. I wondered whether I should wake up Edgar Allan and take him back outside. Or sneak into Cristofer's room and climb into bed with him.

Then over the drip drip drip from the roof and the dying wind another sound came. It came from far away like the sound of motorboats out on the ocean. It was there and then not there and then there again. The sound came from down-island by the bridge. Engines without mufflers. Beating the moist air. It came close and closer. It rose to a roar. Then it was out on the road alongside our land.

The noise died. And the night was quiet again except for the dripping roof and the breeze. Then there was a slamming. Metal breaking. And the engines roared.

A jacked-up yellow pickup came over the top of the hill into the yard. With oversized tires. A roll bar over the bed. Floodlights mounted on the roll bar. Followed by a red pickup and two motorcycles. The headlights glistened off the black dirt and the standing water. Spray shot from the tires.

Doors slammed shut throughout the house. I ran into the hall and tried Mom's room but she and Walter had locked themselves in. I pounded and asked, 'Is Cristofer with you?'

They didn't answer. I ran downstairs. The pickups and motorcycles circled the house. Their headlights flashed into the front room. Then dropped it back into darkness. I crouched by the window and watched through the lights. Two thick-legged men

111

rode the motorcycles. They wore blue jeans and black jackets. Soaked with rain and mud. A woman with a black ponytail drove the yellow pickup. Three German shepherds rode in the bed of the red pickup. I couldn't see inside the dark cab of that truck until one of the motorcycle headlights flashed on it. Paul the driver was at the steering wheel.

I checked the lock on the door. Went through the rooms downstairs. Locked the windows.

I ran back upstairs and pounded on Cristofer's door. Then went to my room and looked out my window. One of the men got off his motorcycle by the tar kiln. He took off a pair of black gloves and reached inside his jacket. He pulled out a cigarette. He flared a lighter and sucked the flame until the tip of the cigarette turned into a little red sun. The night air smelled like gas.

My bedroom door opened. Edgar Allan stood in the hallway. He said, 'How do we get into the attic?'

'What?'

'The attic,' he said.

I looked out the window again.

The biker with the cigarette picked up the can of kerosene that Walter used to fire the kiln. He drew a kerosene circle on the ground. Flicked his cigarette into it. Flames jumped.

The red pickup stopped and Paul the driver got out and talked to the biker. Then Paul opened the tailgate and the German shepherds jumped to the ground and ran through the yard.

'What's Paul doing?' I asked.

'I don't know,' Edgar Allan said.

'Why is he with them?'

'I don't know,' he said.

'You're lying,' I said.

'Come on,' he said. 'We need to get somewhere safe.'

I said, 'I need to find Cristofer.'

'He's OK,' he said.

'How do you know?'

'Trust me.'

'But I *don't* trust you,' I said.

'Let's go to the attic.'

I said, 'We need to get help.'

He took my arm as if he would drag me. 'The phone is down,' he said.

'You checked?' I asked. 'Or you cut it?'

'The storm must have brought down a lot of lines,' he said.

'That's not an answer.'

The yellow pickup stopped next to the red one. One motorcycle still circled the house. Its engine ripping into the night. Then it shot out to the oak tree and past Cristofer's trampoline. Its rear tire slid on the ground where Mom's studio had stood but the rider hit the throttle and the motorcycle flew into the dark. The dogs chased after it. Barking and biting at the wheels and engine. Lunging at the driver. The motorcycle was a big animal that they needed to bring down. The black-haired woman yanked the ripcord on a generator in the bed of the yellow pickup and turned on the roll-bar floodlights so that they shined hot on the house. She climbed down and talked with the others. Then climbed up again and opened a lockbox next to the generator. She pulled out the biggest gun I'd ever seen. A black-barreled thing that looked like it could shoot the stars out of the sky.

113

'Show me the attic,' Edgar Allan said. 'You're safe with me.'

'I don't think so,' I said.

He held my eyes with his. 'Trust me.'

'No,' I said. But what else could I do? I led him to the hall closet where a panel lifted into the attic. He boosted me up and then pulled himself through. I found a flashlight that I had left by the boxes of my dad's books. I shined it on him while he closed the hatch. Vents at the far ends of the roof opened into the air outside the house but the attic was dry and hot and smelled like pine and tar and dust.

We moved boxes of books so we could rest our backs while we sat. Then I asked, 'Who are you and what do you want here?'

He said, 'Give me the flashlight.'

I did and he shined it around the attic. Into the corners. Up at the beams.

'What do you see?' I asked.

'Nothing,' he said. And he laughed. He turned off the light and gave it to me. 'Keep it off,' he said. 'Or we'll have no batteries when we need them.'

'Who are you?' I asked.

'Now we wait until morning,' he said.

'Who—'

'Once upon a time there was a boy,' he said.

Twenty-Three

Oren

'And that boy's name was Oren,' I said.

'Is that your real name?' Lexi asked.

I sighed in the dark. 'Yes, my real name is Oren.'

'Prove it,' she said.

'I can't prove a negative,' I said.

'What do you mean?'

'That's what I'm trying to explain,' I said. We sat and listened to the muffled roar of Jimmy's motorcycle circling the house. Then I said, 'The boy's name was Oren, and he grew—'

Lexi said, 'I want to go back down and find Cristofer.'

'He's safe,' I said.

'You say it like your words make it so. How do you know?' she asked.

'As you say, my words make it so. Now, stop interrupting.'

'I'm not—'

'Shh,' I said. We listened again to Jimmy's motorcycle circling and circling. I said, 'Oren grew up in circumstances that were unusually trying—'

She said, 'I always think it's strange when people talk about themselves in the third person.'

'Fine,' I said. '*I* grew up in the kind of

115

circumstances that lead to violence beyond anything you've ever heard of or imagined.'

'Have you been in prison?' she asked.

'Shh,' I said. 'Before we talk about me, we need to discuss Amon.'

'My dad?' she said.

'Is that your dad's name?'

'Don't do that,' she said.

'Why not?' I asked. When we planned this trip, Paul said, *You've got to disorient if you want to reorient*.

'Because I'm scared,' she said.

'Nothing to be scared of,' I said. 'I'm here with you.'

'That scares me,' she said.

'Amon grew up in Waycross, Georgia,' I said. 'This was in the nineteen-fifties. His father was a banker and a member of the Rotary Club and the First Methodist Church. His mother smelled of talcum powder and lilacs. Have you heard about this?'

'No,' Lexi said. 'My mom doesn't talk about my dad.'

'That's what I thought,' I said. 'Amon's mother – your grandmother – was a lovely woman, fleshy and warm. She called her big hips her *peach cobblers*, which embarrassed Amon when he brought friends home as a teenager, though even as an adult he thought of her as the embodiment of sweetness.'

'This is necessary?' Lexi asked.

I said, 'They lived in a big wooden house – painted yellow, according to his mother's wishes – near the center of town, when downtown Waycross

116

was still the place to live. Amon's father was the kind of man who said, *Belts are for whipping children*. But he rarely whipped Amon because Amon was a good and kind-hearted child who rarely broke the rules and almost never found trouble.'

Lexi said, 'My father grew up in Waycross.'

'Of course he did,' I said.

'But he wasn't good or kind-hearted,' she said. 'Mom says he was a bastard.'

'I thought she doesn't talk about him,' I said.

'She likes to call him a bastard,' Lexi said.

I said, 'So Amon lived what one might think of as the ideal small-town life of a child in the nineteen-fifties. The big world still loomed outside without threatening to disturb his family and families like his. A neighbor talked of moving outside the town limits to avoid change, but Amon's father only laughed at him. Progressive thinking had yet to reach into places like Waycross and shake men like Amon's father out of their backward little desk chairs and expose them to the world's contempt. Although Amon's mother poured her first drink each afternoon at four thirty and she and Amon's father, who arrived home at five fifteen, continued drinking steadily through the evening until they stumbled upstairs to bed, they didn't think of themselves as alcoholics. There were a few known alcoholics in Waycross, but they were public drinkers and spent regular nights in the town jail.'

'You're making this up,' Lexi said.

I said, 'I'm filling in the gaps.'

'Don't,' she said.

I said, 'Amon had a happy childhood. He rode

117

his bicycle to school. After school he and his friends played football in the fall and winter, baseball in the spring. In the summer they rode their bicycles to Herrin Pond out by the cemetery and they fished with worms for croakers. Or they rode farther out of town to the Satilla River, where they poked through the long grass for alligators and water moccasins, which they threw rocks at.'

'Where did you get all this?' Lexi asked.

'They threw rocks at them,' I said, 'but Amon, being a good and kind-hearted child, never wished to hurt them. When he was thirteen years old, his father bought him a deer rifle – a two-eighty Remington – and they drove out to a place north of Dixie Union. The sun was rising through the mist in the forest, soft like it could have been the first day of the world. They walked through the trees and came into a clearing, the dry grass breaking under their feet, then stepped into another grove. Amon and his father said nothing to each other but walked hip-to-hip, shoulder-to-shoulder, like they were on a pilgrimage. More than at any other time in his life, Amon felt a deep love for the trees and the dirt under his feet and the man beside him. When they came to a second clearing, they saw a deer. It was a yearling, and though it didn't seem to have smelled them, its tail hung down between its hind legs like a guilty dog's. The meadow grass was so long it brushed the yearling's belly. Its nose was so narrow it could have been carved from a stick. Its shiny black eyes looked like blown glass.'

'Yeah, right,' Lexi said, like I was telling a lie. Outside, Robert's motorcycle revved. Then

118

Jimmy's revved too. Then they revved together. I knew they were sitting side-by-side on their bikes – I'd seen them do it a thousand times – and when they hit the gas they would race, side-by-side, out to some point they'd decided on and then they would spin and race back. They hit the gas. Carol whooped. Beside me in the dark, Lexi jumped.

So I said, 'Standing at the edge of the grove, Amon's father helped him position his rifle, whispered in his ear, instructing him how to line up the shot and squeeze the trigger slow, then whispered again, like an eager lover, "Do it, boy. Do it."

'But Amon couldn't.

'Whether the deer heard Amon's father as he told his son to shoot or it smelled danger as the wind shifted in the trees, it raised its head, darted through the grass, and disappeared into the next grove.

'Amon's father swore at him. He said he wouldn't have a coward for a son. Amon knew that in refusing to shoot he had dishonored his father and that if he was to repair the bond between them, he must do so right away. But when they saw another deer later that day, he again couldn't bring himself to fire a bullet at it. He hated killing.'

'Nope,' Lexi said. 'Not true. My dad had a lot of guns. He loved to shoot.'

'Later he did,' I said. 'That's right.'

'You're wrong about him,' she said. 'He was in the army. He went to war. Mom says he volunteered.'

'Yes, he did,' I said. 'Again, that was later. Where are his—'

'This is ridiculous,' she said. 'How do you know all this?'

'He told me,' I said.

'You know my dad?' she asked.

'I've had long talks with him,' I said.

'Right,' she said. 'Where is he?'

'Do you want me to tell the story or not?' I asked.

The motorcycles stopped racing and Robert and Jimmy cut the engines. Only the generator in back of the pickup stuttered and hummed. 'It's quiet,' Lexi said.

'Where are the guns now?' I asked. I couldn't see Walter getting rid of them. I figured he'd hidden them. He would oil the black gun barrels in the dark. He would love and caress the guns as he loved and caressed himself.

Lexi said, 'Mom didn't want them in the house after my dad left.'

'I think you're lying,' I said.

'What are you talking about?' she said. 'Why would I—'

'That's what I'm wondering,' I said.

'You're insane,' she said. 'Are you going to tell your story or am I going to climb down?'

So I said, 'Much more than hunting, more than throwing rocks at alligators and snakes, Amon loved to read.'

The engine on Robert's motorcycle roared again.

'You're like him that way,' I said. 'By the time he was fifteen he was skipping football and baseball games to go to the library. There was a bookstore a couple of blocks from his house, and on the third Saturday of every month a truck arrived with new books. Whenever Amon had money, he would wait for the truck, offering to help unload it, offering to open the boxes inside

120

the store. He was book crazy, his mother said, but he believed that she secretly approved of his love of reading as much as his father feared it.'

Carol, Paul, Jimmy, and Robert started whooping and yowling outside in the yard. They laughed. Carol's laugh was light and high and easy.

'Will you get to the point?' Lexi said.

'Am I going too slow?' I asked.

'Uh-huh,' she said.

'What if there *is* no point?'

She said, 'Just move it along.'

'Fine,' I said. 'The abridged version. On Christmas morning when Amon was seventeen, his father shot Amon's mother in the head with a pistol. It seems that she'd been sharing her peach cobblers with their next-door neighbor. Then Amon's father put the hot end of the barrel in his own mouth and pulled the trigger. Three weeks later, Amon enlisted in the army and soon after that he was deployed to Vietnam. Maybe he enlisted to compensate for a sense that he had failed his father. Maybe he had other reasons too. Whatever led to it, the experience changed him forever. This was nineteen-sixty-nine.'

'Jesus,' Lexi said.

'You asked for it.'

'Maybe not quite that fast,' she said.

Then there was a gunshot. One of my friends was shooting at the house. No one was supposed to do that until Walter shot at them. Carol laughed – light and high and easy.

'We've got to get down from here,' Lexi said, and scrambled toward the attic hatch.

But I held her, loosening my grip only when

121

she stopped struggling. What good would come of going down before I finished the story?

I said, 'Amon's superiors put him in a non-combat position. He clearly wasn't fit for fighting.'

'I've got to check on Cristofer,' Lexi said.

'Because Amon was good with language,' I said, 'they made him an assistant information specialist at the Bien Hoa military base in Dong Nai, across the river from Saigon.'

Lexi kicked at me but I held her.

'Cristofer is fine,' I said. 'I promise.'

'How do you know?' she asked.

Because unless my friends had burned our plan, they would protect Cristofer as carefully as they would protect each other. 'I know,' I said.

She stopped struggling.

'On Amon's first weekend leave,' I said, 'some of the other guys from the base took him to the Hall of Mirrors brothel. This was the biggest brothel in Saigon.'

Lexi said, 'Why do you think I want to know this about my dad?'

'It's not about what you *want* to know,' I said. 'There were more than two hundred whores – and more mirrors than whores. There were more opportunities for pleasure and pain, for the making of dreams and nightmares, than Amon had ever thought possible. He stumbled out of the brothel on Sunday morning with a mixture of pride and guilt.'

Outside in the yard, Carol laughed – high and hard.

'He couldn't find his friends,' I said, 'so he wandered through the city. The Tet Offensive had ended. The communists had drawn back to the north. Except for occasional shootings, peace had returned to Saigon. Now the streets were filled with scooters and pared-down motorcycles, little German cars, three-wheeled *tuk-tuks*, and bicycles. Exhaust and dust filled the air. A tangle of electric and telephone wires hung overhead like a wrecked spider web. Children watched Amon from the glassless windows in concrete tenements. Everywhere there was the noise of motors and horns, people shouting, people laughing, babies crying. Everywhere there was the smell of fish oil and salt, rotting vegetables, and the wet decay of buildings. Against all odds and for reasons that he was at a loss to explain to himself, for the second time in his life, as he walked through these streets, Amon felt a deep love for the earth and the people who lived on it. Maybe it was that he had just lost his virginity. Maybe it was that he was so far from home and he'd experienced a total freedom from all that had weighed him down. Whatever the cause, he felt himself falling in love with life in a way that he'd believed impossible after his parents' murder and suicide.

'So,' I said, 'he wasn't surprised that when he turned a corner on to Tu Do Street he found several bookstores along with a mix of bars, newsstands, and hotels, or that when he walked under the awning of the first bookstore – a place called Tin Nghia that had huge stacks of Vietnamese and Chinese books on plywood tables – he saw behind the counter a girl he thought he would spend the rest of his life with.'

'And they lived happily ever after?' Lexi said.

123

'The girl's name was Phan Thi Phuong,' I said, 'and, like him, she was eighteen years old. She spoke a little French but no English, and when he came to the counter with a Vietnamese book that he was incapable of reading, she laughed at him because he had chosen a novel called *Plum Blossom Love* that had been popular mostly among middle-aged women.

'Somehow the hungover American soldier, smelling of whorehouse sex, managed to convince the bookstore clerk to have lunch with him before he returned to base. On his next leave, he skipped the Hall of Mirrors and headed straight to the bookstore. Not only was Phuong waiting for him, but she had learned a few words of English, which, along with Amon's growing Vietnamese vocabulary, kept them happy for his full forty-eight hours. Over the next several months, Amon spent all of his leave time with Phuong and volunteered for any assignments that might take him off base so that he could see her, if only for a few minutes or an hour. Phuong's father, who came from a family that had been wealthy before the war, owned the bookstore, which he also used to run a black-market money exchange and small-scale weapons depot, so she had a set of keys, and when there were no customers, she would lock up and they would have the store to themselves. When the monsoons came and the streets flooded, they made love behind the plastic curtains that kept the books dry, but, after a close call when one of Phuong's uncles arrived as Amon was zipping his pants, Amon rented a room in a nearby apartment building and they met there as often as they could.'

Lexi said, 'Why do I need to know this?'

'It's who you are,' I said.

'I don't think so,' she said.

'You'll never love him unless you know who he was,' I said.

'Why should I love him?' she asked. 'He ran away. He left us here.'

I said, 'If you're going to hate him, you should know who you're hating.' She stopped arguing, so I said, 'Phuong's uncle must have seen more than she and Amon thought he did, because one afternoon when Amon arrived at the store, Phuong's father stood behind the counter with a friend. Amon knew better than to ask where Phuong was. She had told him that her father's only politics were that he despised the Americans and the Viet Cong equally, and his only interest was in protecting his family – his wife, who had gone to live in the country, and his daughter, who had refused to leave. As Amon thumbed through the books on the plywood tables, Phuong's father, who was as handsome as his daughter was beautiful, nudged his friend, a short man with little teeth. The friend approached Amon and asked, "What do you like?"

'Amon, thinking he would break the tension, said he wanted a copy of the book that he had tried to buy on his first visit – *Plum Blossom Love*.

'The friend showed him his little teeth and pulled a snubnose Baby Browning from a pocket. He said, "Come with me, funny man."

'Phuong's father and his friend took Amon into a back room where there was a rusting hotplate and, for reasons Amon never figured out, a crate of tongue depressors. The friend held the gun

125

against Amon while Phuong's father talked. The father said, "Because my daughter loves you, I give you a chance. One. You go away. You will not see my daughter any more. This is your chance." He looked at Amon hopefully.

'Amon asked, "What happens if I don't go away?"

'Phuong's father said, "What happens? I have a gun. Many guns. I buy guns. I sell guns. You want to buy or sell guns – that is good. You want to be with my daughter – that is bad."

'"I love Phuong," Amon said.

'"No," her father said. "You do not love Phuong. No more. You go."

'The friend crammed the snubnose into Amon's ribs.

'"Fine," Amon said. "I go."

'He left, and after that he and Phuong were careful. They met in the apartment that Amon rented or at hotels in parts of the city that they believed were safe from her father and her father's friends.

'Then,' I said, 'Phuong got pregnant.'

'Wait,' Lexi said. 'My dad had a kid in Vietnam?'

'Just listen,' I said. 'When Phuong's father found out, he threatened to kill her. He threatened to castrate Amon. He went to the gates of the Bien Hoa military base and threatened to shoot himself if the sentries didn't turn Amon over to him. Phuong left the city and hid with her mother. Now Amon saw her only once every month or two, when he had enough leave time to travel into the countryside, and on each visit Phuong's belly swelled and the skin tightened until it

126

seemed they would need a knife or a razor to relieve the tension.

'They had a daughter,' I said, 'and they named her Lang. Even—'

Lexi said, 'I have a sister? That's ridiculous.'

I said, 'Even at a glance, it was clear from the baby's skin, her face, and her brown hair that she was Amerasian. That was bad for family peace. When Phuong's mother showed her husband a picture of the baby to try to reconcile him to reality, he just added Lang to his list of people to kill. They kept the baby and Phuong out of sight when he visited. Phuong's mother learned to avoid even mentioning them in his presence, treating them as if they were – as he wished to think them – dead. But one day during the next monsoon season he arrived unexpectedly at the country house and found the baby alone. In one of those moments that should lead to happy endings, he looked at the child and his anger seemed to break inside him. He stood, stunned, alone with this baby whose eyes and face were at once so familiar and so foreign, and then he went to Lang, picked her up, and held her to his chest. When Phuong's mother came into the room, she thought that he was suffocating the child, but then she saw tears on his handsome face.'

'Nice,' Lexi said.

'Only a little,' I said. 'After that first moment of amazement, life became complicated in the family again. Phuong's father still struggled with the fact that Amon was an American. He blamed him – as he blamed all Americans – for bringing death to Vietnam. He still struggled with the knowledge that Phuong had betrayed him,

127

humiliated him in his own eyes and, he was certain, the eyes of both those who had respected him and those who were happy to see weakness in him.

'But Phuong returned to Saigon and worked in her father's store once more. In the evenings she would go to the apartment that Amon had rented, and, whenever he could, Amon would spend a few hours or a night with her. Because of their fears of another attack by the Viet Cong, they left Lang in the country with Phuong's mother, but each month, on a weekend when Phuong's father remained in Saigon, Phuong and Amon went to the country house and lived for two or three days as a family.

'Never in his life had Amon been happier. Never had he felt more at home than in this place nine thousand miles from where he grew up. He re-enlisted after his twelve months ended, then re-enlisted twice more. As the United States drew down some of our troops from South Vietnam in nineteen-seventy-three, he arranged to move Phuong and their daughter with him when his fourth tour ended. But those plans reignited the anger that had always smoldered in Phuong's father.'

Outside, Jimmy's motorcycle droned and droned as it circled and circled the house.

Lexi asked, 'Why are you telling me all this?'

I said, 'I want you to know what you lost.'

'OK,' she said, 'but why?'

I thought, *Because it hurts too much to hurt alone.* I said, 'Two weeks before Amon was scheduled to fly out of Saigon, to be followed by Phuong and their three-year-old daughter, he was alone in the rental apartment, packing the

128

few belongings he would take with him, when there was a soft knock.

'When he opened the door, Lang was standing outside alone. She was wearing a red dress that Phuong had sewed for her third birthday and that already looked too short because the girl was growing so fast. Now her brown hair had been roughly cut off. Strands of the cut hair clung to her dress and to the little red socks that peaked out of her shiny black shoes. She had her hands behind her back as if holding a secret gift, and, despite the violence that had been committed against her hair, she looked excited to see her dad. Amon stared at her, confused. She was supposed to be at the country house with her grandmother. Even if there had been a change in plans, there was no reason for her to be here alone, wearing her best dress, and with her hair tattered.

'But Amon stooped low to hug her and said, "Come here, baby."

'Lang went to him, but as she exposed her hands he saw that she had in fact brought a gift. She held – like it was a doll – an M-twenty-six fragmentation grenade, its safety pin-ring removed. At the Bien Hoa base he had heard drunk soldiers laughing as they'd described the damage the grenades had done to the Viet Cong, and later, after they'd sobered up, he had heard them crying as they'd described the same damage.

'Amon rolled backward on to the floor, skittering away from his daughter.

'She giggled at the game he seemed to be playing.

'He asked, "Where did you get that?"

'She held up the grenade as if it was as harmless as a lemon. "*Ông nôi*," she said – "grandpa" – like that was part of the wonderful surprise. She presented it to him then, as her grandpa must have told her to, setting it on the floor between them, admiring it, and running to Amon.

'He pulled her to himself so tight he knew that she couldn't breathe. He wished that he could pull her into his own skin. He never could explain what he did next. Maybe he panicked. Maybe the anger and fear he'd felt when his father killed his mother had broken something inside him. Maybe he acted according to the warped logic of instinct. Maybe – and this was the thought that haunted him most – he was, as his father had thought he was, a coward. But he threw Lang down on the grenade and fell on top of her. It was an insane act at an insane moment in an insane part of the world. The explosion ripped through the girl and lifted them both into the air. For what seemed a long time, Amon felt that he was flying – hovering in the air in the middle of the apartment, a spray of blood, skin, and bone hanging in the air with him, his daughter's red dress seeming to drift on a brown wind – and then he fell to the floor, torn and lacerated by shrapnel that had passed through Lang's body and into his own.'

Twenty-Four

Lexi

'You asshole,' I said.

'I didn't do it,' Edgar Allan said. Or Oren. This man who called himself Oren. '*He* did.'

'I've never heard any of this,' I said.

'How much has your mother told you about him?' he asked. 'Other than calling him a bastard.'

I didn't answer.

He asked again, 'How much?'

'I told you. Almost nothing.'

He said, 'So do you want to hear or not?'

I didn't know. 'Does it get worse?'

'It has its ups and downs,' he said.

'My dad told you all of this?' I asked.

'Yes,' he said.

'When?' I asked. 'Where?'

He said, 'I'll tell you everything if you want to hear.'

The wooden roof beams in the attic ticked as the night cooled outside. The voices of the people in the yard had fallen to a murmur. A motorcycle circled the house. And circled. The generator in the back of the yellow pickup hummed. Stuttered. Hummed again. One of the German shepherds barked. A light glowed outside the vent at one end of the attic where the floodlights shined at

131

the house. I listened for Mom or Walter or Cristofer. Heard nothing.

'Tell it,' I said.

Twenty-Five

Oren

'Good choice,' I said.

'Or not,' Lexi said.

'Amon spent two months in the military hospital,' I said. 'The doctors removed part of his intestines. They had to fight down a lung infection. But the biggest problems, as you might expect, were in his head. The nightmares – where he relived Lang's arrival at his door, her happiness as she gave him the live grenade, his impulse to throw her on to it, the minutes that he seemed to float above the apartment floor after the explosion – got worse and shaded into daytime hallucinations when he learned that the Vietnamese police were refusing to charge Phuong's father. The man had spared his wife and Phuong, and the only witness who could say that he sent Lang to the apartment had been Lang herself, a three-year-old who now was dead. The police said that Amon's claim that Lang had told him that her *ông nội* had given her the grenade was suspicious. Since the M-twenty-six was American ordnance, they thought that Amon more likely had brought it to the apartment himself.

'"Mr Phan is a peaceful man," the police said. "He operates a bookstore."

'Amon told them, "He's a black-marketer."

'"These are difficult times," they said.

'Amon said, "Search his store. Search his house. He buys and sells guns. You'll find grenades—"

'"Go home, Yankee," they said, "or we will charge you with your daughter's death."

'He boarded the transport plane, leaving the antiseptic smells of the hospital and the salty sewage and rotting vegetation of the city behind. Back in America, waiting for his discharge, he wrote letter after letter to Phuong. He told her about his healing injuries, his worsening nightmares, the American food he was eating. He told her about Waycross, where he would return as soon as he received his papers and where they could build a life together in the house where he grew up. Aside from the descriptions of his nightmares, he never mentioned Lang. That pain was too deep. The pain and the guilt were. The closest he came to mentioning her was when he wrote, *I want a big family. When you come, we'll have children.* He asked her when she was coming.'

Lexi said, 'This is screwed-up.'

'Yeah,' I said. 'Phuong never answered the letters. Did her father intercept them? Did she decide on her own that she couldn't face the pain of being with Amon? Amon never knew.

'When the army discharged him, he went to Waycross and on his first night back in his childhood house he realized that he didn't want to be the person he'd been in the past. When he came through the front door, unopened during the four

133

years since he enlisted, he scuffed a path through the dust, and in the morning he scuffed back out, went to a realty office, told a broker he wanted to sell the house at a price that would move it fast, then checked into a motel east of town.

'Six days later, he drove toward the coast, with a bank draft in his pocket and his car trunk loaded with his favorite books. When he reached the Atlantic, he turned right and headed south past the chain of outer-bank islands. He wanted to find a place where nothing would remind him of the man he had been. He expected he would find such a place in the Florida Keys, but just after crossing the Georgia–Florida border he tried an unpaved road that wound over old, blown sand dunes and through a pine forest that was being cultivated by a paper mill. The road ended at the bridge to Black Hammock Island. A tropical storm had washed out most of the bridge. You could walk across it, but cars and trucks were prohibited. Amon parked his car and walked across, waving aside a curtain of yellow flies. He walked until he saw a sign – *For Sale by Owner* – advertising an up-island plot of three acres, two of them marsh. The place was about as isolated as you could stumble on to in the Southeast without swimming or hiring a boat. Amon had found a new home.'

Outside, the generator stuttered and hummed.

'For thirteen years,' I said, 'Amon lived alone, speaking to others only when necessary, which on an island like Black Hammock was seldom. He paid a company to dig a well but built his own house from lumber that a flatbed truck delivered after the bridge was repaired. He fished in the tidal waters and grew vegetables in a garden that he planted between the marsh and his back door. In the first sign that he had succeeded in forgetting the boy he once had been – the one who had refused to shoot a deer and had managed to make love not war even when he was in the middle of the hottest conflict since the end of World War Two – he started buying guns. At first he bought a pistol and a rifle to scare away the raccoons that raided his garden and dug up the kitchen scraps that he buried in the yard. Then he bought another rifle and a shotgun to shoot squirrels and birds when the fish weren't biting. Then he bought more and more guns just because he could.

'Soon, a neighbor accused him of stealing and slaughtering a hog. Although the police dropped the charges, Amon developed a reputation on the island as a man not to be trusted and, after a second incident, involving a goat, as a man who lived by knife and gun.'

Lexi said, 'I've heard some of this before.'

'Yes, we're getting close to home,' I said. 'Around the time of the goat incident, Amon realized the house that he had built with his own hands was rotting. The planks he had used for siding felt damp and soft even in dry weather. Rats had chewed a hole under the eaves and were living in his roof. Insects were eating their way up from the wooden foundation and had bored into the floor.

'Amon knew that the other islanders painted their roofs and outside walls with pine tar, though until his own house started to fall down, he hadn't understood why. Now, he could let his house disintegrate

135

and disappear into the sand and dirt, a prospect that also had attractions for him, or he could do as his neighbors did. After about a month of indecision, he visited a family that was famous for making tar – out of a mix of sand pine, slash pine, and longleaf pine, with some loblolly mixed in.'

'Ah,' Lexi said.

'Yes, *Ah*,' I said. 'Amon told the man who made the tar – a man named Henry Jakobson—'

'My grandfather,' Lexi said.

'Yes, your grandfather, who, it's said, along with his yardman – an often underestimated man named Tilson – made the richest, smoothest tar in the Southeast. Amon told your grandfather what was happening, and your grandfather sold him ten gallons of tar, enough to coat the house twice. That would have ended the encounter, except that a teenaged girl was sitting on the front porch.'

'My mom?' Lexi asked.

'She was just fifteen and Amon was thirty-five,' I said. 'She was heavy-boned and had acne, and she also used a pair of scissors to cut herself, sometimes on the hands and arms, more often on her face.'

'Oh,' Lexi said.

'Few would have called her beautiful,' I said. 'That would come later. She was a strange girl. She watched the world wide-eyed, as if it held no danger for her, and on the morning that Amon visited she had drawn a line of tar down each cheek, here' – I touched Lexi's face and drew a line down from her left eye – 'and here' – I drew a line down from her right eye. Lexi pulled away into the dark.

I said, 'Your mother looked nothing like Phuong and nothing like Lang, but at that moment Amon saw in her face both his lover and their daughter.

'He stood in the yard, his eyes locked with hers. The heat of the morning seemed to lift and he felt ice on his skin. He thought that he might fall to the ground, colder than anything that had ever lain there.

'Your grandfather watched him and your mother with alarm. He said to Amon, "That's my daughter, Kay."

'Stunned, unaware of what he was saying, Amon asked, "Might I visit her some time?"

'Amon was almost as old as your grandfather, and your grandfather knew the stories of the slaughtered hog and the missing goat. He'd heard that Amon was collecting weapons. "Get the hell off my land," he said. "I'll have my yardboy deliver the tar tomorrow. If you need more after that, you can send a messenger. I don't want to see you back here."

'But it was your mother who pursued the relationship,' I said. 'A week after Amon bought the tar, as he was painting a second coat on the last section of his roof – naked except for his underwear since he owned just two sets of clothes and didn't want to ruin either – he felt eyes watching him. Your mother had crept on to his land and was sitting with a sketchpad and a pencil in the shade of a hoptree. He asked her what she was doing, and his words caught in his dry throat.

'Instead of answering, strange child that she was, she just touched her pencil to the pad.

'He asked, "How long have you been watching?"

137

'She kept drawing.

'He climbed down from the roof, wrapped a towel around his waist, and went to her. He said, "If your daddy found you here, he would dunk me in his tar box, roll me through your chicken yard, and chase me over the bridge and off the island. That's what I think. And he would lock you in your room and take away your shoes. I think he would consider you guilty of bad judgment."

'Your mother looked at him, tipped her head to the side as if trying to square the way his nose aligned with the rest of his face, and touched the pencil to the pad.

'"You think you're an artist?" Amon asked.

'"Take off the towel," she said.

'"*What?*" he said. She'd succeeded in shocking him.

'She said, "Take off your underpants too. I'm not done with the picture."

'"You're done enough," he said. "Let's see."

'She handed him the pad. What he saw shocked him again. Your mother's drawing showed him as he'd forgotten that he had ever been. In lines and shading that were startlingly true, she had drawn his muscular sunbaked body, showing strength where he had seen only weakness.

'Amon balled up the drawing and said, "I'm keeping this."

'"I drew it for you," your mother said.

'"Don't come around here anymore," he said, and he went into his house.

'For a couple of weeks, his life returned to normal. He fished. He gardened. He shot at seagulls and egrets with a variety of weapons, some of them leaving little more than feathers that snowed from the sky. In the evenings, he read his books or he stood in his yard, looked up at the Milky Way, and listened to the callings of frogs in the marsh and the skitterings of animals in the grass. But he couldn't get your mother out of his mind. He couldn't get rid of the feeling that he saw in her both his daughter and Phuong. Sleepless at night, he wanted to sneak to your mother's house and look up at the windows to see if she would be looking back, and he dug his fingers into the skin on his legs to keep himself from going.

'Then one morning,' I said, 'he found a new drawing tacked to the outside of his front door. In this one, he was standing, thigh-deep in an inlet, throwing a cast net for bait fish. The sun shined on his shoulders and he seemed to have a lithe strength that in reality he didn't feel. Three mornings later, another drawing was tacked to the door, this one showing him on his hands and knees in his garden. He seemed to be crawling, seeking something. The next morning produced a fourth drawing. In it, he was standing in his yard, staring at the sky.

'He started watching for her, gazing into the shade as he stood in the sunlight and into the darker shadows after the sun set. He *expected* her. He desired her.

'But he never saw her.'

'Weird,' Lexi said.

'He was in love,' I said.

'I know,' she said.

'Finally, in the middle of another sleepless night, he couldn't help himself. He stopped digging his fingers into his skin, got up in the dark, and bathed his face and arms in a bowl of well-water that he kept on a table. He dressed in the cleaner of his two pairs of pants. He became aware of the sweat, oil, and dirt that were as much a part of his skin as the sun-browned cells. He would present himself outside the windows of your mother's house, and if desire had the power to pass through the air as smoke or fog did, she would know he was there and would come to see him.

'But when he opened his door to leave, she was already standing in front of him. The skin on her face was mottled and shiny. She wore a cotton dress and sandals. In her hands she held a drawing and a tack.

'The sudden opening of the door surprised her, and she turned and ran.

'Amon stepped outside and called her back, the words sticking in his throat. Moonlight was turning the whole world slate-blue – the dirt yard, the hoptree, the grasses out by the marsh.

'Your mother stopped running.

'"Come here," Amon said, his throat dry, his tongue thick.

'She came then. She came until she stood toe-to-toe with him and looked him in the eyes.

'He knew she was waiting for him to touch her. "Why me?" he asked. "I'm broken. Can't you see that?"

'She said, "I like broken things."

'He felt tears rising in his eyes, tears that seemed as miraculous as water rising up from a dry creek bed. He felt that your mother was a gift. Because he had suffered enough.

'They met often after that, always in the middle

140

of the night. She would tap on his door, and he would open it, half expecting to see Lang wearing her too-short birthday dress, her hair roughly cut, her hands hiding a secret behind her back – and thrilled that your mother was standing there instead. He would pull her inside, lift her cotton dress over her head, and carry her to his bed.

'One night, he asked, "What would your father do if he found out?"

'"Kill you," she said, with a calm that made him think she was serious but wasn't worried.

'"And you?" he asked. "Would he kill you too?" That possibility bothered him more than thoughts of his own death.

'"No," she said, and she ran her fingers up his thigh from his knee. "He forgives me for every-thing I do."

'So, for the second time in his life, he was making love to a girl whose father would kill him if he had a chance. But he knew that he would die if he had to give up a love as powerful as this again.

'Remarkably, considering how many nights they spent together, a year and a half passed before your mother became pregnant. She—'

Lexi said, 'My mom got pregnant? At seventeen?'

'A month before she turned seventeen,' I said. 'Yes.'

'She had an abortion?' Lexi said.

'Her father opposed that kind of thing,' I said. 'Just listen to the story.'

'She kept the baby?' Lexi asked.

'*Kept* might be too strong of a word,' I said.

141

'She had the baby?' Lexi said. 'Eight years before she had *me*?'

'Roughly,' I said.

Lexi was quiet for a moment, then asked, 'Why would my dad tell you all of this?'

'Vested interest,' I said. I felt like I was stepping into space and falling.

'An interest in *you*?' she asked.

'Yes,' I said. 'Me.'

'Oh Jesus,' she said, and I knew that she knew.

She fumbled in the dark until she found the flashlight. She turned it on and shined it at me. I didn't blink.

'If what you're saying is true I'm going to throw up,' she said.

'Listen,' I said. 'Your mother was wrong about her father killing Amon. Instead, he got him charged with statutory rape. He— Would you turn off the flashlight?'

'No,' Lexi said.

I said, 'Would you at least stop shining it in my face?'

'No,' she said.

I tried silence but she kept the light on me. So I said, 'The police threw Amon in jail with the rapists and the child molesters – because they considered him one of them. Amon admitted to everything, but your mother claimed he'd never touched her. She blamed a boy her own age, then said a stranger raped her, then said that her own father got her pregnant, though the investigating detective's anger made her go back to the story about the stranger. At home, she stopped eating and started cutting herself again

142

– on her hands and arms, her face, and now her belly.

'Eventually, the police gave up and her father gave in,' I said. 'The police released Amon with the understanding that if he ever tried to see your mother again, her father would shoot him, and if he ran out of bullets, the police would give him more, free of charge, and if his body was ever found, the coroner would declare he had died of natural causes because what could be more natural than killing a man like him?

'The night that he got out of jail, after he unlocked his house, checked the garden, pumped water from his well into his bathing bowl, and climbed into bed alone, your mother came back and tapped on his door.

'"Go away," he said, digging his fingers into his thighs.'

'I know,' Lexi said. As if she'd been there. As if she'd done this herself.

I said, 'Your mother tapped again.

'Amon shouted, "Go away."

'She knocked.

'He jumped out of bed and yanked open the door. Again he wouldn't have been surprised to see Lang in her red dress and her rough-cut hair. He also wouldn't have been surprised to see your mother's father and Phuong's father standing shoulder-to-shoulder with guns in their hands. He owned ten or fifteen guns himself by then, but he wouldn't have shot back.

'Instead, your mother stepped into the house and asked, "What took you so long?"

143

'So he lifted her cotton dress over her head and carried her to his bed.

'As they lay together afterward, he asked, "What will they say? What will they do?"

'She gazed at him as happy as he'd ever seen her, as happy as *he* wanted to be, and said, "They can do nothing to us."

'They got married on the day she turned eighteen, and – believe it or not – her father went with them to the courthouse. If your grandfather never really liked Amon, he at least got used to him and even learned to respect him as a man who had suffered great losses and had worked with what was left to the best of his abilities. He learned too that although Amon wasn't educated, he was well read, and if your grandfather had little interest in books himself, he recognized that Amon shared something of the temperament of his artistic daughter.

'He had allowed Amon to visit and sometimes even spend the night. By the time that the baby was born, they all were on good enough terms that your mother and Amon asked her father to name him. And he did.'

I stopped. The roof beams ticked. Carol and Paul were talking quietly outside.

'Say it,' Lexi said.

'You're sure?' I asked.

'Just say it.'

I said, 'He named him Oren.'

'Like you,' she said.

'Exactly like me,' I said.

'You're lying,' she said.

I asked, 'Where's the box?'

'What box?' she asked.

'Of photographs from when Amon was here.'

She shined the flashlight on a stack of cardboard boxes that contained our dad's books and then on a smaller box wedged at the side of the attic where the roof met the ceiling supports. I crawled to it. It was shiny with oil that had leached from the tar on the outside of the roof and seeped through the layers of shingles and plywood. I brought it back and wiped my hands on an exposed wooden support beam. I broke the masking tape and opened the flaps. The box belched a chemical smell. Years and years of oil had bled in and mixed with the photographic paper. 'I'll show you,' I said, and pulled out a pile of photos that stuck together with a thick paste.

When I peeled the photos from the pile, I showed her nothing. The pine oil had turned against the processing chemicals and the images had burned. The colors and shapes were gone. The people looked as if they had evaporated in the sun. I checked each picture – each piece of greasy paper – and threw it into the dark. I pulled out another pile and threw it. I gave Lexi just one photo, which seemed to show someone standing next to a child. 'There,' I said.

I pulled out a third pile and a fourth. Three photos showed Kay at about twenty sitting on my dad's lap, but the other shots were washed out and as gray as ash.

I reached into the box once more and found a waxed-paper envelope. I opened it and pulled out a brittle lock of hair. 'There,' I said again, and held the lock against the hair on my head.

'Maybe,' Lexi said. 'I don't know.'

'What isn't to know?' I asked.

The sun was rising outside and the attic vents glowed like electric burners. We sat in the quiet, and I let her think about the story I had told her. But then there was a gunshot from inside the house. One shot. Small caliber. Walter's .22. Almost quiet.

It didn't matter how quiet, though. Walter had shot, and that meant Carol, Jimmy, and Robert would be loading rifles and pistols – automatic, semi-automatic, and manual. They would be aiming the guns at the house. I could have done a countdown. Four, three, two, one.

Gunfire exploded in the yard and a spray of bullets hit the outside of the house, punching into the tarred planks, bouncing off the stone chimney, sinking into the oily dark shingles, ricocheting into the sky.

'I can't stay here,' Lexi said, and scrambled for the attic hatch.

'We're safe,' I said, and tried to hold her.

She slipped from my hands and yanked open the hatch.

'You can't tell them what I've told you,' I said.

'Why?' she asked.

'Give me the flashlight,' I said.

She did, and I shined it through the attic. Again I saw none of my dad's guns. I saw only boxes and boxes of his books. I said anyway, 'If Walter learns who I am, he'll kill me. You can't tell them my name.'

'Why have you come?' Lexi said.

'Do you really need to ask?' I said.

Another spray of bullets hit the house.

She lowered herself into the hatch. 'Who are the people outside?' she asked.

146

'I'm inside with you,' I said. 'I'm here because of you and Cristofer.'

'We don't even know you,' she said.

'We'll know each other now,' I said.

Another spray of bullets.

'Who are those people?' she asked.

'They're outside,' I said.

'That's not an answer,' she said.

Another spray, and a flash of light burned through the hallway. Dirt and sand showered down on the outside walls and roof, and Lexi climbed out through the closet and stepped into the hallway.

Twenty-Six

Lexi

And Oren came tumbling after.

'I'm not leaving you alone in this house,' he said.

I said, 'It's *my* house.'

'You think so?' he said.

We went downstairs. Bullets hit the outside walls. A haze hung over the furniture. The air smelled like sweat and splintered wood and tar. Mom sat on the floor by the kitchen doorway. Cristofer jumped up and down on Walter's green chair. Grunting. Walter kneeled by the window with his .22. Squeezing one shot for every ten that the people outside fired. The

147

German shepherds barked and barked and barked.

The green chair was safe from the window but I yelled at Cristofer to get down. He kept bouncing and grunting. Dust pumped from the split cushion. I grabbed him but he swatted my face.

'Hey,' Oren yelled at him.

Cristofer kept bouncing.

'It's all right,' I told Oren. 'He didn't mean to.'

But Oren yanked the chair out. Cristofer hit the edge and fell. Oren stood over him like he would crush him. I yelled, 'Don't.'

Cristofer looked at Oren and keened.

Oren bent over him. Whispered something. Then sat in the chair. Pine oil from the box of photos had stained his sleeve. Cristofer smiled at him and stayed on the floor. Oren stared at the clouds of dust in the morning sunlight. As if he could read a message in them. Then he looked at me and said, 'Anyone for breakfast?'

I gave him the meanest look and crawled to the window where Walter was kneeling with his rifle. The sun was rising over the hill. The ground was wet and glistening from last night's rain. And breathing out a vapor. The people in the yard had parked the pickups end-to-end by the tar kiln. The bikers stood behind the yellow truck. They were thick-chested and square-faced and tan. The black-haired woman wore a black T-shirt. Grinning.

Walter squeezed the trigger of his .22 and sank a bullet into the rear panel of the yellow truck. Raising a yellow-paint mist. The woman finished saying whatever she was saying. Then lifted a

148

black semi-automatic above the truck bed. Shot at the house.

When the sound died and the shock passed Walter shouted into the yard, 'What do you want?'

No one answered.

He shouted again, 'Whatever you want you can have it. What do—'

The woman shouted, 'Your daughter.'

Walter stared at me. Considering. Then he shouted back, 'I have no daughter.'

One of the bikers shouted, 'Your wife.'

The other shouted, 'Your son.'

Walter shot another bullet into the side of the yellow truck.

The woman shouted, 'Your life.'

'Why?' Walter yelled. But soft. Like he was afraid of the answer.

Paul the driver stepped from behind the red truck. Big. He was trying to pass for human but not making it. He cupped a black pistol in his hand. 'Your blood,' he shouted. 'Your wife's. Your—'

Walter shot at him. Paul's pant leg twitched and a spray of blood came from his thigh. The bullet had grazed him. Stung him. He shouted, 'Never wound a predator. Kill him or hide from him. If you wound him—'

Walter shot again. Missed. And Paul yelled and shot his pistol four times at the house. When I looked back outside he had ducked behind the truck. The woman and the bikers had also disappeared.

But then Paul laughed and ran into the open. He threw a jug of something burning which shattered in front of the porch. Exploded. The house groaned. The walls and floor and ceiling shifted and settled. In the kitchen a shelf broke and glass shattered. Flames licked from the dirt in the yard and then died.

Walter said, 'Jesus Christ.'

Mom started crying.

Cristofer keened.

Oren sat in the green chair. Calm. Dabbed at the oil on his sleeve with his handkerchief. When he saw me watching he said, 'I really could use some breakfast.'

'Asshole,' I said.

He frowned at the handkerchief. Spat on it. Dabbed the sleeve.

Walter seemed to notice him for the first time. Squinted through the hazy light and said, 'What the hell are you doing here?'

'Apparently not eating breakfast,' Oren said.

Walter went to him with the rifle. 'Did I or didn't I tell you to leave yesterday?'

'You did,' Oren said. He dabbed the sleeve. 'I found it insulting. Paul must have too. You read about this kind of thing. Guys getting kicked out of parties and then coming back and burning down a place. Until now I didn't think it really happened.'

'Did I or didn't I say I would shoot you if you came into this house?' Walter said.

Oren looked bored. 'You did.'

Walter gripped the rifle barrel and swung the wooden stock so it hit Oren in the head. A crease of blood welled over his eyebrows. Walter tried to hit him again. But Oren grabbed the stock and twisted the gun from his hands. Oren stood.

150

Mom who was sitting in the kitchen doorway said, 'No.'

And Cristofer stopped keening.

Walter backed away.

Oren sighted the gun at the floor. 'How many rounds does it hold?' he asked. No longer bored.

'Go to hell,' Walter said.

Oren chambered a bullet. Raised the gun. Pointed it at Walter's head. 'How many rounds?'

'I modified it,' Walter said. 'Thirteen.'

'Enough for everybody,' Oren said. And lowered the rifle. He gripped the barrel and gave it to Walter. He said, 'This isn't the time to kick guests out.'

'You aren't a guest,' Walter said, and grabbed the gun. 'Why are you doing this?'

Oren looked surprised. 'Me?'

'You and your friends,' Walter said.

'What makes you think they're my friends?' Oren asked.

Walter pointed the gun at the floor. 'You're saying they aren't?'

'I'm inside with you,' Oren said. 'If they were my friends, wouldn't I be out there with them?'

Walter aimed the rifle at him. 'True enough,' he said. 'That's where you belong.'

Oren went back to the chair and sat. 'If I walked out the door, they would shoot me just as they would shoot you.'

'Why did they come here?' Walter asked. 'Why is your driver with them?'

'You treated Paul badly,' Oren said. 'As for the others, you're an unpleasant man. I'm sure you've made unpleasant enemies.'

Walter pointed the rifle at Oren's face. He said,

151

'Why did all sorts of evil start happening when you came?'

'Is that when it started?' Oren asked.

'Why did you come?' Walter's fear was gone.

Oren said, 'Because I appreciate fine painting and have a special interest in portraiture.' The crease of blood over his eyebrows had swollen into a half-moon.

'Get out,' Walter said.

Oren said, 'As far as I'm concerned, right now this house is as much mine as it's yours.'

'I already shot your driver – your *friend*,' Walter said. 'You *know* I'll shoot you.'

'Once again,' Oren said, 'you're calling him a friend.'

'You say he isn't? Let's give it a try,' Walter said. 'Get up. Let's see just how friendly you and those people are.'

Oren shook his head. Hardly tolerating him. And stood.

Walter poked him with the rifle. 'Move.'

'You do that again, I'll break it over your back,' Oren said.

Walter pointed the gun at him. 'To the window,' he said.

'This is a bad idea,' Oren said. But he lifted his hands over his head and moved in front of the window.

Bullets pelted the outside of the house like metal hail. Ricocheting off the chimney. Sinking into the walls.

Oren knocked the rifle from Walter's hands and dropped to the floor. The guns outside stopped. 'Satisfied?' Oren asked.

'Not hardly,' Walter said. 'They didn't come close to hitting you.' And he picked up his rifle and aimed it at Oren.

'You're wasting time,' Oren said. 'While these people are shooting at you and generally kicking your ass you're chasing me around with a squirrel gun. You could be getting ready for a fight. These people look like they're planning to stay awhile.'

If Walter pulled the trigger he would shoot Oren in the eye.

'Don't tell me that's your biggest weapon,' Oren said.

Walter only stared at him.

Oren laughed and said, 'How about knives? Do you have rubbing alcohol? Peroxide? Bleach? You can improvise – a man like you with a modified rifle magazine. You must know how to make things and break them. The rules don't apply to you. Right?'

I said to Walter, 'Listen to him.'

'Shut up,' he said. 'You brought this man into our house—'

Oren said to him, 'You're wasting time. I've never seen a man who acts more like he's got it coming to him. You might as well walk out and get it over with.' He went to Mom. She was weeping in the kitchen doorway. 'And *you*,' he said. 'What's wrong with you? What makes you give up so fast? What do you have to cry about?'

'Shut up,' I said to him.

He stared at me. The wound on his forehead was bright with blood. His eyes were flat.

I said, 'Don't do this.'

He turned back to Mom. 'These people have

153

restrained themselves so far. Do you want to take it to the next level?'

Mom wiped her chin with the back of her hand. 'We're not taking it to any level,' she said. 'They brought this to us. We've never seen them before.'

'You must have done something to bring it on yourself,' Oren said.

'Stop it,' I said.

He looked at me. 'What?'

'Stop this from happening,' I said. 'Tell them to stop. They'll listen to you.'

He shook his head.

'Tell them,' I said.

Then from upstairs there came a grinding of metal on metal. And wood on wood. Old bed springs. The guns outside opened up. The front of the house clattered with bullets. The chimney stones pinged. The grinding got louder. I looked around the room. Cristofer was gone. A spray of bullets hit the house. High above the front porch.

I yelled, 'Cristofer!' And ran for the stairs.

Oren passed me before I reached the landing. Ran into Cristofer's room. Cristofer was bouncing in a cloud of plaster dust. Twirling his fingers through the cloud. Bullets hit the walls outside of the window. One had come through and pocked the ceiling. Oren tackled Cristofer. Throwing him on to the mattress and falling with him on to the floor. Cristofer laughed and laughed. He ran his fingers through Oren's hair. Like Oren was a dog.

Oren looked up at me.

Blood from his forehead had smeared across Cristofer's face.

Twenty-Seven

Oren

'This will be a long day,' I said to Lexi when we were out in the hallway. 'I'll need your help.' Cristofer rocked on his feet as if the house was swaying.

'Not *my* help,' Lexi said. In Cristofer's room the sun was glinting through a white haze. She asked, 'Can you stop them?'

'I don't think so,' I said. Now that we'd started, I would shake the boards of the house until the light shined through.

'Why not?' she said.

'Are you sure you want me to?' I asked.

She almost yelled. 'Yes.'

'Sorry,' I said. 'The bubble's in the vein. It's just a matter of time.'

'What bubble?' she said. 'Whose vein?'

'Walter's,' I said. 'Your mother's.' I would shake the house until the nails popped out.

'You mean *our* mother's?' she said.

'Sure,' I said. 'Why not?' I would shake Kay and Walter until their bones pulled from their joints.

'Stop it,' Lexi said. 'Tell those people to go away.'

'I can't,' I said. I was an honorable man, I told myself. I wanted to believe it.

155

'I'll tell Mom and Walter who you are,' Lexi said.

'Then we're all screwed,' I said.

'As opposed to now?' she said.

'That's right,' I said. 'As opposed to now.'

We went downstairs. Kay was bringing her kitchen knives into the front room. She already had put a half-gallon bottle of Crisco by the green chair.

When Walter brought in a long extension cord, I said, 'Good man.'

'For what?' Lexi asked.

I said, 'Walter is an innovator, a creative thinker – isn't that right, Walter? Don't you have more guns?'

Walter ignored me but said to Lexi, 'Fill the bathtub.'

'This isn't a hurricane,' she said, and sat on the bottom stair.

'Could be worse than one,' I said. 'I admire your thinking, Walter, and I'll be happy to help.' I went back upstairs and turned on the water in the bathroom. 'Tell me if I can do anything else,' I shouted.

Walter yelled up the stairs, 'Bring down the mattresses.'

'Don't be a fool,' Lexi said to him.

'That's one thing I've never been,' Walter said.

Outside, Jimmy fired up his motorcycle and started circling the house. Then he opened the throttle and roared up the hill toward the gate, turned, and roared back. Carol whooped.

156

I dragged a mattress down the stairs and asked Walter, 'Where do you want it, chief?'

He eyed me but said, 'Cover the window.'

'Good thinking,' I said. I leaned it so that a couple of inches of light came in at the top.

'Because this will keep them out?' Lexi asked.

I said – for Walter's sake – 'It might make them think twice about coming in since they won't know what's waiting for them.'

'They could've broken through the door any time they wanted,' she said. 'They still can.'

'But now if they do, we'll have surprises waiting for them,' I said. 'Isn't that right, Walter? You have more than the squirrel gun, don't you?'

'No other guns,' he said.

I stared at him. He stared at me. 'What the hell,' I said, and I grinned.

'Get the other mattresses,' he said.

'Yes, sir,' I said.

Walter said, 'Is this all a joke to you?'

'It's what they call deep play, sir,' I said. 'A high-stakes game.'

'I can't say I know what you're talking about,' he said. He sat down on the green chair with a kitchen knife and the extension cord. He sliced off one end, separated the strands, and scraped the insulation off the wires.

I stopped on the stairs. 'I think you do,' I said. 'I would never underestimate you. I think you've known this has been coming for a long time.'

The engine on Robert's motorcycle roared outside, and soon both motorcycles were racing around the house. Then one of the trucks joined

157

them. The house shook with the noise, and Cristofer started keening.

I would shake the house until Kay's and Walter's sinews ripped into threads that blew out through the window and fell like snow in the yard.

After I brought the other mattresses and put them on the floor by the bookshelves, Walter asked me to get a hammer and a screwdriver from one of the kitchen drawers. Then he and I went upstairs, unhooked Cristofer's door from the hinges, carried it down, and propped it against the mattress covering the window.

'I'm impressed by your thinking, chief,' I said.

'Shut up,' he said.

As we came down with the second bedroom door, the motorcycles and truck stopped racing around the house, but Paul's German shepherds barked and whined like they'd found meat. Lexi shoved the mattress away and looked out. Carol was lying on the ground by her truck, laughing, playing, rolling in the dirt with Cereb and Flip. Carol wore knee-high black boots, and Cereb bit at her ankles.

Walter said to Lexi, 'Don't blame me if they put a bullet in your head.' We carried the door into the kitchen and set it by the window to the side yard. Then we went back upstairs and brought down the third door, which we set against the wall by the shelves.

Although we had blocked most of the openings to the front, when Robert pulled a cooler out of the bed of the red pickup and lit a fire, the smell of cooking meat came into the house. We hadn't eaten since the day before, and hunger twisted in my belly.

158

It must have twisted in Lexi too. She brought a bunch of cans from the kitchen cabinet, opened some kidney beans, and ate the food cold with a spoon. Afterward she went upstairs and got her Bible, brought it back to the dinner table, and told Cristofer to sit with her so she could read to him.

Walter smiled grimly at her as if reading the Bible was the first sensible thing she'd done in her life. But she pulled out *Great American Stories* and read out loud, '*Here comes a raging rush of people with torches, and an awful whooping and yelling, and banging tin pans and blowing horns; and we jumped to one side to let them go by; and as they went by I see they had the king and the duke astraddle of a rail – that is, I knowed it was the king and the duke, though they was all over tar and feathers, and didn't look like nothing in the world that was human – just looked like a couple of monstrous big soldier-plumes. Well, it made me sick to see it; and I was sorry for them poor pitiful rascals, it seemed like I couldn't ever feel any hardness against them any more in the world. It was a dreadful thing to see. Human beings can be awful cruel to one another.*'

I said, 'No one will ever buy it.'

'It's a great American story,' Lexi said.

'They just say that to sell books,' I said. 'It's trash.'

Then Walter said, 'Listen.' And when we didn't, he said it again – 'Listen!'

A diesel engine sounded from outside, different from the generator or the motorcycles and trucks. It made a musical rattle and hum.

'Lane Charles's tractor,' Walter said.

159

He pushed the mattress from the window and crouched so he could see. Carol and the others were standing behind her yellow truck, cooking over the fire. Lane Charles's tractor rolled out of his field and into the yard.

Walter laughed. 'That sonofabitch is coming. First thing he's ever done. About time.'

Lane Charles wore black pants and a white button-up shirt as if he'd been away on business or at church. His glasses reflected the sun.

I wanted to yell at him to stay out of it, but now Paul, Carol, Jimmy, and Robert stepped into the open and watched him come. Paul's biggest dog, Flip, ran to greet him, whapping his tail like he was swatting flies.

'That nosy sonofabitch, God bless him,' Walter said, and he yelled, 'Hey.'

The tractor engine drowned out Walter's voice or else Lane Charles just ignored it. The tractor drove toward my friends.

Walter stood up at the window. 'Hey,' he yelled again, 'Over here, you sonofabitch.'

The tractor bee-lined at Carol's pickup, black smoke hiccupping from the exhaust stack. When it reached the truck, Lane Charles climbed down, leaving the engine running. Paul talked with him. He shook his hand. Paul pointed at the house and then at the back-acre pine woods and explained something we couldn't hear.

'Goddamn it,' Walter yelled. 'Don't listen to him. Get help.'

Lane Charles nodded at something Paul said.

Since Lane Charles had gotten into the middle, it seemed like a good time to show Walter how

160

helpless he was. I said to him, 'Get the man's attention.'

'I'm trying, damn it,' Walter said.

'No, *get* his attention. Let him know you're here,' I said.

Walter got an idea. 'You're OK,' he said, and he pointed his .22 at the sky and fired.

Paul looked at the house, but Lane Charles didn't seem to notice.

Walter chambered another bullet.

'That's enough,' I said.

But Walter lowered the rifle barrel and shot again. A flower of yellow paint burst from the hood of Carol's truck. Now Lane Charles stared at the house. Walter waved at him and yelled again, 'Get help.'

Lane Charles scrambled on to the tractor. Paul spoke to him, but he shifted and opened the throttle. The tractor jerked and bumped and then rolled across the yard. Lane Charles sat tall in his seat, his back straight, as if he was too proud to bend. But he ran the tractor full.

'Goddamn it,' Walter muttered, and chambered a bullet.

'No more,' I said.

'One shot into the engine casing,' Walter said. 'He'll come back.'

I said, 'You've done enough.'

But Walter sighted the gun and shot. The bullet went low.

'Don't,' I said.

Walter yelled at Lane Charles again, 'Hey.'

In a few seconds, the man would disappear into his field.

Walter chambered a bullet and sighted the rifle again.

'Don't —' I said.

He did, and his shot missed the tractor again.

Lane Charles hunched low in his seat.

'Goddamned fool,' Walter said, and chambered another bullet.

I tried to knock the gun from his hands.

But he shot.

Lane Charles's head snapped back. Blood lit up the air above him.

'What did you do?' I yelled.

The tractor veered back into the yard and careened out toward the hill, spitting dirt from its tires, then turned back toward the pickup trucks and motorcycles. Lane Charles lay on the steering wheel, his body hard against the throttle. The sun glinted off his glasses.

'What have you done?' Kay shouted at Walter.

He stood, shocked, with the rifle in his hands, as if someone had tricked him into holding it. 'Not my fault,' he said.

I knocked the gun from his hands.

Outside, the tractor arced short of the pickup trucks and headed for the house. It seemed it would hit the porch and come through the door. Walter looked terrified. Paul, Carol, Jimmy, and Robert watched. The sun flashed off the tractor and Lane Charles's bloody shirt.

I watched the tractor come. It would hit the house. My head was buzzing.

Then Paul stepped behind the yellow truck and came back with a shotgun. He aimed at Lane Charles.

162

'No,' Lexi said.

I wanted to shout out the window at Paul. But I said to Lexi, 'He's already dead.'

Paul squeezed the trigger.

Lane Charles's body jerked.

I felt sick.

But the tractor seemed to figure out where it was going. It passed by the side of the house and bumped and rattled across the yard toward the pine woods. I listened for a crash when it hit the trees, but only quiet followed and an uncertainty worse than sound.

Walter picked up his .22 and said, 'I'm ending this now.' He headed for the door.

Lexi stepped in front of him, blocked him.

Walter looked like he would hit her. 'They've got their hands on our necks,' he said. 'I won't stand it. I'm—'

Out in the yard, Paul yelled, 'Go,' with such strange force that Walter went to the window instead, to see what he was doing. Paul's German shepherds streaked across the yard toward the house, Stretcher leading. They turned and ran along the porch, turned again, sprinted to the side and around the back, and came again to the front. They circled the house, the sun sparkling in their gray fur, turning it silver, clouds of dirt and dust rising from their feet. They circled the house a second time and a third, and then Walter raised his rifle to his shoulder and tracked Stretcher's movement as the dog came around to the front. I ran to him to take the gun. I was ready to shoot *him*. He wanted to end this and I was ready to end it for him.

But he pulled the trigger.

A spot of blood shined on Stretcher's haunches. The dog spun and for a moment stood still. Then it tried to bite the bullet wound like a gaffed shark turning on itself.

'Ha,' Walter shouted out the window.

I ripped the rifle from his hands. 'Enough,' I said.

But Stretcher wasn't done. The big dog turned toward the house, smelled the air, and sprang on to the porch. His feet hardly touched the planking before he leaped through the window. He came at Walter, knocking him to the floor, making noises made only by predatory animals – muscle noises, noises from deep in the throat, deep in the chest, skin slapping against skin.

Then Flip and Cereb came through the window, ripping and yapping. Stretcher closed his jaws on Walter's leg, and Walter screamed. Cereb cornered Kay, growling low from the belly, and Flip, his ruff high, stood by Cristofer, watchful.

Walter screamed again as Stretcher tore at his leg. I set Walter's gun down against the wall. Lexi went for it, but Cereb turned from Cristofer and backed her away with his teeth. She shouted at me, 'Shoot it.'

I caught my breath, dizzy. But I put a finger to my lips. 'Shh,' I said, and I went to the green chair and sat down. *Close your eyes*, Paul had said. *Let it happen.*

I closed my eyes – then opened them again.

Walter screamed again when Stretcher's teeth found his leg bone.

Lexi ran across the room, grabbed the rifle, and swung the butt down on the head of the dog.

'Don't,' I said, too late – for a third time, too late.

The butt came away sticky and gray, and Stretcher fell, his teeth caught in Walter's leg.

Flip went after Lexi, and she prodded him back with the gun. Flip lunged, and she jabbed him. He sprawled, got to his feet, and lunged again. She knocked him down again. When he got back to his feet, I whistled once, high, and Flip's muscles relaxed. Cereb trotted over from Kay and licked Flip on the ears, as if neither one ever had known meanness.

Then, out in the yard, Paul whistled too – long and low – an answer to my high whistle. Cereb turned and leaped out through the window, jumped from the porch, and raced across the yard toward the pickup trucks. Flip sniffed at Stretcher's body, looked at me. I pointed at the window and he leaped out.

Kay went to Walter. One of his pant legs was ripped. His shin, up to his knee and down to his work boot, was covered in blood, his pale flesh ripped and ragged. His face was gray, and for the first time I knew what he would look like when he was dead.

'Get towels and water,' Kay said.

Lexi went to the kitchen and brought back a bowl, towels, and turpentine. Kay had Walter lie on the floor with his hurt leg on one of the dinner chairs. She bathed the torn skin, touching it with the softest part of a towel, tipping water from the bowl to rinse it. Walter moaned until Kay screwed the cap off the turpentine and shook the bottle over his leg, and then he screamed again, louder than when Stretcher was

165

biting him. His face looked feverish. His jeans were damp with sweat. A foul smell rose from him as she bandaged his leg with a clean towel.

'Hush,' Kay said. 'Hush.'

But as the first and worst of the pain lifted, he looked around the room savagely. When his eyes landed on me, sitting on the green chair, he said, 'Why didn't you shoot it?'

I looked down at him. I said, 'It wasn't bothering me.'

'It was trying to kill *me*,' Walter said.

'You shot it,' I said. 'It didn't shoot *you*.'

Walter grimaced, as though a sudden pain had shocked him. 'Why didn't any of the dogs go after you?' he asked.

'I showed no fear,' I said.

'And why not?' he said. 'Unless you knew they wouldn't attack you.'

I said, 'They looked more like the kind of dogs that would attack *you*.'

Walter tried to push himself on to his elbows, scowling as his leg dragged on the floor. 'You're with those people out there,' he said.

'I thought we'd been through that already,' I said.

He said, 'Let's go through it again.'

I'd underestimated him. Stretcher had worked hard on his leg, but his ligaments still held him together and he was still capable of anger. So I got up from the chair and went to him. I nudged one of his elbows with my shoe. I blamed him for Lane Charles's death. And Stretcher's. And my dad's. And for all but killing me. 'Some men see straight,' I said to him. 'Some men have such great eyes they seem to see around corners. But others – they're so preoccupied with themselves it's like they live in a house of mirrors. I think you're that third kind of man.'

'I see clear enough,' Walter said.

I sighed. 'Where's your duct tape? Do you have rope or twine?'

'Why?' he asked.

Because I want to finish tearing you apart, I thought. I said, 'Because you don't seem like you'll be very steady on your feet right now. Someone's got to get the house together.'

Walter shook his head. 'You just go on making yourself comfortable,' he said. 'We'll tell you when this is over.'

But I crouched so that I could look into Stretcher's dead eyes. Then I pushed the mattress to cover the window, went into the kitchen, and dug through the drawers and cabinets. I brought back tape, two screwdrivers, a ball of brown twine, three Bic lighters, an aerosol can of roach spray, another of white spray paint, two candles, and a rusty flashlight that glowed dimly when I tried the switch and shined it at Lexi. I pushed the dinner table against the front door and stacked the dinner chairs on top of it.

Because the tighter you pack an explosive, the harder it explodes.

I went up to Kay's bedroom and then inched her bureau down the stairs, resting each time it thumped on a step and, when I got it to the first floor, shoving it against the dinner table. I got Walter's hammer and went back upstairs. I smashed the bathroom mirror. I came down with

167

the pieces of glass in a bundled towel. I opened it and poured the glass out at Kay's feet. 'Do with it what you will,' I said to her.

'What?' she said.

'Make weapons,' I said.

I sat down on the green chair with one of the kitchen knives, sliced the towel into strips, and tied the strips together end-to-end.

'What are you doing?' Walter asked.

'In general, tearing your house apart,' I said, but added, 'We don't know what we will need.' I stretched a length of the ripped towel between my hands as if it was a rope.

Twenty-Eight

Lexi

The heat rose inside the house as the afternoon passed. Walter unbuttoned the top of his jeans. He was lying on the floor bare-chested next to the dead German shepherd. Mom sat in the kitchen doorway with her legs spread and the front of her dress unbuttoned to her belly. Ignoring the broken mirror. Cristofer stood in a corner like a scared animal. His hair slick with sweat. I sat by the shelves where the room was darkest. The hem of my dress rolled up. If the people outside didn't kill me I would sweat to death. Oren kept preparing the house. Carrying in scissors and a cutting board and an old razor and a box cutter and a broom handle. Anything bladed. Anything blunt.

Walter pushed himself to sitting. Stared at him like he wanted to kill him. Tried to get to his feet.

'What are you doing?' Mom asked him.

The leg that the dog bit wouldn't hold him. He looked around the room for help. I watched and wouldn't mind if he fell. But Oren brought him the broom handle. Walter used it like a staff. He went to the mattress that covered the window and shouldered it aside. The sun shined sharp into the room. The people in the yard were resting. An airplane hummed high and lonesome overhead. Beyond the hill a locust whined.

Walter limped to the dead dog. Grabbed its hind legs. Almost fell. And said to Oren, 'Help me.' Oren stared at him until Walter asked again. Then Oren picked up the dog's front legs and he and Walter carried it to the window. Walter said, 'On three.' On *three* they threw the carcass out over the porch into the yard.

As the sun set the people cooked another meal over the open fire. The smell of meat drifted into the house. And the sweet smoke of roasting corn. The people talked and laughed. The woman's laughter rising high and fearless over the voices of the others. The darkening sky looked like it would weigh the whole world into silence.

Walter stood by the window. Leaned on the broom handle.

'You're an easy target,' Oren said.

But Walter yelled out into the yard, 'What do you want?'

169

The talk and the laughter carried on.

Walter yelled, 'I'm coming out and I'm going to shoot each one of you.'

The people kept talking.

Walter yelled, 'I need air.'

They ignored him.

'You understand?' Walter asked.

Paul the driver stepped out from behind the yellow pickup with a black semi-automatic. He pelted the outside wall with bullets. Walter dropped to the floor like someone had kicked the broom handle. Or punched him in the liver.

He was panting. Broken or almost. He said to Oren, 'Cover the window.' Oren did and the room was dark. Walter crawled to one of the mattresses and was quiet. After a while Mom spread out beside him. Cradling his sweaty back against her breasts. Then Cristofer sat down. Rocking and grunting.

Oren came to me and took my hand. He led me upstairs. Through the hall. To the attic hatchway. Without a word. He boosted me through and pulled himself up after me. He put the board back over the hatch. Whether to keep everyone else from coming up or me from going down I didn't know. The last light of the day glowed in the attic vents. Sweat broke from my forehead. My arms. My legs. 'What are we doing?' I asked.

He said, 'Once upon a time there was a boy named Oren.'

'Don't,' I said.

'His mother was a seventeen-year-old girl named Kay,' he said, 'and his father was a thirty-seven-year-old man named Amon which

170

in Hebrew means *Teacher*. I looked it up. It's also Egyptian for *The Hidden One*.'

'As in disappearing from this house?' I asked.

'Now you see him and now you don't,' Oren said.

Twenty-Nine

Oren

As the sunlight at the roof vents dimmed and darkened, the generator in the back of Carol's truck ripped, sputtered, ripped, and hummed. The floodlights went on and the vents glowed again. Cereb and Flip barked, Jimmy laughed, and, right on schedule, music started to play – loud music with a deep beat that entered the old roof beams and made the house tremble.

'When I was born,' I said to Lexi, 'Amon moved into the house with Kay and her father. Kay at this time had been going to school only occasionally and then only so that she could steal oil crayons and paint from her art teacher. Because she lived in such a remote house or because of her strange personality, she had few friends other than Walter, who lived up-island. Walter was a skinny kid given to running away from home but never far, never crossing the bridge from Black Hammock. He slept in the woods in the summer and, on cold winter nights, wrapped himself around the Jakobson's tar kiln

171

for warmth. When Kay went to school, they rode the bus together from the base of the bridge, and in the afternoons Walter lounged on the porch with her, watching her draw or paint. Her pregnancy had brought him still closer. As her belly swelled, he'd spent more time at the house and treated her and the unborn baby as if the baby was his own, as if he would stand between her and any threat to her.'

Jimmy's motorcycle roared, and the speakers in the back of Carol's truck blasted Bachman–Turner Overdrive's 'You Ain't Seen Nothing Yet.'

'After moving in, Amon put an end to Walter's visits,' I said. 'He discouraged Kay from seeing this child who reminded him that he had gotten another child pregnant – and maybe also reminded him of the young man he had been in Saigon, little more than a boy himself – a boy-man who had also believed that he would sacrifice himself to protect his lover and their daughter, but instead had thrown his daughter on to a live grenade.

'Lying in bed with Kay, with their baby asleep in a crib near the open window and the smells of lovemaking and the baby's new life mingling in the night air, Amon should have been happy. When he'd come back from Vietnam, he'd seemed destined for loneliness and misery, and when Phuong failed to respond to his letters, he had learned to expect no more than that. Kay's appearance in his life, her pursuit of him, and the child she had given him had been a great miracle, a miracle no less extraordinary, to his thinking, than the laying of hands on a cripple. He should have been happy.

172

'But as Kay lay naked in bed beside him, her hand on his thigh, her fingers digging into his flesh, he sensed in her a hunger that scared him. When he had first known her, she had wanted to see him naked, asking him to take off his towel and underwear as he'd stood before her. She'd asked him to expose himself to her. She hadn't asked him to do such things again, but she hadn't needed to. He'd taken off his clothes for her and she'd taken hers off for him. But he'd sensed in her eyes and her touch a desire to go deeper, down to the blood and bones, to get into the parts of him where he held his most brutal memories of himself and those he had loved before her, the parts where damage rolled into damage like underwater currents. Seeing his old wounds would not be enough for her. She would want to rip away the scars and see what moved beneath.

'He had read enough books and experienced enough of life to know that he might be projecting his own fears and guilt on to her. If his own sense of himself coursed through his veins as thick and bitter as the pine tar that dripped from the kiln into the box under it, that might not be her fault. But more than once in the middle of the night he had awakened to her touch and had felt as if she were prodding him with a needle or the blade of a box cutter.

'The anger and misery that had lifted when he first had carried Kay into his bedroom, in the house that he'd built with his own hands, now settled back on to him with a weight that seemed all the heavier because he knew it was unwarranted. *Not*

173

her fault, he repeated to himself, but he blamed her anyway. She had made him happy, and if he had lost that happiness, he reasoned, who else could be the cause?

'But me, he loved,' I said. 'When I wasn't in my crib, I was in his arms. He carried me through the house, through the yard, and out into the woods. He introduced me to the smell of the pine trees and the heat of the tar kiln. Instead of a mother's breast, I felt the rough skin and cloth of a man who had rubbed hard against the world.

'Except when he had me in his hands, he turned mean. Kay had re-taught him his strength, and he used that strength to assert himself into the house, starting the kiln fire in the morning before Kay's father was awake, greeting the tar customers who drove over the hill and into the yard, inviting Tilson into the house to drink with him in the late afternoon, and collapsing at the end of each day into the chair that Kay's father always had claimed as his own. Amon took over the responsibilities of the house so fast that by the time Kay's father stopped appreciating the extra help and started to resent it, Amon had completely displaced him. Four months later, Kay's father died from a stroke or a heart attack or something else – no one checked, but it was quick – and Amon suspected that the man had just stopped breathing when he realized he'd become useless.

'At first, Kay was as attracted to Amon's new hardness as to his old wrecked self. She reached for him in bed. She followed him into the pine woods. She pushed my crib out into the hallway, closed the door, mounted Amon, and groaned as if she was singing a song.'

Lexi asked, 'How do you know this? Why would you *want* to?'

'He told me,' I said.

'That's messed-up,' she said.

'He was a complicated man,' I said.

'No,' she said. 'It's just messed-up.'

'So Amon started to push Kay away,' I said. 'The mounting, groaning girl wanted to get inside him, he believed – wanted to see, touch, and smell parts of him that he wished to reveal to no one. So he treated her as roughly as he had treated her father, and though they continued to share a bed, they rarely touched each other.'

Outside, Jimi Hendrix whined his guitar through the 'Star Spangled Banner.'

I said, 'When the sex stopped, Kay went back to drawing pictures of Amon – Amon sleeping, Amon holding me against his sweaty chest, Amon shooting one of his guns into the air, Amon standing by the kiln with red-streaked eyes and soot- and tar-stained arms and cheeks – and she gave each picture to him, as they previously had given their bodies to each other. He took the pictures and, she thought, hid them – an act that would have had its own intimacy and that, while it lacked the pleasure of sex, made her think that, in spite of the torment that was driving him away physically, they still shared a bright place that excluded everyone else. But one morning she saw him in the yard with a charcoal drawing. It showed him standing shirtless in the sunlight with an axe in his hand. Now, in the yard, he looked identical

175

to the drawing except that instead of an axe he held the picture. She watched, wondering if she would see where he was hiding her gifts. Instead, he ripped the picture and put it into the kiln. He loaded pine strips on top of it, added Spanish moss, and covered the pile with soil. He threw dry brush into the bottom oven, poured kerosene on to the brush, and tossed in a lighted match.

'After that,' I said, 'Kay made only self-portraits and kept them for herself.'

'Oh,' Lexi said.

'See?' I said. 'Amon was no hero. His meanness was bigger than other men's meanness. But so was his love. Shortly after I could walk, he tried to teach me skills that few children are capable of learning at a young age and that few parents are interested in having them know. How to sharpen a knife and use it on rope and wood. How to fish and clean out the organs with the scoop of a finger. How to dig trenches and build fences. How to sleep in the open air with only an embankment of earth and a blanket of pine needles to stay warm and keep off the insects. When I turned four, Amon taught me how to shoot a rifle and a pistol. It was as if he was preparing me to survive on my own, not only without the help of others but despite their hostility to me. He seemed to feel a jealous love for me, a love so strong that he feared it had to come to a bad end.'

'You remember this *how*?' Lexi asked.

'I remember everything,' I said.

'You're making it up,' she said. 'Or someone made it up for you.'

'Just go with me,' I said.

176

'That depends on where you want to take me,' she said.

I said, 'When a social services worker came to the house shortly after I turned six, Amon panicked. The lady brought a questionnaire that asked about vaccinations and health, schooling, household conditions, and parenting. Amon had good reason to worry, but the lady showed no real disapproval. When she visited my room, she picked up an open pocketknife and a spent shotgun shell from my bed and placed them in Amon's hand without a word. When she asked why I hadn't started kindergarten, she quietly wrote down Amon's answer that he was teaching me all that I needed to know at home. She complimented Kay on her pictures before driving out over the hill.

'But her visit was like pushing Amon down the stairs. He wondered if she would try to take me away from him, and he decided that she would. So that same night, as Kay slept, he stuffed our clothes and the money that remained from his parents' house behind the passenger seat of the Chevy pickup that Kay's father had bought in the early seventies. He wrapped a few of his best guns in a plastic sheet and put them in the bed of the truck. He ripped the phone line from the outside wall to slow Kay when she tried to report him—'

'This is when he left?' Lexi asked.

'The first time,' I said.

'It happened more than once?'

'Just listen,' I said. 'Amon carried me downstairs, still wrapped in my blanket, and put me in the passenger seat. By the time that Kay awoke at the house, we were driving across the Panhandle with the sun shining through the rear window, Amon white-knuckling the steering wheel, and me with my blanket draped around my shoulders. I knew that the world had begun spinning in a new direction during the night.

'Amon's paranoia rose with each mile that we drove, and so we left the highway and took rural routes through small towns, bypassing cities entirely or else driving into them and circling through the tangles of streets as if doing so would shake our scent.

'The first night, we camped inside the truck, tucking our clean clothes against the doors to make ourselves comfortable. The next day, Amon bought a tarp at a hardware store so that we could sleep in the truck bed. By the end of the third day, the pickup cab smelled of our bodies and breath and of the roadside food that we were eating. It was easy to forget the house on Black Hammock Island – or to see it as a dream and my present situation in the truck with Amon as my only possible reality. I didn't ask where we were going or why we had left. I knew we were going where we needed to go.

'We zigzagged north and then west toward California. When we needed breaks, Amon drove through small towns until we found playgrounds – the first that I had ever seen. I would go down the slides time after time, or swing on the swing sets, or pull myself to the tops of jungle gyms and sit on the metal bars, while Amon lay on park benches staring at the tree branches or the sky.

'During the long daily drives, Amon told me about meeting Kay and the history of their relationship and my own history with him. And he

178

told me about Vietnam, about the woman he had loved there, and about the sister I would never meet. He told me place names – Saigon, Bien Hoa, Dong Nai, Phu Nhuan, Nha Trang – and the names of people, and asked me to repeat them to him, quizzing me, repeating parts of his story as if it would make me understand who and what I was, where I had come from, and where I was going.

'As we drove from Kansas City to Tulsa, the clouds, which had hung low and brown for the past hundred miles, turned green, and, though rain had fallen and dampened the ground, a wind kicked dust into the air. I asked if we could look for a playground, but Amon just looked up at the sky and accelerated as if the forces that he had feared were following us through the maze of American roads had collected above and would come down on us like a fist. The wind died and the air seemed clenched as we drove out of town. The clouds darkened over the farm fields to the east. Amon rolled down his window and bent low to watch the storm as it moved overhead.

'When a tornado dropped from one of the clouds, Amon let out a short laugh, as if the storm had confirmed all that he'd suspected since the social worker came to our house. If he had accelerated, we could have driven away from the tornado. Instead, he took his foot off the gas and glided to a stop on the road shoulder next to a hayfield. He told me to get out.'

'Stupid,' Lexi said.

I said, 'We walked together into the field, the green hay mashing under our feet. We walked

179

toward the tornado, which darkened as it picked up dirt and debris.

'"Dad?" I said.

'"Shh," he said, as if he expected the tornado also to speak and he wanted to listen.

'The tornado grew and blackened. Shingles and pieces of plywood and barn siding rose through the funnel and flew out when they reached a certain height, but still the tornado pulled more dirt from the ground. Wind started to whip around us. Overhead, a set of telephone wires throbbed.

'"Lie down, son," Amon said.

'"Dad—" I said.

'"Do as I say," he said.

'We lay together on the rough hay, and the sky seemed to tilt above us.

'"Hold my hand," he said. I did, and he said, "*Listen*."

'Then I heard the tornado. It was a low rumble. Then it was a roar. Then it was a sound like the sky and the ground were tearing at each other. I gripped Amon's arm and climbed on top of him, clutching his chest, and he was laughing, and his laughter was as terrifying as the storm.'

'How close did it come?' Lexi asked.

'A hundred feet?' I said. 'Or a hundred yards? It came close, but it passed.'

'He was stupid,' Lexi said.

'Maybe,' I said. 'But how was he to interpret the passing? Had the tornado been a warning that worse would come? Or had it purged Amon of his past, freeing him? Had it meant something else, or had it meant nothing at all? Amon said it must mean something.

'He carried me, still clutching his chest, out of the field, set me on the passenger seat of the pickup, and closed my door. That day, we drove until we left the storm clouds far behind and long after the sun set. When we pulled over and drew our tarp over the truck bed on the bank of the San Gabriel River in Texas, the stars shined hard against the blackness. The next morning, when we awoke still in the dark, Amon pointed to the one constellation that he knew – Orion – not quite my namesake but, with its shield and sword, enough to reassure me that the universe might protect as well as destroy me.

'Over the following days, we drove west into New Mexico, up through Albuquerque, and into Colorado. We drove up the valley of the northern Rio Grande, past the foothills of the Rocky Mountains, and with each mile Amon became more sullen and silent. At night, lying in the truck bed under stars that seemed brighter and colder as we drove higher, I clung to him for warmth and comfort, and he clung to me too as if we risked flying apart. But during the days, Amon stopped looking for playgrounds, and he stopped telling stories of the places he had been and the people he had known.

'After crossing the border into Wyoming, just short of Cheyenne, on a strip of rough concrete road that paralleled the Interstate, Amon pulled the pickup on to the shoulder, turned around, and, without a word, began driving south again, back across the border into Colorado, and down toward New Mexico. If I had been older, I might have questioned Amon's sanity. As it was, I pulled my

181

blanket around myself in the passenger seat and looked forward to the night-time when I would lie in the warmth of his muscular arms.

'Between Santa Fe and Albuquerque, Amon turned the truck on to a road that headed to the north again, but the next day we swung to the west and crossed into Arizona. We dropped to the south, and two days later, sixty miles short of Tucson, we turned west and drove into the desert, which, with its emptiness, terrified me as much as the tornado.'

Outside in the yard, one of my friends shot a gun. Shot it again and again and again. It popped like a string of firecrackers. Lexi jumped. The speakers in the back of the truck started to play 'Reptile' by Nine Inch Nails. The music sounded like ripping metal and machines that ate ripped metal.

I said, 'When we reached San Diego, Amon's mood lifted. Maybe being close to an ocean again after all the miles we had driven gave him a sense of peace. Maybe he was just happy to be at the end of the journey. For a week, we parked at a campground above the beach. In the mornings, while the air was cool with the salt breeze, I played on a rusting slide outside the park reception office and swung on the one swing that still hung from the swing set. In the afternoons, we waded into the cold Pacific Ocean water, shivering and laughing as the waves slapped against our skin and the salt stung our eyes. On our fourth day at the campsite, Amon bought a boogie board for me and a fishing rod for himself, and that evening, with my skin sunburned and scraped raw by the sand, I ate white seabass that Amon had caught in the surf and then cooked over a charcoal grill that he'd rented from the park office.

'For a long time, I blamed myself for what happened next. After all of our days on the road, being stationary made me think of home. The charcoal grill reminded me of the tar kiln, and the comforts of the park made me think of the comforts of Black Hammock. As Amon pulled the tarp over the bed of the pickup that night and a filmy layer of clouds crossed the rising moon, I told him that I missed my mother.

'When he said nothing, I told him again.

'In truth, I couldn't remember ever having been happier than I'd been that afternoon as the waves lifted me on my Styrofoam board and carried me on to the beach, or that evening as I ate dinner with Amon at a picnic table. But I was six years old and at that age happiness was enough reason to cry, and so the tears came and I cried quietly and, when Amon still said nothing, cried more loudly.

'What did I want? I wanted Amon to pull me into his arms and hold me. If he had done that, my day would have been perfect.

'But instead Amon tore the tarp from us and climbed out of the truck. I sat up and Amon spun on me as if he would climb back in and kill me. In the moonlight, his eyes shined with an anger unlike any I had ever seen – the anger of betrayal, the kind of anger that might lead a man to throw his own child on to a grenade.

'I backed away. I wanted to say I was sorry. I wanted to reverse time and erase my tears and my words about missing my mother. Instead, I said, "I want to go home."'

Lexi said, 'That bastard. He totally brainwashed you.'

I said, 'I don't want you to think of him that way. He was a good man but—'

'He completely fucked with your head,' she said.

'These were difficult times,' I said. 'For the next three days, Amon stayed at the truck when I went to the playground by the reception office or sat on the beach while I swam. He brooded, and the weight that he had shed as we drove into San Diego lowered upon him again.

'When I woke on the eighth morning at the campground, Amon was already out of the truck picking up the clothes that I had left to dry on the hood overnight and gathering the odds and ends that we had accumulated and left outside. Amon picked up the boogie board, snapped it in half, and stuffed it in the garbage barrel at the side of the campsite. He stuffed his fishing rod in too. He carried the rented charcoal grill to the reception office as if it was the only object in Southern California worthy of care. When he got back to the pickup, I was sitting on the passenger seat, my blanket close around my shoulders.

'We drove up through Los Angeles and on to the Pacific Coast Highway. The mountains climbed over rockslides and mud runs outside of my window. The ocean waves pounded against stone cliffs and washed in and out of rock basins outside of Amon's. When I saw sea lions lying on a spit of sand, with the sea mist sparkling in the air above them, I begged Amon to stop. He accelerated around the next bend. "I want to go home," I said, and he accelerated again.

184

'That night, we slept by Limekiln Beach, south of Carmel.'

Lexi said, 'None of this really happened. Did it?'

'Shh. Some of it did,' I said. 'When the damp and cold woke me in the dark, Amon was crying silently, his tears shining in the moonlight.'

Lexi asked, 'How much of it happened?'

I said, 'Everything that matters is true.'

'Why should I believe you?' she asked.

'Because,' I said, 'I watched Amon crying, and I was unsure and scared, and so I climbed on top of him and held my face close to his wet cheeks. I wanted to kiss the tears – to take his salt – but instead I touched the skin under one of his eyes with a finger.

'"No," Amon said, and lifted me off him, setting me on to the cold metal truck bed.

'In the morning, neither of us mentioned the crying, and Amon even seemed cheerful. "You want to go home, son?" he asked.

'I said nothing. I was unsure what I wanted.

'"That's fine," Amon said. "That's what we'll do. We'll take you home."

'I was only six years old and I not only loved my dad, I had a kind of crush on him, but I knew he was lying.

'He bundled the sleeping tarp and put it in a garbage can, and I climbed into the pickup and wrapped myself in my blanket. Amon spun the tires of the pickup in the gravel and dirt as we pulled from our camping spot back on to the highway.

'Late that morning, we arrived in San Francisco. We cruised through the streets and up and down

185

the hills as if we were tourists. Then we drove through the Presidio and on to the Golden Gate Bridge. Amon slowed until the other cars honked and sped around us. He peered past me, out the passenger-side window, and down to the churning water of the bay. "That's something, isn't it?" he said.

'"I'm hungry," I said.

'"Soon," he said. "Real soon."

'When we reached Sausalito, on the other side of the bridge, Amon turned the truck around and took us back over to San Francisco. Then we drove across the city and got on the highway to Oakland. We climbed the ramp on to the Bay Bridge, and Amon again slowed and peered through my window. "That's more like it," he said, and when I said nothing, he asked, "Isn't this more like it?"

'"Yes," I said, wanting to please him, though I was unsure what *it* was *like* or even what *it* was.

'Amon pulled the pickup to the side, and as cars blew their horns and whipped past, he got out and came around to my door. His eyes were wet but he smiled and said, "You ready to go?"

'He climbed over the metal rail and lifted me after him. We stood with the cold metal behind us and an expanse of open air in front, the concrete bed of the bridge ringing under the tires of the passing cars and then going silent as traffic stopped and people got out and spoke to us – dozens of frightened voices calling over each other. A cold wind blew my hair back and whistled in my ears. A brown gull hung in the air as if gravity was only a thing of the human imagination. The sun glimmered on the water below, and the surface looked as permeable and harmless as light itself, as if an object could pass through and arrive in another realm that was invisible only because of the glare. Amon held my hand, and though only a thin ledge kept me from falling, I felt safe.'

Lexi said, 'You've got to be kidding.'

I said, 'This is how it was with him then. Fearless.'

She said, 'I wouldn't want it.'

'Pretty terrible,' I said. 'But in its way, I've never known anything better.'

She said, 'Definitely wouldn't want it.'

I said, 'So Amon asked, "Are you ready?"'

'I was ready for anything he wanted me to do. But a voice that came from a place inside me that I hadn't known existed said, "No."

'"Come," Amon said, and inched close to the edge.

'"No," I said.

'"It's nothing," Amon said. "Like flying."

'"I don't know how to fly," I said.

'The people who had gotten out of their cars moved closer, almost to the rail, but Amon gave them a look that made them stop and back away.

'"There's not much time," Amon said. "We'll miss it."

'"Miss what?" I asked.

'He said, "Our one chance."

'But I pulled my hand from his and sat down on the ledge, my legs crossed under me. He easily could have picked me up, thrown me off the bridge, and jumped after me, but he sat next to me, his legs dangling over the edge. He put an arm around my shoulders.

187

'Sirens approached from both ends of the bridge, and megaphones told drivers to move their cars out of the way. A helicopter swooped in and hovered a hundred yards away, the pilot, visible through the windshield, wearing a white helmet and sunglasses that made him look like a hard-headed insect. By the time a San Francisco Marine Unit boat and a Coast Guard cutter arrived, the police had put all the onlookers back into their cars and made them drive away and had barricaded the bridge entrances. A plain-clothes officer climbed over the bridge railing and sat a few feet away from us on the ledge – with his legs, like mine, crossed under him.

'"Why are you out here, sir?" the officer asked.

'"Taking the scenery," Amon said.

'"Better places to do that," the officer said. "What do you mean to do now?"

'Amon said nothing.

'The officer looked at me. "Are you all right?"

'I looked at Amon, and he nodded.

'"Yes," I said to the officer.

'For an hour or more, the officer talked with Amon, asking where we were from, who we had left behind, why Amon had chosen to come to San Francisco. When Amon stopped answering the questions, the officer talked about the weather, a visit that he had made to Florida with his family when he was a boy of about my age, and then about hope, love, and his belief in humanity – matters that belonged on the earthward side of the glaring water. Then, in the same calm, matter-of-fact voice that he'd been using since he joined

188

us on the ledge, he told me to stand up and climb over the railing on to the road.

'Amon, who had seemed not to be listening, gripped my shoulder, though I hadn't tried to follow the officer's instruction.

'The officer said to Amon, "If you look behind you, sir, you will see a policeman with a rifle aimed at you. You can make a decision about your own life. But you will not take your child with you. Do you understand?"

'I looked and saw that what the officer had said was true.

'Amon didn't look, but after a few seconds he eased his grip on me. Then he stood and climbed back over the railing on to the road, where two policemen rushed to him and handcuffed him.

'The plain-clothes officer grinned as if he had won a game. "Climb over, son," he said.

'I stood and peered over the side of the bridge. With Amon's steadying arm gone, I tottered as I watched the slow eddies behind the Marine Unit and Coast Guard boats. The water seemed to pull at me and I leaned toward it. I heard Amon's voice telling me, *It's nothing*.

'But a policeman's hands reached over the railing and sucked me back. In a moment, I was on the other side, and a second policeman was wrapping a blanket around me – not the blanket that I had carried in the pickup from Black Hammock Island but a clean one – and I was shivering, though I felt a fever rising from my chest to my head.

'Afterward, Amon denied that he ever meant to jump or to harm me. The court hospitalized him for evaluation and sent me home on an

189

airplane. Kay looked at me as if she was unsure whether I had caused or was the victim of Amon's flight, and, though we had never had as close of a relationship as most mothers and their children, I felt a new coldness. In San Francisco, the doctors dug up Amon's records and said that he had suffered from a breakdown triggered by the visit from the social worker, which had made him fear losing me as he had lost his daughter Lang. It was a sympathetic story once the newspapers, magazines, and television news retold it. The doctors reassured Amon that rest, therapy, and, most of all, an encouraging letter from the state Department of Children and Families would restore him to mental health. Photographers from *Newsweek*, *Time*, and the *San Francisco Chronicle* snapped pictures of him as he walked out of the hospital, wild-eyed and bearded, his long hair uncombed. Amon had broken no laws, except maybe negligent driving and criminal trespassing for crossing the guardrail and the law of common sense for running off across the country the way he did with me. The police made a collection, bought another plane ticket, and sent him home.'

'Christ,' Lexi said.

Out in the yard, the music had stopped, but the generator hummed and Jimmy's motorcycle droned far and near as he rode out over the hill and back toward the house.

I said, 'For about a week after Amon returned, we were famous, though Amon chased away the reporters who made the trek to Black Hammock Island. But one of the soldiers who'd known him at the Bien Hoa military base – a man named Eric

Cantrell – saw a *Time Magazine* article and got to thinking. He'd been among the guys who'd taken Amon to the Hall of Mirrors brothel on the weekend when he met Phan Thi Phuong, but Cantrell had left the service after one tour and, until reading the article, had heard only rumors about the death of Amon's Vietnamese daughter. Now he lived in New Orleans and owned a bar that he had decorated to look like a miniature Hall of Mirrors, though the two Cambodian hookers he'd convinced to run their business from his bar stools in the early nineteen-eighties had been arrested and then had disappeared. Decades had passed since he'd left Vietnam, but he still met with other Bien Hoa vets every six or eight months. He rode a Kawasaki Eliminator, and the others owned a variety of bikes ranging from the barely street-legal to a grandpa-and-grandma thing with a homemade sidecar. One man was a real estate lawyer, another a high-functioning addict who shot up in gas station bathrooms as they traveled, a third a high school history teacher, another a roofer.

'When Cantrell called to tell them he was riding to Black Hammock Island to see Amon, only two of them could join him – Rob Terrenbaum, the realtor, and Stevie Abbott, the addict, who said he was bringing his sister, Denisa, even though she'd caused problems on earlier rides. Terrenbaum rode from L.A. to Taos, where Abbott met him with Denisa sitting behind him on his bike.

'"Is she necessary?" Terrenbaum asked.

'"Can't trust her alone," Abbott said, though in truth on her last trip with them it was his own

191

need for drug money that resulted in her getting beaten up.

'When they arrived in New Orleans, Eric Cantrell left the keys to his bar with one of his bartenders, and the next day, five hundred miles to the east, the motorcycles roared across the bridge to Black Hammock Island.

'As Amon's friends expected, Amon was a mess. On returning from San Francisco, he'd stuffed the packet of phone numbers and psycho-therapy resources into the kiln. He'd stopped bathing and mostly stopped eating. He was living in the yard, unwilling – it seemed, unable – to step on to the front porch. He was cared for only by Tilson, who had brought a plastic sheet from his own house for him to sleep under when it rained. I went outside to him when I could, but Kay mostly kept me upstairs.'

'Did *this* really happen?' Lexi asked.

'Every bit,' I said.

Lexi said, 'Mom never told me any of it.'

'No,' I said. 'She wouldn't. During Amon's absence, Walter had begun coming to the house again. He was no longer a skinny boy but a man nearly as large as Amon, and Amon seemed to lack the strength or the will to chase him away. Early one morning, a week after Amon returned, I was watching from a window as he slept under Tilson's plastic sheet. Walter walked into the yard, eyed the sleeping heap, stooped by it, and spoke so quietly that I couldn't hear. Amon showed no sign of hearing either, and Walter spat on the sheet, then crossed the yard, climbed the porch steps, and came into the house without knocking. He went upstairs, walked into Kay's bedroom, and closed the door.

'I ran out to the yard and shook Amon, telling him where Walter was. But he said nothing, did nothing.

'When Amon's Vietnam friends roared into the yard and found him flea-bitten and stinking, they sat by the kiln with him and got him drunk – blackout drunk, vomiting drunk, drunk into oblivion. Then, after listening to his drunken, disjointed mumbling, they beat the hell out of Walter.'

'Good,' Lexi said.

I said, 'The next morning, when Amon sobered up enough to stand, Stevie Abbott's sister went to him and kissed him with her hard, thin lips. He shoved her away. She came back and kissed him again and kept coming back until he stopped shoving her. She took off her shirt and stood, skinny and hard-breasted in the shivering morning light. So he unzipped her jeans and lowered them to the dirt. As Kay watched from her bedroom window and I watched from mine, he turned her around and pushed her to her hands and knees.

'Apparently, he felt better afterward,' I said. 'He drew water from the well and bathed. When Eric Cantrell went inside to the kitchen and brought back the turpentine, he scrubbed the deepest stains from his skin. He poured the remaining turpentine into his bowl of well-water and slicked back his hair. Only then did he realize that these men, who had disappeared from his life more than twenty years earlier, had come to save him.

'Amon's friends spent nearly a month at the

house. Mostly they stayed drunk. When the liquor ran out, Cantrell or Terrenbaum would ride over the hill on a motorcycle and return an hour or two later with new supplies. Abbott found a dealer a couple of islands up the coast. His sister sometimes wandered into the woods for a day or two or walked out on the road and crossed the bridge, but when she came back she would go to Amon and they would find a hidden spot or sometimes stay right out in the open, and afterward Amon would eye Kay like a housecat with a bird in its mouth that it was unwilling to give up. The men invited Tilson to join the party, but though he would pick up their spent bottles and trash from the yard, and even bring them new bottles when they called for them, he stayed sober, as if he knew that they needed someone to watch over them. Lane Charles, though, came from next door and drank as hard and laughed as loud as the rest. Walter appeared twice at the edge of the pine woods, watching and waiting, until Stevie Abbott got on his motorcycle and chased him into the trees.

'Terrenbaum left first, and a week later Cantrell rode out, followed by Abbott with his sister behind him hugging him with her skinny thighs. Denisa had spent the previous night with Amon, but when she climbed on to the motorcycle, she gave him the finger as if to say he should expect no tears.

'When Amon's friends left, the battle between him and Walter flared. Walter tried to go back to the behavior he'd adopted when Amon was gone. He walked out of the pine woods, crossed the yard, calling to the chickens as if they were his own, mounted the front porch, and entered the

194

house without knocking. But now Amon stood inside with a club of pinewood that he'd picked from the kindling. He split Walter's head with it, and Walter jumped on him and threw him to the floor. As blood came from the wound, turning Walter's face into a red mask and dropping from his eyes like tears, the two men wrestled, gripping each other by the throat, pounding each other's head on the floorboards, silent except for moans, as if their fight was about something more than sex or territory – about more than themselves.

'Kay watched from the kitchen doorway – holding me behind her – and though blood smeared across Amon's and Walter's faces and arms and stained their clothing, though they knocked over chairs and lamps and broke the table, she never tried to stop them. When they exhausted themselves, they lay in each other's arms, breathing each other's breath, drenched in each other's sweat and blood, until one of them drew enough energy to throw an elbow into the other's cheekbone or to raise the other's head and slam his skull against the floor. It seemed that they wouldn't stop until one of them was dead.

'But then Walter pulled himself from Amon's hands, got up with great difficulty, and, instead of dropping on to Amon again and crushing him, turned away. Without a glance at Kay, he walked to the door and went out. Amon lay on his back, breathing hard through his torn and bloody lips. A broken tooth – Walter's – clung to his forehead. His eyes focused on the ceiling as if he was looking for stars. He clenched and unclenched his fists, though his fingers were broken.

'Then Kay went to Amon, dropping to her knees. She said his name and said it again, and though his eyes remained on the ceiling, he raised a hand and searched the air until he found her and gripped her.

'"I'm sorry," he said.

'Tears filled Kay's eyes.

'"So sorry," Amon said.

'She kissed his wrecked lips, and he tried to pull her to him.

'But first she said to me, "Go." The kiss had smeared Amon's blood on her face. "Go," she said again as Amon tried to bring her body to his own. "To your room," she said, and she let herself be drawn down to Amon.

'The next two years were calm,' I said. 'Amon moved back into the house and shared a bed with Kay. She set up an easel and a mirror in the front room and painted the self-portraits that made her famous. He shaved his beard and cut his hair short. In the mornings, he tended to the chickens or, with Tilson's help, cut kiln wood in the back acres. In the afternoons, he collected the drippings from the tar box and sold pails of tar and jars of turpentine to customers who drove over the hill and into the yard. Many days, Lane Charles came with a bottle of vodka. In the early evenings, Amon would sit in his chair reading one of his books, or he would set up a target and shoot at it with one of his guns, or he would walk with me through the pine forest, telling me stories about the life he had lived. Shortly after sunset, he and Kay would tuck me into bed and then disappear behind their bedroom door.'

Jimmy cut the engine on his motorcycle.

196

Everyone in the yard was quiet. Only the generator hummed, dull and constant, boring into the night.

I told Lexi, 'When you were born, Amon loved you with the same intensity that he loved me, but he also seemed to fear you. Maybe you reminded him of Lang. Maybe he'd learned the danger of loving a child too much. And when Cristofer was born, Amon started spending more time in the yard again, but each night he came inside and locked the door behind him, and before disappearing into his bedroom with Kay, he stood for a long time in your doorway and Cristofer's and mine. As much as the family ever had been – as much as we ever could be – we were happy.

'Once when returning from the woods, though, I thought I saw Walter slipping away from the house. And sometimes when Amon was cutting wood with Tilson, Kay set down her paintbrushes, put you and Cristofer into my care, and left the house for a morning. I would follow her until she walked out over the hill and turned up-island on the road toward Walter's house.

'The night that Walter came back for good had been no different from the months and months of nights before it. Amon had knocked back a bottle of Smirnoff with Lane Charles in the afternoon and had invited Tilson to join the family for dinner. We were eating big meals in those days, but dinner was done now, and the table was covered with greasy plates, platters with bones and the tendon remains of a chicken, the head of a red fish that Tilson had contributed, and bowls with the last, uneaten greens from a kitchen garden that Kay had started.

197

'Amon, Tilson, and I remained at the table. Kay had taken you and Cristofer upstairs to put you in your cribs. Amon and I watched as Tilson gathered the bones from the chicken legs and thighs, used his teeth to scrape off the remaining cartilage, and sucked away the specks of blood.

'Amon said to him, "I'm not much given to the fine points of table manners, but do you want to explain what the hell you're doing?"

'Tilson wiped the grease and saliva from the bones on a pant leg. "Seem to me you get luck now," he said, and he cupped the dry bones in his hands, shook them, and cast them like dice on to the tabletop. Then he gathered them and cast them again. Though he hadn't drunk Lane Charles's vodka, he stared at the bones with glazed eyes.

'Amon asked, "They say I'm going to be lucky?"

'Tilson swept the bones into a pile. He said, "Good luck, bad, or something else, sure."

'Kay came down the stairs. But instead of joining us at the table, she stood holding the bottom of the banister. Amon patted his lap, inviting her to sit, but she stayed where she was.

'The look in her eyes scared me, and though I had no reason to, I looked from her to the door. Outside, the sun had lowered through the pine woods, but the frogs and locusts that usually sang after dark were silent. Still, the house felt safe and tight.

'Then Walter walked in. He was wearing his work overalls, a pressed white cotton shirt, and on his feet a pair of polished black dress shoes. "Good evening," he said, calm and easy, as if he expected a warm welcome and a hot plate of food.

'Kay stayed at the banister, and Amon, surprised but sure of his power in the house, remained in his chair. I was too scared to move. Only Tilson shoved back from the table.

'Amon cupped his chin in his hand and said, "What can we do for you, Walter?" If he'd gotten up and gone for one of his guns, everything would have been fine – he must have owned forty by then, and he kept some of them loaded.

'Walter came to the table and stood by him. "I've come to tell you it's time for you to go," he said.

'"*Go?*" Amon said, and he grinned.

'"Go," Walter said. "Time to leave. You did it before. No one missed you. I didn't."

'"You didn't, no." Amon nodded at me, as if he had everything under control. "No, you moved right in. A man might forgive another man for walking into his house uninvited once. He might even forgive him for walking into his bedroom. But twice? That wouldn't be a man. That would be either a saint or a man with no self-respect. A coward. And I'm none of those."

'"I'm sorry, Amon, but you can't stay." Walter almost managed to sound apologetic.

'"That's your decision, is it?" Amon grinned around the room – at me, at Tilson, at Kay.

'"It's *our* decision," Walter said. "Kay's and mine."

'Amon's grin cracked. He looked at Kay.

'She said, "You've exhausted me, Amon. There's too much of you. Soon there will be nothing left of *me*."

199

'Walter said, "We'll give you one chance, Amon. You can walk out now. If you don't—"

'Amon bellowed, his chest and face swelling in his rage. He looked as if he would vomit, as if tears would shoot from his eyes. He rose from his chair and turned over the dinner table. Plates, bowls, and glasses shattered on the floor. At that moment, I knew that someone in the room would die that night.

'Walter backed away one step, but one step only. Kay moved from the banister and threw something to him. It was one of the splitting chisels that Amon used to hack pine logs into strips for the kiln. Until that afternoon, the chisel had been rusty and dull, but Kay had taken a stone to it, and it spun as bright as a star into Walter's hand.

'Tilson rushed him, but Walter went to Amon and sank the chisel into his chest. The chisel made a sucking noise as Walter pulled it out. Each time that he thrust it again, it cracked bones and ground against something inside of Amon. Amon fell to the floor, and Walter mounted him. Amon must have died fast, but Walter kept plunging the chisel into him until his chest and stomach were a black bloody hole.'

'That's a lie,' Lexi shouted. 'My dad ran away. He'd done it before.'

I said, 'That's what Kay told the police when Lane Charles reported him missing. She didn't call the police herself. When they asked her about that, she said that Amon had left once and she'd taken him back. Now that he'd done it again, she said, she didn't want him back.'

'No,' Lexi said. 'Why would the police believe her?'

'Why wouldn't they?' I asked. 'As she said, he'd left before. They knew he'd been unstable, and a quick check – if anyone bothered to make one – would show that he had never gotten the treatment that the doctors in San Francisco had said he needed. It seems that only one young cop thought something was wrong.'

'Daniel Turner,' Lexi said.

'That's right,' I said. 'And Lane Charles also knew in his heart that his friend was dead, though he had no more proof than Daniel Turner did. He'd seen Kay walking up-island toward Walter's place all those mornings when Amon was cutting wood, and he'd kept a close eye on the house. But when Daniel Turner asked, Walter admitted to the affair and hinted that learning of it might have sent Amon running for a second time. When Daniel Turner pulled the charred scraps of a bloody dress from the tar kiln, Kay pointed out that, with all the axes, chisels, and saws, everyone in the house bled from time to time. When the police – who, in an unrelated case, were searching a section of South Georgia woods along the Interstate Highway – found the burnt-out car that Amon supposedly left in, Kay and Walter could offer no explanation and acted like it wasn't their obligation to offer one.'

'How about Tilson?' Lexi asked. 'He saw—'

'He saw everything,' I said. 'He knew everything. He buried Amon's body by the chicken pen.'

'Why would he do that?' she asked.

'Self-interest? Self-preservation?' I said. 'He

201

knew that justice is slow and it takes years and years to get rid of the blood of a killing like Amon's. Tilson is smart. He knew that you can scrub the floorboards with bleach and a wire brush, and you can rub pine oil and pitch into the rest of the floor so it takes the same color as the stain, but those are superficial cures. Tilson disliked Kay and Walter. Walter treated him badly, and Kay mostly ignored him. Only Amon had been good to him. But the best he could do for Amon was to dig a hole for him in the yard so he could be close to the house when justice came. That and he could protect me.'

'What happened to you?' Lexi asked.

'When Amon was lying on the floor, I climbed on top of him the same way I'd climbed on to him when we were driving west. The pool of blood and broken bones where his belly and chest should have been felt hot, and if I could have, I would have climbed into his skin and stayed. When Walter pulled me away, I bit and scratched him. I tried to kill him. But Walter threw me down on the floor and left me there.

'However much planning Kay and Walter had done before killing Amon, they'd failed to figure out what to do with me. I might be old enough to be believed by the police and the courts, and I wouldn't be coaxed or threatened into silence. But Kay had drawn the line at killing me. Walter could torture Amon if that's what it took for him to feel free. He could cut off Amon's arms and legs. He could stir his insides with a wood chisel. But I was a child – *her* child, even if I didn't act like it. Walter

202

had reasoned with her. He'd countered every scenario she had offered where they remained safe after Amon's murder with a scenario of his own where I betrayed them. Still she had refused to let Walter hurt me. Even when Walter came into the house that night – even when she held the wood chisel to her thigh as she stood by the banister – she had convinced herself that there was another way.

'But as I lay on the floor where Walter had thrown me, covered with Amon's blood, Kay knew that Walter was right. She watched me lying on Amon's body, burrowing into it. She must have thought that I was irretrievable. Amon had taken me, made me his own and no one else's. If Amon had to die, then I did too. I was no longer her child. Outside, the frogs and crickets began to sing. The air in the house smelled of brine, the first smell of death. "Not here," Kay said.

'Walter sighed with relief. *Not here* meant *In another place*. He asked, "Where?"

'"In the woods," she said. "I don't want to see it. I don't want to hear it."

'He came to me and picked me up – like a father picking up a sleeping child to carry him to bed.

'But Tilson, who had stood by Amon's book-shelves as if he wished to be forgotten, said, "*I* do it."

'Walter and Kay stared at him.

'He said, "You never trust me again if I don't. You think I tell the police unless I got blood on me too. I do it, then you don't got to worry."

'They stared at each other, and Kay nodded.

203

Walter said to Tilson, "Take a shovel. Do it where the soil is wet."

'Tilson said, "I live here my whole life. I know where to put him."

"'Don't tell me where," Kay said. "I swear, if I hear anything—"

'Tilson said, "I know how to be quiet. All you life I been quiet. That ain't no problem for me."

'Tilson carried me out into the night, across the yard, and into the pine woods. Maybe I should have panicked but I felt as secure in the arms of this man who had just promised to kill me as I'd felt in my dad's arms. A yellow crescent moon, as sharp-ended as a bull's horn, was rising through a cloud, and I watched it over Tilson's shoulder. "It all right, boy," Tilson said as he walked. "Ain't nobody but nobody, yeah, it all right."

'In the woods, Tilson circled to a path that ran along a rise that separated a grove of slash pines from a stand of loblollies. A night bird dropped from a low branch and swept past us, and then the only sounds were Tilson's heavy breathing and the crush of pine needles under his feet.

'The path left the woods and cut across a low meadow. Tilson carried me through long grasses and over the tops of sand dunes, then into neighboring woods and back out into another meadow.

'Tilson lived in a windowless shack under a pecan tree, and the ground around it was covered with dried husks and split shells. The shack was made of weathered wood that Tilson had mudded to fill the cracks. A padlock held the door shut.

"'Hush now," Tilson said, and set me down. He unlocked the door and hurried me inside.

204

'The floor was made of wooden planks laid side by side, swept clean of dirt and dust. The bed – a mattress on a thin wooden frame – was covered with cotton sheets and a piece of carpet. Glass jars – holding stones, small branches, and dried leaves – lined one of the side walls. The facing wall was pasted over with the yellow sheets of an old newspaper. The air smelled of animal skins and rotting wood and cheap wax. Tilson said, "I come back tomorrow, maybe next day, maybe day after. You don't make a sound, you understand? They water in the jug if you got to drink. They meal and biscuit in the tin. You got to piss or shit, you do it inside against the wall. We worry about that later. You understand? I come back when I can." He went outside then, closed the door, and snapped the padlock on it, locking me inside.

'He returned three nights later, at which point I was more than half insane with fear, filth, and hunger. I had wrecked the inside of the house so badly that the best that could have come to it was burning, but Tilson just helped me clean myself, fed me half of a sandwich, and, with neither anger toward me nor an apology for being away so long, led me away from the shack, across some fields, and to a road that reached from the interior of the island to the bridge. There, a brown sedan was standing on the shoulder with a woman at the wheel. "She take care of you, OK?" Tilson said, and pushed me toward the passenger door. "You keep you mouth shut. You understand? You do that for you daddy. And you never come back. You understand? You come back and someone got to die, and I think that someone be you."

'I asked, "Where is she taking me?"

'"Far away, boy," Tilson said. "Farther the better."

'The woman in the brown sedan was a cousin of Tilson's mother, and she lived outside of Atlanta. Her name was Bessy Ross – "like the flag," she said – and she was big-boned and diabetic and suffered from ulcers. She was tough, though, and when her neighbors asked what a sixty-year-old black, Southern woman was doing with an eight-year-old white boy, she let them know it was none of their damn business, and when whites on the bus or on the street looked at her with suspicion, she gave *them* a look that made them turn away in embarrassment or shame. She wasn't loving toward me, but she was caring. I had never been to school, though Amon had taught me to read, so, after teaching me the basics of addition and subtraction, she found a place that would take me. After my second day, I told her, "The flag isn't *Bessy*. It's *Betsy*."

'"No, child," she said. "They've got that wrong."

'She bought me good-enough clothes and fed me good-enough food. When I cried at night, she closed the door so I could have privacy.

'She cleaned house and cooked meals for a divorced lawyer and her two sons, and on days when I had no school she brought me with her to the woman's house. She put a broom or a dust rag in my hands and she didn't complain when I left my work unfinished and played with the lawyer's younger son, who was my own age. One evening, after she had finished cooking the lawyer's dinner, the lawyer asked her to sit at the table with her and then said, "Now, Bessy, tell me about this boy."

206

'Bessy Ross shooed me out of the room, and for two hours she and the lawyer talked. After that night, I often caught the lawyer watching me as I swept the kitchen floor or played with the younger son. I learned fast. If nothing else, after living in the house with Amon and Kay, I'd figured out how to pay attention. I caught up with the other children in school, and when I was at the lawyer's house, I copied her sons' manners.

'Then Bessy Ross got sick with cancer, and on a Saturday morning, two months after the diagnosis, the lawyer pulled up in her Audi and helped me carry my belongings to the trunk. "You're going to live with us for a while as Miss Bessy takes care of herself and gets healthy," she said. "Would you like that?"

'I said I would.

'Three weeks later, Bessy Ross died.

'A careful lawyer would have turned me over to child welfare. But, like Bessy Ross, this lawyer was more interested in being charitable than careful. For the next nine years, I shared a bedroom with her younger son, Jimmy. On my last night on Black Hammock Island, I had slept in a windowless shack, and now I woke each morning when sunlight shined through a clean window in an air-conditioned house that smelled of furniture polish and lavender soap. Downstairs, the cook would be setting bacon and toast on the kitchen table, and a woman who I barely knew but who treated me more gently and kindly than anyone else I'd ever known would be reading the newspaper and drinking coffee. As if this was the way real people lived.

'When the lawyer's sons became teenagers, they

turned wild, the way that kids with parents who are more generous than sensible sometimes do. They talked their mother into buying them a dirt bike, which they rode on a local trail. Once, while stoned, they jumped from their second-story roof over a tile patio into the deep end of their backyard pool. I took a hit from the joint and, closing my eyes, jumped from the roof into the air after them.

'Neither of my brothers – that's what I came to think of them as – went to college. Their interest in dirt bikes grew into a love of motor-cycles, and, after some long arguments, the lawyer agreed to give them money to open a dealership, which, by the time that Jimmy turned twenty-two, had expanded into three dealerships and an offshoot repair garage.'

Outside, a heavy piece of metal slammed against the roof at the back of the house. Unless Paul had changed our plan, that would be a ladder.

Lexi and I listened. There was no more noise. Lexi asked, 'Are the men outside the lawyer's sons?'

'Yeah,' I said. 'Jimmy and Robert.'

'Who's the man who drove you here?' she asked.

'Paul. A friend of mine.'

'The woman?' she asked.

'Carol. I'm going to marry her,' I said.

'This is screwed-up,' Lexi said.

The ladder scraped against the roof.

'What are you going to do?' Lexi asked.

'What would *you* do?' I said.

More scraping.

'I don't know,' she said.

'Yes, you do,' I said. 'And you think I'm right to do it.'

'What about me?' she asked. 'And Cristofer?'

Footsteps went up the roof above us. Robert and Jimmy were climbing on to the house. If I punched through the plywood, the shingles, and the tar, I could have grabbed their ankles.

'What are they doing?' Lexi asked.

'It's moving day,' I said.

'What does that mean?' she said.

Then, down inside the house, the front door slammed.

'Are they coming in?' Lexi asked.

'No,' I said. Not unless they were innovating.

They weren't. Walter had gone out. In the yard, his .22 popped twice, three times, twice more. Then the heavier guns shook the house. The door slammed again. Walter was back inside.

'Why are you doing this?' Lexi asked.

'Don't you think I deserve it?' I asked.

'No,' she said. 'Not this.'

'I'm doing it for you too,' I said.

'Don't,' she said.

The footsteps went down the roof. The ladder scraped. Then the house was quiet.

Lexi flipped on the flashlight and slid to the attic hatch. 'I'm going down,' she said.

I repeated what I'd said the first time we came to the attic. 'You can't tell Walter and Kay who I am.'

'Or what?' Lexi asked.

'What will they do to me if they know?' I said.

'What will you do to us?' she asked.

'I won't hurt you,' I said.

209

'Cristofer?' she asked.

'Never,' I said.

'Mom?' she asked.

I turned my eyes away.

'Walter?' she asked.

I said, 'What do you expect?'

'Not this,' she said.

'You could help me,' I said. 'You should. Walter has hurt you. They both have.'

'No,' Lexi said.

'Are Amon's guns really gone?' I asked.

She gave me a look that could have pitied me. 'A long time ago,' she said. 'Mom made Walter dump them.'

'Where?' I asked.

She said, 'In Clapboard Creek.'

I saw no reason for her to lie.

'We're defenseless,' she said. 'You can do whatever you want with us.'

I said, 'You should help me. I'm your brother.'

'I don't know *who* you are,' she said.

Thirty

Lexi

Death smells sweet. As if sweetness met sweetness and met sweetness again. Until all that sweetness got sick and choked on itself. It gets in your nose and throat. A leech. It goes only inward. You try to blow it out. You hold your

210

breath. You run outside into the air. But it goes up to your brain. And down to your belly.

I dropped from the attic hatch. The smell bristled on the inside. Licked against the top of my mouth. I gagged.

I went downstairs. Oren behind me. The smell fingering down my throat. I pulled my dress to my face. Breathed through the cotton.

But Oren said, 'In my job you get used to it. I mean you never *really* get used to it but . . .'

In the front room Walter was shoving a mattress across the fireplace. He favored the leg that the dog had bitten. He looked feverish. Cristofer sat on the floor by the bookshelves. Keening. His eyes wide. Mom was carrying chicken carcasses from a pile by the fireplace to the front window. Wearing rubber kitchen gloves. She had a cigarette between her lips. She breathed in through it and breathed out from her nose. As if the smoke could filter the stink of death. Oren's friends had dug up the pit where Tilson had buried the chickens. They had lugged the rotting meat on to the roof. They had dumped it into the chimney. I recognized Goneril the gray.

'Wait,' Oren said to Walter. But Walter squared the mattress against the fireplace bricks. Oren went into the kitchen. Came back with a mop. Pushed the mattress away. He stuck the mop handle up the chimney and stirred. Feathers and flesh fell out of the flue. Bounced off the damper. Broke apart on the grate. The sour smell of spoiled chicken. And sugar. And acid. Oren poked and pulled the mess. He moved it out alongside the dead birds. He said to Walter, 'If you get all panicky you'll miss what you need to see.'

Walter shoved the mattress back over the fireplace. And said, 'Where the hell were you last night?'

'You look like you didn't sleep,' Oren said.

'I slept fine,' Walter said. 'Always do.'

Oren went to the window and looked out. The first sunlight was turning the sky orange. The pickup trucks and motorcycles were dark and quiet. Oren's friends were invisible in the yard.

'What did you do to deserve this?' Oren asked Walter.

'Go to hell,' Walter said. He limped across the room. Collapsed into the green chair.

Oren said, 'People don't attack others like this without a reason.'

'Why don't you go out there and ask?' Walter said. 'If they won't tell you, maybe at least they'll shut your mouth so I don't have to listen to you.' He looked at Oren square. Like he was fighting to recognize the boy he thought was dead. And fighting against recognizing. Because of what that would mean.

Mom carried the rest of the chickens to the window and heaved them out. One by one. Then went into the kitchen and came back with a jug of vinegar. She sprinkled it on the hearth. Scrubbed the hearth stones with a rag. Threw the rag out the window. The room smelled like death and vinegar.

She went to the kitchen doorway and sank to the floor. And lit another cigarette. Oren sat down next to her and cocked his head. 'Right after your first husband disappeared you painted your best self-portraits,' he said. 'The reviewers called that work a breakthrough and I agree with them. One said you painted *the symmetry of chaos*. Another said you found *balance in disproportion*. One said something about old ideas of *discordia concors*. My favorite said that you arrange *fragments of a broken woman so perfectly that we might think that we're looking at an unblemished beauty*.'

'I don't feel like talking about painting right now,' Mom said. Her eyes were sunken.

'I think you need to,' Oren said. 'I have the feeling that you're about to have another breakthrough.'

She said, 'Why are you doing this?'

'Doing what?' he asked.

'You need to stop,' she said. 'You need to—'

'I don't know what you're talking about,' he said.

He looked at me and got up. He went into the kitchen and found a knife and came back to Mom. As if he would cut her.

'No,' I said.

'No?' He eyed me. Curiously.

'*No*,' I said.

'OK,' he said. He sat in the doorway again. Shoved one sleeve of his suit jacket up to his elbow. Unbuttoned his shirt cuff and shoved up the shirt sleeve. He held the knife blade against his arm. And jerked it back. Blood rose through the split skin. 'Yeah,' he said to Mom. 'You're on the verge of a breakthrough.' He dipped a finger into his blood. Drew the rough outline of a face on the floor.

'Don't,' Mom said.

But he finger-painted a picture with his blood.

213

A stick figure with breasts. Then he finger-painted a boy.

'What's that?' Mom asked.

'What's it look like?' he asked.

'I don't recognize them,' she said.

'It's a still life,' he said. 'Call it what you want.'

She took a deep breath and gagged. Dry retched. Spat out white flakes of saliva.

Oren got up. He bandaged his arm with the handkerchief from his suit pocket. Buttoned his shirt sleeve over it. Straightened his jacket.

I grabbed his sleeve and pulled him into the kitchen. 'Stop it,' I said.

'Stop what?'

'I'll tell them who you are,' I said.

He ran a finger down my face. 'Why haven't you already?'

I hit his hand away. 'I don't care what they did to you. You can't—'

'And your dad?' he asked. 'You don't care what they did to him?'

'All I know is what you've told me,' I said. 'Nobody else thinks anything bad happened to him.'

'Except your next-door neighbor,' he said. 'And the police detective. And you. You've always known that something was wrong. If you didn't you would have told them about me as soon as I told you.'

'Until a couple of days ago I didn't know you existed,' I said.

'But you were waiting for me anyway,' he said.

'I've never needed you. Never missed you,' I said. 'I've taken care of myself.'

'And of Cristofer too,' he said. 'You're a good

person. More than good. That's why you've waited for me. It's why you need me.'

'Because you're not good?'

'I am what Amon made me,' he said. 'I'm as good as I can be. I'm what Walter and Kay tried to destroy.'

'What are you going to do to them?' I said.

'What wouldn't I be justified in doing?' he asked.

'That's not an answer.'

'I'm supposed to forgive them?' he said. 'I'm supposed to walk away? I don't think that's what you really want.'

'Then you don't know me,' I said.

He said, 'When you were a baby and Kay left the house to see Walter I would pick you up and carry you around the way that Amon used to carry me. I would tell you the names of the household objects. I would read Amon's books to you. I saw the hunger in your eyes. I saw the anger. I've known you since before you knew yourself.'

I said, 'You don't know anything about me.'

'I'm sorry,' he said. 'I won't walk away.'

'Then I have no choice.' And I went back into the front room. 'Mom,' I said. 'Walter—' But Walter was at the window with his .22. And Mom was carrying rag-wicked jars of turpentine to him. 'What's happening?' I asked.

'Get the jars,' Walter said.

I stood in Mom's way. 'What's happening?'

She nodded at the window. 'They're coming,' she said.

The generator in the bed of the yellow pickup ripped and hummed. Floodlights burst on and made the early morning sky bright. The pickups stood end-to-end. Forming a barrier wall for anyone on the other side. Walter squeezed two shots from the .22. The bullets hit the side of the yellow truck. A ball of flame rose from the yard beyond the trucks as if the gunshots had triggered an explosion. A wave of light and heat rolled over us.

Walter shot again. And a second ball of fire rose in the yard.

He set down the .22. He lit the rag on one of the turpentine jars and threw the jar out the window. It bounced on the ground and went out. He lit a second rag and threw the jar. It sailed over the first one. Broke in the yard. Made a pool of flame.

Out on the hill another ball of fire erupted. Bigger than the others. Lifting into the sky. Blocking the rising sun.

Walter fired the .22 wild until he spent the magazine. And still he kept pulling the trigger against the empty chamber.

Oren said, 'Walter?'

Walter kept at it.

Again, 'Walter?' Oren held a box of .22 bullets.

'Give them,' Walter said.

Walter crammed the bullets into the magazine. But there was a new knocking and scraping against the roof in the back of the house. Oren's friends were climbing the ladder again. Heavy steps crossed the roof.

'Goddamn it,' Walter said. Tears and sweat filled his eyes as he tried to load his gun.

From behind the mattress covering the fireplace there was a noise of sucking air. And a crash. Flesh against stone. Walter's eyes turned bright with fear.

Cristofer keened.

Oren went to the mattress and shoved it.

'Don't,' I said.

Oren said, 'Don't you want to know?' He pushed the mattress from the fireplace.

Lane Charles's body lay on the fireplace grate. His head was crushed. His neck broken. One of his shoulders was dislocated and thrust to where his chest should be. One knee still in the chimney. The other jammed into his ribcage. Insects working on his face.

Cristofer keened. Walter panicked. And made a sound like Cristofer's. He raised his rifle and shot a bullet into Lane Charles's body as if it might crawl into the room. The corpse made a rotten sigh. Walter shot it again. He swung the gun barrel around the room. Aimed at me. At Oren. At Cristofer. Then he limped to the open window and yelled, 'No more.'

The window framed him. They could have shot him. He seemed to forget himself. The way some scared people lose muscle and mental control. 'What do you want?' he yelled. The sun rising over the hill shined on his chest and face and made his skin golden. 'What do you want?' he yelled again. His eyes were watery and red.

Outside in the yard Oren's girlfriend yelled back, 'I want you, baby.' And she laughed.

One of the men yelled, 'And your wife. I want your wife.'

That more or less slapped Walter. He ducked so that the lower wall shielded him. He jammed the rifle barrel out the window. And squinted

217

into the sunlight. He yelled, 'I'll give you our girl.'

I needed a moment before I knew that he meant *me*. I said, 'You coward.'

Mom said, 'No.' But quiet.

Cristofer stood by the shelves.

I rushed Walter. If I'd been stronger I would have thrown him out the window on to the porch. I would have climbed out after him. And kicked him into the yard with the rotting chickens. And the dead dog.

But he pointed the rifle at me.

'No,' Mom said again.

Walter yelled through the window, 'I'm bringing her out. We have nothing more to give you. I'm bringing her out.' He nudged me toward the door with the rifle. 'Go.'

'You're weak,' I said. 'If you don't get what you want you take it from others. You're a thief.'

'Go,' he said. And jabbed me.

Oren's girlfriend called from the yard, 'Send her out.'

Mom got to her feet. Said, 'No.'

Walter ignored her. For the first time ever. 'I don't like you,' Walter said to me. 'You're filthy and you have filthy habits. I've put up with you. Now get the hell out.' He thrust the barrel at me.

I looked at Oren. He said, 'Your turn.'

I looked at Mom. She was terrified.

Cristofer keened.

'Shut up,' Walter said to him.

He keened louder.

Walter aimed the gun at him. And squeezed the trigger. The bullet cracked a shelf behind him.

218

Cristofer stared at Walter. And made no more noise.

'I'll go,' I said. I moved the furniture that blocked the door. But I told Walter, 'I know what you did. I know why these people are here. They don't want me. They want you and Mom.'

'Get the hell out of the house,' he said.

Then Cristofer charged across the room. He grabbed Walter's rifle. Wrested it from him. And swung it at him. Missed. But he'd knocked the wind out of Walter's anger.

Cristofer dropped the gun on the floor. Went back to his corner.

Oren clapped his hands. As if Cristofer had put on a show just for him. Oren said, 'It's about time.'

Walter sank to the floor. Like he was horrified by what he'd done.

Oren's friends turned on their music. Playing it through speakers in the truck beds. They kept the sound low. Hardly got into the house. But Oren stood up and danced around the room.

Walter glared at him.

When Oren passed me he took one of my hands. Pulled me to him. Tried to dance with me.

I was still trembling from Walter. I asked, 'What are you doing?'

He tried to spin me. 'It's the symmetry of chaos,' he said. 'It's balanced disproportion. Unblemished fragmentation—'

I pushed him away.

He went to Mom. He held one of her hands. Put an arm around her waist. Danced again. He could have danced as easily with a stone. He let her go. Danced on his own.

219

'What have you done?' Walter asked him.

Oren just danced.

The song ended. The people turned up the next one. Screamin' Jay Hawkins. 'I Put a Spell on You.' Oren danced over to Cristofer and bounced to the beat. A smile spread across Cristofer's face. He bounced too.

'What have you done?' Walter asked again.

Oren danced over to him. Followed by Cristofer. Oren mouthed along with the music.

Walter said, 'I'm going to kill you.'

Oren laughed. And said, 'When are you going to learn? You can't kill a man twice.'

A glimmer came into Walter's eyes. Understanding? Fear? But he said, 'You're insane.'

The people cranked up the Rolling Stones. 'Sympathy for the Devil.' Oren and Cristofer bounced and raced around the room. In the wash and rush of sound. Jumping over the green chair. Slamming against the walls. Shouting and laughing and keening. If there was symmetry in that chaos I missed it.

The sun rose high and the house warmed. Thousands of flies came down the chimney. Buzzing and darting. They landed on Lane Charles's body and crawled on his face. And in and out of his shirt. They drank from the cuts on his skin. They flashed through the room. Drunk on blood and pus. Landed on our arms and legs. In our hair. Tasting us for later eating. A swarm clung to the rag bandage on Walter's leg.

Oren went to Lane Charles and bent low to him. He waved the flies away. Touched Lane Charles's

220

skin. Ran his fingers through his hair. A mother with her sleeping child. Oren mumbled a prayer. Or something that sounded like one. Then he left the body and sprawled on the green chair. His legs splayed. King Oren. Cristofer sat on the floor leaning against him. Oren ruffled his hair with his fingers and Cristofer laughed. Then Oren stopped ruffling and started tapping his fingers on Cristofer's head in time to the music. Nine Inch Nails. Nirvana. Metallica. Slayer. Korn. On and on and on. As drilling as the buzzing flies.

Mom sat on the floor by Walter. Her eyes frantic. She let a fly crawl across her ear. 'Someone say something,' she said.

No one did.

She stared at me as if talking was my job. She got up. Shook a cigarette from her pack of Newports. She paced from the kitchen to the bookshelves. She said, 'If we all went outside together all at once what would they do?'

No one answered.

Mom stared at me. I stared at her. Walter swatted at the flies. A fever shined on his face. Cristofer laughed at Oren.

Mom threw her cigarette to the floor. Kept pacing. 'Someone,' she said. And crossed to the kitchen. 'Talk. Someone.' She crossed to the shelves. 'Say something.'

Oren said, 'Once upon a time—'

'Shut up,' Walter said. Oren was quiet. For a couple of minutes. Then again, 'Once upon a time—'

Thirty-One

Oren

'No,' Lexi said. 'Seriously. Shut up.'

'And far, far away in the land of California,' I said, 'there was a grave robber who—'

'Stop it,' she said.

'This is a true story,' I said. 'In the late nineteen-nineties, he cut up—'

'I mean it,' Lexi said.

'What?' I said. 'Too close? Too recent? Fine. Plenty of other examples. These things are surprisingly common. Let's return to an old one. Up until the early nineteenth century, do you know what they did with the bodies of executed criminals – let's say the body of a woman who had killed her husband and child?'

'Enough,' Lexi said.

Kay's eyes were wide. She said to me, 'I know you now.'

'Nonsense,' I said. 'No one knows anyone. You said it yourself. We don't even know ourselves.'

She pulled another Newport from her pack with trembling fingers, hung it between her lips, and flicked her lighter three times before it lit.

'Until the nineteenth century, they gibbeted the bodies,' I said. 'You know what gibbeting is? Do you know exactly what's involved?'

'We don't want to know,' Lexi said.

'To gibbet a corpse,' I said, 'you dip it in tar – pine tar works well – and hang it up in an iron cage. It's all about the spectacle. The tar keeps the body from rotting too fast. You want to give the townspeople plenty of time to see it. And the crows don't mind. They peck right through.' I ruffled Cristofer's hair with my fingers, and he laughed. 'But nineteenth-century medical sciences advanced as the medical sciences will, and doctors needed the executed bodies for anatomical study. The doctors convinced politicians to change the law. So no more gibbeting, which saddened many members of the public, especially the tar makers.'

'You talk like a snake,' Walter said.

I said, 'Then, with an eye toward the popular vote, politicians – being politicians – passed new laws saying that the worst criminals would be publicly dissected, which made the public happy again since everyone likes a corpse. But if for each problem there's a solution, for each solution there's also a problem, the problem in this case being that a dissection is much quicker than a rotting, and the public was hungry – I don't think that's too strong of a word – for the flesh and bones of criminals.' I looked at Kay to see if she was listening. 'As a quick aside, when we prepare bodies for medical study today, we use the chemical *phenol*, which also comes from tar, and along with keeping a corpse fresh, the phenol has a smell that makes you salivate. So every time medical students cut into cadavers they daydream about cheeseburgers—'

'Will you be getting to the point of this?' Walter said.

'The first point – and there are two –' I said, 'involves supply and demand. Nineteenth-century scientists had eager or, if you will, hungry crowds, but they quickly ran out of dead criminals for dissection. That left the scientists with limited options. They could stop studying human anatomy and take up plant biology, for example. Or they could lobby the government to pass laws that would criminalize more behaviors – say, sex with another man's wife or even simple trespassing – and increase the number of executions. Or they could find new sources of bodies. I don't think that the scientists voted, but the last option won the day. I'll give you another example. Once upon a time—'

'Please don't,' Lexi said.

'There were two canal diggers,' I said. 'Stop me if you've heard this one. There were two canal diggers with time on their hands. Other canal diggers with time on their hands might go to the pub or gamble or, if they were inclined differently, attend church services, and in truth these two did have a taste for whiskey and dice, but while they had time *on* their hands, they had little money *in* them. So, having tastes but no means of satisfying them, they kept their eyes open for any opportunities that might present themselves, whether in the form of a careless lady's silver necklace or a drunk with a pocketful of coins – nothing that would get them gibbeted or dissected but enough to buy them a night or two of pleasure.

'The wife of one of the canal diggers ran a boarding house and, late on a winter evening, the oldest of her tenants died – without paying his bill. Who could blame the canal diggers if

224

they saw opportunity? Who could blame them if they wrapped the man in a blanket, threw him into a wheelbarrow, and pushed him over the cobblestones to the house of a doctor who had advertised his need for bodies – big and small, young and old – and his willingness to pay top dollar, no questions asked. Who could blame them if, after giving the canal digger's wife the money that was due to her, they spent Sunday in whiskey, dice, and whores? Who could blame them if, on Monday morning, they failed to show up at the canal and instead went on the prowl for bodies – big and small, young and old – and, when they discovered a scarcity of already dead ones, living too, because, as far as they were concerned, a living body was just a dead one in the making.

'The doctor paid them twenty dollars a pop – not bad for the time, though now if you cut up a body right, you can do much better. Strip out a spine today and you can get three or four thousand bucks. A cornea, four or five hundred. A knee, seven hundred.

'Over the next year, the canal diggers lured most of their victims into the boarding house and smothered them – vagrants, poor widowers, old prostitutes, anyone who might disappear with little concern from the neighbors. Some, though, they killed out in the open. Once, they found an eight-year-old orphan and broke his back in an alleyway. His body weighed so little that they didn't need the wheelbarrow. One of the canal diggers slung him over his shoulder like a sleeping child and a half-hour later they were knocking at the doctor's

225

door.' I looked from Lexi to Kay to Walter. 'Have you heard this before?'

Lexi said, 'I've read something.'

'Sure, they were famous,' I said. 'Their mistake, like the mistakes of most criminals, was in getting sloppy, though it's unclear whether their sloppiness resulted from overconfidence or from guilt over what they were doing. The fact is, though, that they rushed some jobs. And they sometimes got drunk before a killing instead of after. And when they had killed all of the least visible people in the neighborhood, they turned to others with closer social connections – young prostitutes with watchful pimps, old men known on the street for their talkativeness. They got caught after stowing a girl's body under the bed of one of the boarding-house tenants instead of taking her straight to the doctor.

'But – and this is where we can learn some lessons – only one of the canal diggers was found guilty – the one whose wife owned the boarding house. See, there was very little evidence. The doctor had chopped up the bodies in public dissections and then fed the pieces to his dogs. He had burned the clothes.

'A crowd of twenty thousand came to watch the execution of the one convicted man. The next day, another crowd rioted when the police turned away those who had no tickets to see the dissection of the corpse. At the dissection, the anatomist poked a feather into the executed man's skull and held the quill high so that the crowd could see the gore. Then he wrote with it on a piece of parchment, "This is written with the blood of a

226

hanged man. This blood was taken from his head." Which shows that every fool wants to be a comedian.' I looked from Lexi to Kay to Walter. 'The end,' I said.

'That's the other point of your story?' Walter asked, scornfully. 'Every fool wants to be a comedian?'

'No,' I said, 'The point is, what goes around comes around, because where there's a will, there's a way, and when opportunity knocks, don't necessarily open the door, but if at first you don't succeed, try and try again.'

Thirty-Two

Lexi

'That's a lot of points,' Walter said.

'Yes,' Oren said.

'And if where there's a will there's a way what's *your* will?' Walter asked.

'I was thinking,' Oren said, 'about escape.'

'Yes,' Mom said.

'There's no escape,' Walter said.

But Oren got up from the chair. And clapped his hands. 'Come on everyone,' he said. 'We leave tonight. Go upstairs and get your clothes. Get your pillows and sheets and towels. There's work to be done. Come on.' He clapped again. 'Come on.'

None of us moved. Not even Cristofer.

227

'You're pathetic,' Oren said. And he went upstairs alone. A few minutes later he came down with an armful of Walter's and Mom's clothes. Which he dumped on the green chair. He went back up and got Cristofer's clothes and mine. Then went up again and came down with pillows and bed sheets and towels. The room stunk of sweat and rancid chicken. And the rot of Lane Charles. Through the hot middle of the day Oren sat on the green chair and gutted the pillows with a kitchen knife. He dumped feather-down and cotton threads on to a bed sheet. He shredded the pillowcases. And a towel. And cut the shreds into cotton fluff and dust.

'What are you doing?' I asked. My belly was clenching.

'Creating a diversion,' he said. 'Want to help?'

We watched as he started on another towel. Like a weaver at a loom. But he pulled apart instead of making the cloth. Outside a breeze blew clouds from behind the house to the ocean. By the time the sky darkened with afternoon thunderheads Oren had covered one bed sheet with a mound of thread and fuzz and feathers. And started on a second.

Lightning jagged the sky. Fat raindrops fell. Oren's friends ducked under tarps tied to the pickup trucks.

Oren gathered the clothes he had brought from upstairs. He chose a pair of Walter's jeans and a flannel shirt. He chose a pair Mom's pants and a blouse. He stuffed the pants and shirts with other clothes. Tied the shirt tails through the belt loops. Propped the headless dummies against the

228

bookshelves. Then he made two more dummies out of Cristofer's clothes and mine.

'How about you?' I asked. 'Aren't you going to make one for yourself?'

'No one cares about me,' he said. 'Where's your vacuum cleaner?'

'We don't have one,' I said.

'No vacuum cleaner?' he said. 'Who ever heard of that? How about a window fan?'

'Uh-uh,' I said.

'There's a broken fan in the kitchen pantry,' Walter said.

'Can you fix it?' Oren asked.

Walter glared at him. 'Bring it to me,' he said. 'And a screwdriver.'

While Walter repaired the fan Oren bundled the sheets that he'd filled and took them upstairs. Then came down and dug through the pile of bottles and aerosol sprays and cleaners that we'd brought in from the kitchen. He found a can of roach spray and another of white spray paint. Which he also took upstairs. He came back and watched Walter work and handed him a pair of pliers when he needed it. So Walter screwed the wire grill over the fan box and tested the plug in an outlet. And Oren took the fan upstairs too.

I followed him up and into Mom's bedroom. Outside the window the rain was driving so hard that the two pickup trucks disappeared. The room inside was almost dark. Oren had put the bundles of feathers and shredded cotton on the bed. Now he pushed Mom's dresser lengthwise against the window. He set the fan on the far end. Plugged it in. Tested it. Turned it off again. He set the

229

cans of roach spray and spray paint on the floor next to the dresser. I asked, 'What are you doing?'

'Like I said. Creating a diversion.'

'No, what are you *really* doing?' I asked. 'Why are you doing this?'

In the dim light his eyes were kind. He said, 'They were looking like they'd almost lost hope.'

'Mom and Walter? What do they have to hope for?' I asked.

A gust of wind slapped rain against the front of the house.

'Almost nothing,' he said. 'You heard Walter. He said that there's no escape but now I have him fixing a fan because I let him think it might get him out of this. I tease him with ideas of escape and then tear apart his bed linens and bath towels for reasons that he can't possibly understand or appreciate. Nothing could look more useless and ridiculous to him. But what does he come away with?'

'A little hope?' I said.

'That's right. It's the dirtiest word I know. As a kid I had hope. I hoped all over the place. I hoped all the way to California with Amon. I hoped as I rode on an airplane back here after they put him in a hospital. I hoped when I was locked in Tilson's shed. I hoped when Bessy Ross was dying of cancer in Atlanta. All of that hope got me worse than nothing. You know what happens when everything you've hoped for crashes down?'

'Sure,' I said. 'I've hoped. We all have.'

'Then you've died inside too,' he said. 'Because

230

a part of me has been ripped out every time I've hoped. There's nothing worse.'

'What about when hope comes true?' I said.

'I wouldn't know what that feels like,' he said.

'You're going to destroy them,' I said.

'Until there's nothing left,' he said. 'That's the plan.'

Twenty minutes later the rain stopped. As suddenly as it had started. But for another hour thunder rumbled and veins of lightning glowed through the dark clouds. Then the clouds blew out over the ocean. And all that remained of the storm was a soft wind that crossed the yard from the pine woods.

But downstairs we smelled none of the forest peat and hot and damp that such winds usually brought. We smelled Lane Charles rotting.

Walter said, 'Can't we get him out of here?'

Oren tugged on Lane Charles's leg until the chimney let go of the rest of him and he tumbled on to the hearth. Oren dragged him across the room to the window. 'I need help,' he said.

Mom and Walter just looked at him. So I went and together we slung one of Lane Charles's legs over the windowsill. Then the other. Oren lifted his body until we'd propped it in the window. Like it was sitting there.

A gunshot rang from the yard and Lane Charles's body lurched backward. Struck in the chest.

'Jesus,' Walter said.

Another gunshot – and the body lurched again.

'Push,' Oren said. We shoved the body out of

the window. It fell to the front porch. And rested. With one hand reaching over the edge into the yard.

Oren and I sat with our backs against the wall. Catching our breath. 'I don't think we improved matters,' Oren said.

When the sky darkened Oren's friends turned the music loud. They flipped on the floodlights. They yelled and laughed. The men rode their motor-cycles in wild circles around the house. Oren's girlfriend got into the red truck and spun it in circles and kicked dirt into the air. Whooping out through the open window. Like she was riding a bull.

Oren sat in the green chair. Cristofer leaned against him. Walter had pulled his legs to his chest. The hurt one and the good one. He rocked. Comforting himself. Mom sat wide-eyed in the kitchen doorway. She smoked cigarette after cigarette. I could tell that Oren was right and they had about a trickle of hope left between them. Walter looked at Oren. Oren only shook his head.

'When?' I asked.

'Shh,' he said.

A little after midnight his friends turned off the music. They got off the motorcycles. They gath-ered around a bonfire by the kiln. Their hollering stopped and they talked quietly in the warm glow of the floodlights and the fire. They ate meat that they roasted over the open flames. Cristofer fell asleep leaning against one of Oren's legs. Walter stopped rocking and stared at Oren. Mom sucked

232

on a cigarette. She held the smoke in her lungs. Then let it out like it was her last breath.

Oren looked from her to Walter to me. 'Ready?' he asked.

'I've been ready all my life,' I said.

He woke Cristofer. Walter pushed himself to his feet with his broom handle and limped over to Mom. He offered her a hand. Pulled her up. Oren carried the dummies to the window and laid them side by side. He got the bottle of turpentine and poured it over them.

'What are you doing?' I asked.

'Stripping everyone naked,' he said. Then he said to Mom, 'You first. Give your lighter to Lexi.' She handed it to me. He had Mom pick up one side of the dummy he'd made from her clothes. And he picked up the other side. He looked out through the window. Past Lane Charles's body to his friends at the bonfire. 'OK?' he asked Mom. Then said to me, 'Now.'

I flicked the lighter. I touched the flame to the turpentine-soaked blouse. The cloth and the fumes above it flared. The blaze rippled across the dummy. Oren and Mom flung it out over the edge of the porch into the yard.

The people at the bonfire got up. They stood next to the trucks. They cheered like we'd set off a Fourth of July rocket.

'Why the hell?' Walter said.

Oren just said, 'Your turn.' Together they picked up the dummy made of Walter's clothes. I touched the lighter to the turpentine. And Walter and Oren flung the dummy out after Mom's. Oren's friends cheered louder.

233

'What's the point?' I asked.

'We're giving everyone something to think about,' he said. 'Get yours.'

'Right,' I said. I gave Mom her lighter. She lit the shirt on my dummy. Oren and I threw it out on to Walter's and Mom's. Then Oren and I threw Cristofer's out after it. With each new dummy the people in the yard cheered louder. With Cristofer's the woman gave her bull-riding whoop. The sound felt like ice. Tears welled in my eyes. I watched the burning heap of clothes. Wrapped around bodies that were not ours. I looked from Mom to Walter. Their eyes were wet too. I looked at Cristofer. His face was bright and he laughed.

'Go to the kitchen,' Oren said.

'We're leaving now?' Mom asked.

'Five minutes,' he said.

In the kitchen Oren flipped off the lights. He opened the window that faced the side of the house where he and Mom had hung her paintings on the afternoon before her studio burned.

Mom pulled a cigarette out of her pack. But Oren snatched it from her lips. 'No light in here,' he said. 'From now on you're invisible.' He took Mom's Newports and lighter. Pocketed them.

'Come on,' he said to me. We went upstairs to Mom's bedroom. The room was dark except along the ceiling where the floodlights from outside shined long golden streaks. Oren's friends stood by the pickup trucks. Watching as the flames on the dummies died. And black smoke blew toward them on the breeze.

Oren untied the bed-sheet bundles. He picked up a handful of pillow down and threads and cotton dust. 'Get some,' he said. I scooped the stuff into my hands and arms. When we went to the window Oren's friends were looking up at us as if they'd known we would be there.

Oren threw his handful outside. The breeze caught it and spread it out over the floodlit yard.

'Go ahead,' he said. I did what he had done.

The breeze blew the feathers and dust in easy swirls. The threads fell like snow. The light sparkled and shaded.

'More,' Oren said. We scooped more from the bed sheet and threw it out of the window.

'Oooh,' the people in the yard shouted as the stuff flew from Oren's hands.

'Ahhh,' they shouted as it flew from mine.

I laughed. I couldn't help myself. I'd never seen anything more wonderful. Feathers and cotton threads snowing. Playing in the invisible currents and eddies of wind. Falling and rising. And falling again. As they drifted out toward the hill. There was no sense to what Oren was doing. No sense that I could see. But I didn't care. The light dazzling on the soaring flurry was changing the yard.

'It's like a Christmas movie,' I said.

'Or millions of moths,' Oren said. He went back to the bed. 'Help me with this.'

Together we moved one of the sheets to the end of the dresser. He shaped the pile on top of it with his hands. Mounded it by the windowsill. The men outside stayed by the trucks but Oren's girlfriend ran around the yard like a kid. Trying to catch the falling pieces.

At the other end of the dresser Oren flipped on the fan and shoved it toward the window. A

235

blizzard of feathers and cotton filled the air outside. Oren's girlfriend laughed. The men shouted. They became almost invisible. Oren's girlfriend turned into a black shade that danced and ran. The men hung back. Dark against the pickups.

When the pile was gone Oren turned off the fan and slid it to the far end of the dresser. We brought the other sheet to the window. He shaped the pile like the first one. Slid the fan against it.

'This is it,' he said. And he flipped the fan on high. As feathers and cotton dust shot from the room into the night he grabbed the roach spray from the floor. He pulled Mom's lighter from his pocket. Held the spray can and lighter outside of the window. Lit the aerosol stream. It bloomed orange and red. The blaze spread into the threads and feather-down. Which rose and blew across the yard. Touching other specks. The fire rippled through the air. Waves of fire. Flares raining into the yard.

Oren said, 'Let's go.'

'You'll kill your friends,' I said.

But the men by the trucks shouted, 'Oooh.' And Oren's girlfriend whooped like she was riding a bull.

Oren took my hand and we ran downstairs.

Mom and Cristofer already had climbed through the kitchen window. Oren helped Walter after them. I climbed out next. Oren came after.

The front of the house was bright with floodlights and flecks of fire that rose on the wind and settled to the ground. I couldn't see Paul or the other men. But Oren's girlfriend danced in the fire fall.

236

Spots of flame landed on her shoulders and in her hair. She looked up at the sky. She opened her mouth. She let a flame land on her tongue.

Oren ran toward the back acres. And the rest of us followed. Walter limped behind. Before we reached the pine woods Oren looped toward Lane Charles's house. He headed for the back door. Walter caught up. Grinning. Breathless. Hope in his eyes. He said, 'Why not go for the bridge?'

'Lane Charles had a truck,' Oren said. 'And unless they cut his line he had a phone too.'

We crossed into Lane Charles's yard. Rested by a cluster of wax myrtle trees. Ran to the door.

It was locked. Oren kicked it and it swung open.

We stepped into a small dark room that smelled of burlap. The house was quiet. Other than Walter's breathing. Oren led us into the kitchen. And through a hallway to the front of the house. Walter asked, 'What are we—'

'Shh,' Oren said.

We came to the living room. Which was dark behind curtained windows.

'Sit down,' Oren said. We felt our way through the room until we found chairs and a sofa. But before we could sit there was a flash. The lights in the house went on.

Paul the driver and the other men stood in the room. Paul held a long-barreled pistol. Oren held a pistol that matched Paul's. The other two held rifles. The front door opened. Oren's girlfriend walked in. She walked past Paul and the other men. She went to Oren. Jumped into his arms. Kissed him. Stuck her tongue in his mouth. Like a snake.

Thirty-Three

Oren

I said, 'Once upon a time . . .'
After a certain point, a story tells itself.

Thirty-Four

Lexi

'Once upon a time . . .' Oren said.

Midnight was long gone. After walking us into our yard Oren's friends had cleaned up our house. Like it was their house now. They had carried the mattresses up to the bedrooms. They had scrubbed the hearth and the floor by the window where rotting flesh had leached into the pores of the stone and the grain of the wood planking. They had set the dinner table upright. They had arranged the chairs around it. They had swept the dirt and filth out through the door to the porch. The house no longer felt or smelled like it was ours. Mom and Walter and Cristofer and I were intruders.

Oren's girlfriend had gone upstairs and was moving furniture in Mom's room. Out in the yard

238

one of the bikers was dragging Lane Charles's body toward the chicken pen. The other re-dug the pit where Tilson had buried the chickens. Then he used the heel of his boot to mark a spot to dig a pit for Lane Charles. Paul was cleaning the front porch.

Walter sat at the head of the dinner table. Broken and humiliated. His face greasy and red with sweat and fever. Mom sat at the other end. Her dress hanging low on her shoulders. As if it had become too big for her. Her eyes fiery. Cristofer sat across from me. Smiling.

Oren sat on the green chair and looked worried for the first time since he came.

Then he stood. And walked in circles around the table. Like a zoo cat. 'Once upon a time,' he said, 'a boy died and was reborn. This was no ordinary boy. When he was born the first time he crawled out of a tar box as if it was a womb and his afterbirth was the hot pine drippings. He crawled out and rolled around in the dust and sand, and his father who also was a man of dust and sand loved him though others reserved their judgment. How does one love a child who has crawled out of fire? What does one do with such a child?'

'I loved you,' Mom said. Blankly.

'The child's mother decided she knew what to do,' Oren said. 'She would kill the child.'

'Amon took you for himself,' Mom said. 'It wasn't my fault.'

'Who could blame her,' Oren said, 'with a hot and sticky dust-coated child like that? A child like that belonged in the ground. Dust with dust.

Or buried in a forest where his flesh could feed the pines that grew from the sandy soil.'

'I had no choice,' Mom said.

Walter said, 'Nothing that you think happened really did. Not in my eyes. Not in the eyes of the law.'

Thirty-Five

Oren

'So,' I said, 'the boy died, but extraordinary child that he was, he had a second birth. This second birth couldn't have been more different from his first. Instead of crawling out of a tar box, he crawled into a room with white carpet, white bed linens layered twelve inches deep, and white overstuffed chairs that could swallow a child in comfort. Air conditioning poured from ceiling vents. Happy music piped into the room from a stereo controlled elsewhere.

'You might think that a dusty, tar-coated child would look out of place in a room like that, but this child cleaned up well – so well that you would never know that the room was unnatural to him. It made him itch, though, and it made him sweat, which, in the air conditioning, gave him a chill. If you think that this child was ungrateful for having a second chance at life, you're right. Once a child of tar, always a child of tar.'

240

Walter said, 'You were never my child. Not Kay's rightfully either.'

I said, 'Now and then, a workman who had helped the child escape from his murderous mother would come to visit. He told the child about his little sister and brother. He told him about his mother's growing fame as a painter who pretended that she was a perfect eggshell but whose bloodied yoke showed through the cracks – which made her more famous. He told him about his mother's new husband, a self-righteous man of vicious habits, a man who believed he was doing God's work, but he had no children of his own for a sacrifice so he went seeking another man's.'

'That's a lie,' Walter said. 'I've always only meant to protect your mother.'

I said, 'The workman who gave the child a second life made him promise never to return. *Too dangerous*, he said. *Nothing good would come of it*, he said.

'For a long time – many years – the child kept his promise. He went to school. He played with other children. He slept at night in his fat white linens in his fat white bed in the fat white house.

'Only after he became an adult did he question the workman's reasons for him staying away. *What was wrong with danger?* he wondered. He'd come through more danger by the time he was ten years old than most people saw in a lifetime. He accepted danger as one of the conditions of being alive, whether for a first or a second time. And why should the idea that nothing good would

241

come of his returning stop him? The house where his mother lived had long been a bad place. Why should it change for him?'

Thirty-Six

Lexi

Oren's girlfriend came downstairs. Went outside into the yard. Came back from the trucks with a cooler. Which she carried into the kitchen. She turned on the water in the sink. Pots clanked each other as she put them on the stove. Then meat was frying in a pan.

I pushed my chair back from the table and got up.

'Sit down,' Oren said.

I went to the kitchen door and looked in. Bacon was cooking in a skillet. Oren's girlfriend was unloading ground beef and turkey breasts from the cooler on to the counter. She'd put plastic-wrapped loaves of bread by the sink. And a browning bunch of bananas. A bag of apples. A bunch of carrots.

'Sit down,' Oren said again.

I went to the door to the porch and looked out. The generator hummed in the back of the yellow pickup. The floodlights made the night glow golden. But beyond the hill the sky was black. A sliver moon hung overhead. A bent needle. One of the men was digging in the yard. The other was raking cinders and ash from Oren's blizzard of fire. Paul sat on the porch swing. Rocking and rocking and rocking.

I went back to the dinner table and sat.

Thirty-Seven

Oren

I glared at Lexi. 'When the boy became an adult,' I said, 'the workman visited once more. He retold the stories that he'd told on previous visits, as if he wanted to be certain that the young man knew who he once had been and where he'd come from.'

I repeated the details that Tilson had given me and that, up in the attic, I had told to Lexi. How Kay and Walter had killed my dad. How they had hidden the bloody wood chisel in the tar box afterward, and then years and years of tar sediment had solidified around it. How Tilson, after hiding me in his shack, had gone back to the house and showed Kay and Walter his bloody hands – the blood from a thigh wound that he gave himself – to convince them that I was dead. How, after that day, Kay and Walter had never mentioned me, as if Tilson had buried that part of their memory along with my body. How Kay and Walter had let Lexi and Cristofer live, though Walter treated them as if they were stains on his life, and the best that could be said of Kay was that she neglected them and left them alone.

243

'And when the workman was done telling the stories,' I said, 'he made the young man repeat his promise never to return.'

In the kitchen, Carol was taking plates from the cabinet, and the house smelled of dinner.

I said, 'But the young man was angry. The stories that the workman had told him churned with other stories he knew about himself, and they made a kind of heat inside him. He was angry, and he was impatient, and, if truth be told, even after all of his years away, he was homesick. So, harboring resentments and desires as deep as his tar-marrowed bones, he decided to return home and go into the family business.'

I looked from Lexi to Cristofer, from Walter to Mom. 'And so,' I said, 'here I am.'

Thirty-Eight

Lexi

Oren held his hands out wide like we were supposed to clap.

Then his girlfriend came to the kitchen doorway with a tray of sliced turkey and green beans and corn. She said, 'Dinnertime.'

At three in the morning she brought platter after platter and bowl after bowl to the table. The room smelled of turkey and carrots and butter. She had filled one bowl with lettuce and

244

apple slices. Another with stuffing that she'd made from bread and ground beef and bacon. Oren's friends stayed out in the yard. And a clanging and a metallic chopping started. As if the men were taking apart their trucks. Oren's girlfriend ignored the sound. She put juice glasses on the table. She filled them with red wine.

Oren clinked his glass to hers. Raised it to us. 'To family,' he said.

None of us lifted a glass.

Oren said, 'Eat up.'

Mom and Walter stared at the food. I thought it would taste like tar and ash. But I forked three slices of turkey on to my plate. And spooned stuffing and carrots on top.

Everyone watched as I put the food in my mouth. It wasn't tar and it wasn't ash. I ate the turkey and drank my wine. Then Walter stabbed a slice of turkey with his fork. He frowned. Stabbed another slice. He filled the rest of his plate with potatoes and stuffing. Mom pulled the salad to her. Before eating she picked up her glass and stared at the wine. And drank it.

My belly cramped after three days of mostly scraps and canned food. But I kept eating. I put a piece of turkey on Cristofer's plate. He keened low. He stopped when I tried mashed potatoes. I filled his plate with mashed potatoes.

Thirty-Nine

Oren

'And so here I am,' I said again, 'and, as you fill your stomachs, as you gorge yourselves and make yourselves drunk on my wine, you might ask yourselves, *What are the implications of this young man's return? What possibly can it mean for us in the short term and long run?*

'If I were a prodigal son, *you* would have cooked a feast *for me*. You would have dug the gold rings out of your jewelry boxes and put them on my fingers. You would have filled my pockets with coins. But I'm the unwanted son, the son you thought you had killed. So, along with my good friends, I've prepared a feast for you. *But what possibly can that mean? In the short term? In the long run?*'

I went to the table, picked up a slice of turkey and took a bite. Then I stared at Walter and asked, 'What does it mean?'

Forty

Lexi

Walter put his fork on his plate. He wiped his mouth with the back of his hand. 'It means nothing,' he said. 'Nothing happened here. Nothing. Amon left with you eighteen years ago and now you're back. That's what it looks like.' He tried to smile. 'You're back and we're glad to have you. Welcome back, son.'

'Amon's bones aren't in the yard?' Oren asked.

Walter said, 'Even if a body was there it would've rotted after eighteen years.'

'You know that? Or you hope it?' Oren said. 'What would Daniel Turner think?'

'I don't give a damn what he thinks,' Walter said. 'Unless a court tells him he can dig here he won't. And a court won't tell him he can. Not after all this time. Not unless you've got more than these lies to tell.'

Oren said, 'How about you, *Mom*? Do you mind if I call you that? I mean, that door is long shut. Vines have grown over it and the hinges have locked up with rust. The umbilical cord stopped pumping many years ago. But *Mom* – what can my arrival mean?'

'I've loved you,' she said. 'I did what I needed to survive.'

247

'It's a little late for that don't you think?' he said.

'Too late for love?' she said. 'No.'

'How about you?' he said to me. 'What can it mean?'

'It means trouble,' I said.

He grinned.

'You can stay if you want,' Walter said. 'You can tell your stories to anyone who will listen. If anyone will. But we've been here for a long time. You're wrong if you think we're going to cower. You're wrong if you think we're going to run away. And if you think we're going to say we're sorry for what we've done you're wrong again. We're better off without your father.'

'I don't want you to run away,' Oren said. 'And I don't care if you're sorry.'

'That's good,' Walter said. 'Because you aren't getting either.'

Mom asked, 'What *do* you want?'

'I want you to disappear,' Oren said.

Walter shook his head. 'That isn't happening.'

In the back of the house metal scraped against wood. The men were climbing on to the roof again.

The noise unsettled Walter. 'What are they doing now?' he said.

'Same as they've been doing all night,' Oren said. 'Cleaning up.'

Oren's girlfriend went to the fireplace. Looked up through the flue.

'What's she doing?' Walter said.

She pulled the grate out and leaned it against

248

the wall. Then she sat down on the hearth with her legs crossed under her. She stared into the empty space. As if she knew what was coming.

'What's she doing?' Walter asked again. He shoved his chair back and pushed himself to his feet.

Something fell into the chimney from the roof. Scraping the bricks. Bouncing off the damper. And landed hard on the blackened floor of the fireplace. It looked like it once was a work boot. But little had lasted of the leather and laces. Then another boot scratched and bounced and landed.

'Goddamn it, no,' Walter said. He hobbled over to the hearth.

The rotten end of what could have been a leg bone tumbled through the chimney and cracked on the floor. Two more bones fell. Clanked on the damper. Bounced out of the fireplace on to the hearth. Then a clump of fabric. A rotten ball of denim and dirt. It smacked on the floor. Walter watched. His eyes blazed. And a piece of red-and-black checkered flannel fell from the chimney into the room. The same as the shirt that my dad wore in the photo of him that Mom kept on the bookshelf. Darkened with age and water. And more bones fell. And something else rolled on to the hearth. Muscle or root or meat.

Walter trembled.

But Mom's face hardened. She stood and helped Walter back to the table. She guided him into his chair. Maybe the fluttering and plummeting reminded her of why she had killed my dad. Maybe the toughness that had driven her out of her father's house and up-island to visit my dad when she was only fifteen years old pumped through her veins again. Maybe she felt the force that had driven her to paint thousands of portraits of herself.

She went to Oren. He was so much taller. But she seemed to stand over him. He was an animal that needed to be pushed down before it would submit to her. 'Leave,' she said. 'Take her.' She pointed at his girlfriend. 'Get your other friends and go. This is no place for you.'

Without moving his feet Oren seemed to step back. He started to speak. But no words came.

'Just go,' Mom said.

Then a tapping came at the door to the porch. And the sound seemed to wake Oren.

'Listen,' he said.

'Go.' Mom stepped toward him.

'It was a soft knock,' Oren said. 'Not like all those years ago when Walter came to kill Amon.'

Another tapping on the door.

'Should we let our visitor in?' he asked. 'If it were my friends I think they would come in on their own. Don't you? They've made themselves sufficiently at home. So who can it be arriving in the middle of the night?' He turned to the door and shouted, 'Who is it?'

'Go,' Mom shouted. But she had lost her strength.

Another tapping. As soft as before.

'I think we had best find out,' Oren said. He went to the door and opened it.

Tilson was standing on the porch. His hands and face were grimed with soot and sweat and oil. He held a tar-caked wood chisel. He gave it to Oren.

'Come in. Come in,' Oren said. 'You're as dirty as a newborn baby. But this house has seen worse. Much worse. Take a seat at the table. Have dinner. A meal before you go. Or stay the rest of the night if you like. We have plenty of beds upstairs and we've just changed the sheets.'

Tilson went to Mom's chair and sat. Without a word. And filled her plate with food.

'And what's this?' Oren said. He held up the dirty wood chisel. 'A house-warming gift for an old house and an old family? No house should be without one. You never know when you might need it. Let's say you wake up at three in the morning and find yourself in need of kindling. Let's say you have a husband who needs killing. It's just the tool for the job.' He started to circle the table again. 'Where did you find it?' he asked Tilson.

'In the tar box,' Tilson said. Chewing a bite of turkey.

'The tar box,' Oren said. 'What a place to keep a chisel. I can imagine a *tool*box. Or a work-bench. Even a kitchen drawer if you kept tools there.'

'Nope,' Tilson said. 'Was the tar box.'

'What a place,' Oren said. He ruffled Cristofer's hair as he walked behind his chair. 'Was it hard to get it out? It must have been covered with a lot of old tar.'

'About eighteen years' worth, no more,' Tilson said.

'Well you've done a good job,' Oren said. He

251

put a hand on my shoulder as he passed. My thighs itched. I put my hands between them.

Tilson said. 'Hate to waste a good tool.'

Oren stopped behind Walter's chair.

'I got a suggestion,' Tilson said. 'Now on you keep that chisel in a place you can find it. A place you can get it easy.'

'An excellent suggestion,' Oren said. 'Do you have any ideas?'

'All out of ideas,' he said. 'Sorry.'

Oren looked at me. He looked at Cristofer. He even looked at Mom. 'How about here?' he said. He raised the chisel above his head. And drove it down through Walter's neck.

Walter hardly moved as he died.

He slid low in his chair.

His eyes lost their fear.

Tears of blood ran down on to his shoulders.

Mom screamed.

For him.

For herself.

If she had run for the door she might have gotten to the front porch. Or the yard. But she started toward Walter. As if she could do anything for him. And Oren wrenched the chisel free from the bone. Then Mom did turn toward the door. Oren was waiting for her. She came anyway. As if she was running into his arms. And he drove the chisel through the flesh of her belly. And up under the ribcage toward her heart. She fell on to him as she slid to the floor. Holding him. Her face and mouth pressing against his neck. As if she would kiss or suck it.

Forty-One

Oren

Kay's lips touched my neck.
  Her teeth touched my neck.
  Her tongue touched my neck.
  She seemed to lick the salt from me.
  I twisted the chisel.

Forty-Two

Lexi

Three days later Daniel Turner came to check on us. Oren was out at the road fixing the gate and they drove in together in the detective's car. Cristofer was bouncing on his trampoline. Oren's girlfriend Carol and I sat together on the porch swing.

Earlier that morning Paul and the other men had taken their guns from the truck lock boxes. They had carried them inside and passed them through the hatch into the attic. They had driven out over the hill and come back with the lock boxes steaming in the heat. Packed with ice. Oren had showed them how to wrap and prepare

Mom and Walter so that the ice wouldn't burn their skin or wreck their eyes in the hours between Black Hammock Island and Mercer School of Medicine. He had slapped the tailgate on the yellow truck like it was the rump of a horse. And the trucks had bolted over the hill. Out of sight.

Oren's friends had raked the yard before leaving and now if I squinted I could imagine I was looking through ocean water at a furrowed sand bottom. And Carol and I were swaying and floating far from shore. Away from the breaking waves. Tilson had rebuilt the kiln and was loading it with strips of pinewood. The air smelled of bitter weeds and peat from the pine woods and ocean salt. 'Smells good,' Carol had said when she'd sat down by me on the swing. And she'd put her hand on mine.

I'd pulled my hand away. I'm not that easy. Not after everything else.

Now Oren and Daniel Turner got out of the car. The detective looked around as if he was seeing the yard for the first time. As if it had twisted on its axis. But he couldn't name how.

The place *had* changed. Oren and Tilson and the other men had patched the damage to the house and porch and tarred and painted over their work. They had fixed the poultry pen and bought a dozen new hens. They had shoveled the remains of Mom's studio into the wheelbarrow and dumped them in the woods. They had leveled the ground so that aside from a darkness it looked the same as the rest of the yard.

254

'Look who's come for a visit,' Oren said now. His face and hands were dirty. Sunburn had blistered the skin on his nose and cheeks. For the first time I could see my family in him.

Daniel Turner looked at Carol and me and said, 'Good morning.'

I nodded good morning to him.

'Your mom and Walter here?' he asked.

'No sir,' I said.

He looked at the yard again. Asked, 'When might they be back?'

'No time soon,' I said.

The sun was glinting off the roof of his car. 'They're out for a while then?' he said.

'They went traveling,' I said.

'That's what I told him,' Oren said. 'But he wanted to hear it from you.'

Daniel Turner stepped on to the porch and into the shade. 'Your mother doesn't travel,' he said. 'She's known for staying on this island. I've read the articles about her refusing to go to the openings of her exhibits.'

'Maybe she changed her mind?' I said.

'Maybe so,' he said. 'And maybe one of you can explain this.' He pulled a piece of paper from his pocket. 'See, I've been traveling a bit myself lately – a buddy of mine has a fishing cabin in Tennessee, and if there's one thing I love, it's rainbow trout. But when I came back, there was a note on my desk. It seems your neighbor heard noise here the other night and called to tell me about it. He told the person who wrote the message for me that it sounded like quite a commotion. Do you know what that could be about?'

'My family never has gotten along with Lane Charles,' I said.

'I've seen that,' he said. 'Any reason why he would report hearing gunshots here in the middle of the night?'

'You would have to ask him,' I said.

'Well, you see, I tried that,' he said. 'I called his house and he didn't pick up. And then I drove out here and he's not home.'

'Maybe he went to the city,' I said.

'That must be right. Can you explain what his tractor is doing out there, wrecked, by your pine grove?'

'No sir,' I said. 'I can't explain that either.'

Daniel Turner shook his head. Walked down to the yard. Went to the kiln. He and Tilson talked. Which made him no happier. Then he came back to the porch and said to Carol, 'Might you tell me who *you* are?'

She nodded at Oren. 'I'm with him.'

Daniel Turner asked Oren, 'You're staying for a while then?'

'I thought I would,' he said. 'Good people. A good house.'

'And what's your claim on this place?' he asked.

Oren looked confused. He said, 'Does a man need to have a claim?'

Three weeks later Daniel Turner came back. Leading four squad cars and a forensics van. He drove past our yard and turned on to the driveway leading to Lane Charles's house. All morning they went in and out of the house. Carrying bags. Wearing white shoe covers and gloves. As if life

256

on Black Hammock Island hadn't already contaminated every surface where people had breathed. We watched from the front porch. When Carol touched her fingers to mine I gripped her hand and held tight.

A month passed and then another. Then early one afternoon Daniel Turner came back again. Alone. We were mostly keeping the gate open now and he drove over the hill and stopped in front of the house. He left his engine on and stayed in his car. Waiting until Oren and I came out.

He rolled down his window and told us that the investigators had found traces of blood in Lane Charles's living room. But the blood didn't match Lane Charles. He stared at Oren and me. Like he expected us to ask whose it was. We didn't ask. And I didn't tell him that Walter's dog bite was bleeding and leaking when Oren marched us through the house.

'I have a theory,' Daniel Turner said. 'More than one theory. But my lieutenant doesn't like them. He has a theory of his own. Not enough to act on but more than I have. He's seen the list of calls from Lane Charles to me and the department and he's got it in his head that Lane Charles became obsessed with your family. He thinks that the blood shows that Lane Charles did something to your mom and Walter. He can't explain why you're uncooperative but he thinks that after growing up in this family you probably have your reasons. He thinks someday Lane Charles will turn up because blood always rises no matter how deep you bury it and he'll have stories to tell about what happened to your mom and Walter though he'll probably keep them to himself. What do you think of that?'

'It's a theory,' I said.

'We both know what it is,' he said. 'I agree with the lieutenant on one point though. Blood will rise. When it rises here I'll be here too. You can count on that.' Then he rolled up his window. And drove out over the hill.

Weeds took over Lane Charles's field. Crept up the steps to his front door. Cristofer spent more and more time on his trampoline. As if with each downward plunge he was trying to disappear into the jumping mat. I brought my dad's books down and lined the shelves with them. I read the stories that had made him the man he was. A hard man. I wondered if I could love him.

At night I heard Oren wandering through the rooms of the house. Climbing into the attic to be with the guns. Swinging on the front-porch swing. Sometimes he went into the yard and chopped wood until the sun came up. Then he spent the daytime feeding pine strips into the kiln. Some days he ate nothing. Carol left after six months. If he decided to act sane again he should give her a call she said.

'Don't you understand?' I asked him. 'You're free now. You've done that for yourself. You're free.'

He stared at me as if freedom was a lie. As dirty a word to him as *hope*.

One morning I went into Mom's bedroom which Oren had taken for himself. The room smelled of sweat and acid and sugar. Rotting meat. I found the wood chisel tucked into the sheets on Walter's side of the bed. I ran with it from the room. To wash it. To bury it in the yard.

But Oren was coming up the stairs.

I held the chisel from him. Tried to keep it away.

He grabbed me. Wrestled with me. Took it from my hands.

I thought he would stab me with it.

But he just raised it above his head. And he screamed. Like a bird dropping toward a fleeing animal. Like the animal itself in its last rush before dying.